Dogged

by

J L Wilson

A Remembered Classics Romance

Dogged

Cover Art by *Kim Mendoza*

The Wild Rose Press, Inc.
PO Box 708
Adams Basin, NY 14410-0708
Visit us at www.thewildrosepress.com

Publishing History
First Crimson Rose Edition, 2016
Print ISBN 978-1-5092-1054-1
Digital ISBN 978-1-5092-1055-8

A Remembered Classics Romance
Published in the United States of America

Dedication

To the tireless volunteers
at animal sanctuaries and shelters everywhere,
but especially to those at:

The Wildcat Sanctuary
http://www.wildcatsanctuary.org/

the North American Bear Center
http://www.bear.org/website/

and The Elephant Sanctuary
http://elephants.com/

Chapter 1

"It was murder. I'm sure of it." Mom's voice had that hint of drama she loved to use.

I managed to keep my impatient sigh under control. "Mom, why are you so sure?"

"I have evidence." My mother, Janelle "Jay" Watson, pulled a bright red memo notepad out of her voluminous leather handbag, a purse that could easily qualify as carry-on luggage. She skimmed through a few pages then regarded me with her sharp green eyes. "I talked to Charlie on Tuesday night. He mentioned someone was coming over for a visit."

When no further 'evidence' was forthcoming, I prompted, "And?" I leaned back in my chair and regarded the pile of work awaiting me atop my old oak desk. To my left were mid-terms to be graded and to the right were three PhD theses awaiting my evaluation. The fate of Stoneyburst College's graduate English students was on hold, however, while my mother made her case for murder.

"Well, don't you see?" Mom tapped the notepad against her palm, her bright orange-and-black pumpkin-themed fingernails a clash with the small red memo book. She was ensconced in my overstuffed chintz guest chair, her feet tapping an erratic rhythm on my wood floors. Her white hair was fluffy and poofed just right, as always, and her black slacks and black, red, and white polka-dot knit top looked new. Probably the result of one of those casino shopping trips the residents of the Senior Center always took.

"No, I don't see." I hazarded a glance at the clock over Mom's right shoulder. *Thank you, Jesus.* It was just about time for my Thursday three o'clock class.

"Honestly, Annabelle, you're too practical for your own good."

I raised an eyebrow at her use of my given name. Most people used my nickname, Acie, which was based on my initials. When Mom used my given name, I knew she was trying to obscure whatever issue was at hand. "Practicality can be useful," I said non-committally.

She shot me an admonishing look. "I can't believe I raised a daughter to be so blind to what's around her."

I can't believe you think you raised a daughter, I almost said, but I kept my opinion to myself. My alcoholic father had raised me after Mom ran off with Jimmy Watson. She traded life in Grimper, Iowa, for a life of bouncing from job to job across the United States. I was eight years old when she left and I didn't see her again until she showed up, newly widowed after Watson's death, for Dad's funeral when I turned eighteen. Then I took off for my own career while Mom remained behind in Grimper. She had very little to do with my upbringing—or so I prayed.

"I guess it comes from having to pay the rent every month," I said, gathering my iPhone and iPad and dropping them into my book bag. "That tends to make a person practical."

Mom regarded me with patient good humor. "Just because you have to be responsible doesn't mean you can't be imaginative."

"Good point." I stood, slinging my leather book bag over one shoulder and coming around a corner of the desk. "Imaginative is a good term to describe your so-called evidence. I have to go to class." I glanced at the other occupant of my office. "Come on, Conan."

My nine-month-old bulldog puppy looked up from his bed near the window and yawned, then stumbled to me, black nails clicking on the hardwood floor. Conan was a Dorset Bulldog, an old-time breed making a comeback. He was taller and leggier than most bulldogs with a slender face, beautiful black-and-tan markings, and a big white cross on his tummy. A friend had convinced me to give the breed a try when my Golden Retriever died the previous winter. The puppy earned the name Conan when he destroyed, very barbarically, two dog beds within twenty minutes of seeing them.

After five months with me, he was finally shaping into a good Doggy Citizen, although he had occasional lapses. Luckily for both of us, Stoneyburst allowed faculty to bring pets to class as long as the students didn't object. None of my students did, so I brought Conan with me for my Thursday afternoon class, giving him more opportunity to learn good behavior in the wide world.

I clipped his lead to his collar and we wended our way through my crowded office. Mom stood when Conan and I neared her, angling her metal cane dangerously near my foot. She used the cane more as a fashion accessory than she did for assistance. Today's cane was a dark cherry color which matched her outfit. "Charlie was supposed to meet someone on Tuesday night. What if that person killed him?"

"What if that person didn't show up?" I countered. "Why are you so determined to believe Charlie was murdered? He was an older gentleman." *Like you. No, older than you, I think.* "He had a heart attack. Dr. Mortimer said so."

"Mortimer," she snorted. "He's no better than a vet." Mom tried slinging her black handbag over her shoulder like I did, but it was too bulky. She settled for letting it dangle from her left hand while she followed Conan and me to the door.

"For heaven's sake, why do you say that? Dr. Mortimer is a good doctor."

"If he's so good, why can't he figure out how come my back hurts so much?"

"He told you why your back hurts." I held the door open for her, ushering her and my puppy out into the hallway. My nameplate—*Dr. A. C. Doyle, Room 221*—jiggled when I pulled the door shut. I made a mental note to talk to the department secretary about getting someone to tighten the bolts holding it in place. "You have sciatica," I reminded her. "Remember?"

"Of course I remember," she said. "I'm old, not senile."

I avoided her remark by looking around the hall but it was quiet. My English Department colleagues were either busy in their offices or at class. Baker Hall housed English and Philosophy and neither department was known for their extensive public social gatherings. "Do you want to take the elevator or the stairs?"

"I hate that elevator. The stairs." Mom started off down the hall to the right. I breathed a sigh of relief. The ancient elevator was claustrophobically small and wheezed when it worked. I avoided it as much as possible.

"Mortimer may have said what I have, but why doesn't he fix it?" Mom grumbled, ambling along the carpet-lined hall with me. Like many buildings on Stoneyburst's quaint old campus, this one dated back to the early 20th century, with slightly warped oak floors that creaked when we walked and the high ceilings of the hall creating a tunnel-like effect.

"Heel," I murmured to Conan, although I also aimed the command, hopefully, at my mother. The puppy took up position slightly behind me on the right, pausing once to give his head a good shake. Conan loved the jingly sound of his tags when he trotted. "Some things can't be fixed, Mom. Your back is just wearing out. After all, it's given you good service for eighty-two years."

"There's a cure for just about everything these days, at least that's the way it sounds from TV." Mom stabbed at the carpet runner with her cane. "Mortimer is probably too lazy to figure out how to treat me."

"Lazy or busy. There're only five doctors in town, and that's not really enough to treat seven thousand residents." We approached the polished granite stairway leading to the main level and hence outdoors to the classroom buildings. "Take the railing, Mom." I scooped up Conan and tucked him against my left side.

"I'm fine," she said, although she did grab the rail while I took her left elbow. Her cane dangled from her hand while we started slowly down the stairs.

It was all I could do to keep my squirming forty-pound puppy under control and try to steer both my mother and myself on the slippery steps—slippery and *hard* steps that could easily harm a growing puppy or an elderly woman if one of them took a tumble.

"You have your hands full," a laughing male voice said behind me.

I managed a glimpse over my shoulder. Dr. Isaac "Ike" Adler, professor of Renaissance literature, hurried down the steps behind us. "Here, I'll help your mother," he said, coming around me to stand in front of Mom. "You handle the Hell Hound."

Ever since Conan got loose and startled Ike and several other professors by popping into their offices unannounced, my puppy was known as The Hell Hound of Baker Hall, a poor joke on his name and his namesake's novel, *The Hound of the Baskervilles.*

I welcomed Ike's intervention, if only to keep Mom occupied. My mother loved Ike, as did all women. What wasn't to love? Ike was a broad-shouldered, six-foot tall hunk of man with thick salt-and-pepper tousled hair and deep dimples in an oval face with a strong jaw. His pale blue eyes had a dark blue rim around the iris, making his gaze very intense. Ike always looked a person straight in the eyes when talking, a habit that usually reduced undergraduates, male or female, to stuttering idiocy.

He was also long-divorced, intelligent, a natural athlete, a cunning bridge player, an amateur gourmet cook, and an exceptional gardener, with a landscaped back yard that was the envy of many members of the Garden Club. Ike was a Renaissance man in more ways than one. Like me, he was in his mid-fifties, but he appeared more like forty-something.

I still looked youngish, too, but that was just good luck and good genetics. Like Mom, I was tall and slender, and like Mom I had great skin. All of it kept me looking young, which helped me pass as younger than my age for years when I modeled. Of course, it also used to work against me when I wanted to be treated like an adult.

"Thanks, Ike," I said, relinquishing my hold on Mom's arm and going back up two steps so Ike could take my place.

"No problem." With me on the steps above him, we were almost the same height. "Have you been out in the sun again, Acie?" he asked teasingly then he turned his attention to my mom.

I glared at the back of his head. My fair skin freckled the minute I stepped into the sun and my ex-husband once said I had eyes that were like green lasers when I was angry, which I aimed now at Ike, who loved to point out how I blended in with the student body. *Acie fits right in,* he'd say. *She could be a spy on campus for us.*

As though it was my fault I appeared thirty instead of fifty and I tended to dress a few years younger than my age. A good denim skirt, a couple of pairs of jeans, a few good sweaters and blouses, and I was set.

That was another difference between Ike and me. I used to be a clothing model, with a somewhat successful catalog and print career. When I left the biz I left high style behind me, settling for comfort in my clothing and my hair style. My waist-long blonde (now white) hair was bundled into a multi-layered French braid and I wore my usual low-heeled shoes, a swirly denim skirt, a hastily tucked-in navy knit top, and a white sweater.

Well, it used to be white until I picked up my puppy.

Ike always dressed like a male model. Like now. He was the epitome of College Professor in his dark burgundy crewneck sweater, gray slacks, and black-and-gray sports coat. Even his loafers, casually scuffed, matched the burgundy of his sweater. He looked like he was ready for a Calvin Klein photo shoot at Yale.

"You knew Charlie Baron, didn't you?" Mom asked Ike while they carefully navigated the steps.

I rolled my eyes. *Lord, give me patience,* I mouthed to the ceiling.

"I met him at a fundraiser at the Country Club," Ike said. "I heard he died. I was surprised. He seemed like he was in such good health."

"You see?" my mother demanded, shooting me a reproachful glare over her shoulder. "Even Dr. Adler thinks he was murdered."

"Murdered?" Ike paused on the step to peer back at me.

I didn't realize he stopped until I ran into him, staggering back so I didn't run him over. It caused me to tip precariously. Ike released my mother, put his arms around me and Conan, steadied us on the step, and turned to help my mother again, all in the space of a breath.

"Nicely done," Mom said admiringly. "You have all the grace of a dancer."

This time I let my impatient sigh come out. Mom spent three years as a dance instructor during her peripatetic relationship with Jimmy Watson. She insisted on teaching me every dance imaginable when I came back to town as an adult. I pointed out that I seldom had the opportunity to dance, but Mom was adamant about teaching me, probably out of a misguided notion that it would bring us closer together. It was easier to acquiesce than to argue with Mom so I went along with her.

"I do enjoy dancing," Ike said, steering her down the remaining steps. "I don't get much chance to do it, though. There are so few events any more where people can dance."

I had a sudden image of an old-fashioned Fred Astaire movie, the men in tuxes and the women in gowns, all swaying on glossy floors under gleaming chandeliers. "Nope," I said, setting Conan on the floor near the main entrance. He gave himself a shake, making his tags jingle. "Not much chance of that in good old Grimper."

"There's the Harvest Ball," Mom said.

I almost laughed out loud. "The Harvest Ball is not the event it used to be."

"How would you know?" she countered. "You haven't gone in years."

"True," I conceded.

"But you have to go this year. After all, you're accepting the endowment," Ike said, still holding Mom's arm. "It's a special event this year." He smiled at Mom, little dimples playing around his mouth. The man really was too handsome to be real.

Mom simpered. "You're so right. Everybody will be there." She shot me another reproachful look. "You're accepting the grant on behalf of your department. You have to go."

"Endowment," I corrected, starting for the front door. "I have to go for that part of it. I don't need to stay for all of it."

"Oh, you'll stay," Mom said. "Once they start

dancing, you'll want to stay."

"We'll see," I said.

"I know what that means," Ike said. *"We'll see* means no, right?"

"Oh, look. Speaking of endowments, there's Hank." I nodded at the stylish woman seen through the glass doors that opened onto the campus.

Ike laughed. "She'll hit you if she hears you say that."

"She's too polite to hit me." I shrugged. "Henrietta, Hank. All the same, right?" I hoped my jealousy didn't show. Henrietta Baron was the fashion plate I used to portray on camera, but she lived it in real life. Like me, she had grown up in Grimper, attending the same high school but a couple of years behind me. Like I did, she left after high school, although in her case it was because her family relocated to Chicago. I had old, not-very-fond memories of Henrietta from school.

"I'm off to class," I said, tugging Conan away from his examination of Ike's shoes. "Thanks for stopping, Mom."

She smiled brightly at me but I saw canny mischief in her green eyes. "Sherry wants to go see Lee Street about our concern. We thought we'd stop by on our way back to Elm Grove."

Her words brought me to a halt, as she knew they would. "Again?"

Ike watched us, his gaze bouncing from me to Mom, his hands buried in his slacks pockets. I could tell by his amused gaze I would be teased later about My Mom, the Detective. Everybody in town knew about Mom and my Aunt Sherry Holms, who fancied themselves the Jessica Fletchers of Iowa. The residents of the Elm Grove Home for Seniors were often roped into helping the two old ladies in their investigative endeavors.

"Lee Street is a detective with the Grimper Police Department," Mom said defensively. "He's a public servant. It's his duty to talk to citizens about their concerns."

"Not when their concerns are—" I swallowed the word *idiotic* and substituted, "unfounded."

"Is this about Charlie Baron?" Ike asked, turning his charm on Mom. "Henrietta's uncle?"

She nodded energetically while I edged toward the front door. "Charlie died so suddenly. We think there should be an investigation into his death."

Ike held the door for us, listening to Mom babble on about Charlie Baron and her suspicions. I tuned her out, having heard the story the night before when the two old ladies descended on me after dinner and bent my ear for an hour or more about their latest investigation.

Conan and I emerged into the sunny and chilly October afternoon. My office building was on the edge of the small campus which was centered at the Student Union, a stately old four-story building complete with ivy covered walls. Sidewalks projected out from the Union like spokes on a wheel, leading to the different campus buildings. I started down the steps to the 'rim' of the wheel, a brick sidewalk curving past every building.

I was followed closely by my mother and Ike, who still listened to her but who had his eyes fixed on a spot past me. I followed his gaze and saw the reason for his smile when Henrietta's eyes shifted from me to him.

Henrietta was tall and leggy with abundant black hair cut in a chin-length layered style so it framed her slightly round face. It also emphasized her long neck, today swathed in a dark gray cashmere turtleneck sweater that matched her eyes. She had a curvaceous figure made all the more curvy by her tight jeans and form-fitting sweater. Everything about her seemed casual but I guessed one beauty day at Henrietta's pricy Chicago salon probably cost more than I made in a week as a professor at our little private college.

She was in her early fifties and an alumnus of Stoneyburst, having returned to graduate with a degree in Business Admin. She was also a frequent visitor to Grimper to visit her uncle, Charlie Baron, making the three-hour drive from Chicago often. Now that he was dead, she would inherit his house and estate, or so the rumor mill in town said.

Ike often escorted her to the few social occasions Grimper could boast and they sometimes paired in golf and bridge at the Beacon Golf and Country Club. The rumor mill had them walking down the aisle soon, although Ike had never mentioned the possibility to me or any of our fellow academicians.

"Just the man I wanted to see," Henrietta said in her throaty, low voice, striding forward on impossibly high-heeled black leather boots. "I wanted to talk to Dr. Adler about the ceremony for the endowment."

I saw Ike eye Henrietta's endowments, prominently displayed in her tight sweater. "Well, here he is. Thanks, Ike. See you later, Mom." I moved to the left, heading for Devon Hall and the graduate students who awaited me. Conan veered to my right, puppy curiosity winning out over Canine Good Citizenship. His stubby black tail wagged with enthusiasm while his butt wiggled, all in anticipation of meeting a new friend.

Henrietta Baron took one look at the small puppy and drew back in horror. "That's a dog," she said in a strangled voice.

"A puppy," I corrected. "He's a Dorset bulldog."

"A bulldog?" Her voice rose. "Those are vicious."

I looked at Conan, who still wiggled his way forward, held back by my firm hand on his leash. "Yep. Vicious," I agreed. "C'mon, hound." I tugged him away from the object of his infatuation.

"I needed to talk to you, too," Henrietta said, sidling away from me and my vicious attack canine. She insinuated herself next to Ike, neatly separating him from my mother, who leveled a look at her that would have cut Henrietta off at the knees had Mom's eyes been weapons. "I spoke to Mr. Franklin, Uncle Charles' lawyer. We're examining his will this afternoon."

I belatedly remembered my manners even though Henrietta didn't appear to be mournful. "I was sorry to hear about your uncle's death," I said, keeping Conan firmly restrained. "I'm glad to know you're continuing with his wishes and allowing the endowment to go forward."

Henrietta clung to Ike's arm, her eyes fixed on Conan with fascinated dread. Conan, sensing her interest, struggled against the leash to meet this person who was obviously curious about him. "That's why I wanted to talk to you," she said. "Nothing can be done with the land until the will is read and probated. So there's no use proceeding with your plans for a sanctuary until the legalities are ironed out. It might take months."

"What?" I pulled gently on Conan's lead but my puppy was anxious to meet this fascinating person who kept staring at him. "I'm not sure I understand."

Henrietta pressed hard against Ike, who put his arm around her shoulder, tucking her against his body. She appeared to be trembling, just like Conan, who was so anxious to meet her he was slowly pulling me toward her.

"He won't hurt you, Henrietta," Ike said softly. "He's just a puppy. He wants to be friends."

She shuddered, a reaction which caused her ample bosom to press even more firmly against Ike's arm. "I hate animals," she said in a low, hissing sort of voice.

"That's a very sweeping statement," Mom said. "Most animals are quite benign and are capable of living with humans very harmoniously. It's humans who have created the problems. Charlie talked about it often. He was a passionate believer in animal rights."

Henrietta leveled a contemptuous look at Mom. "That's ridiculous."

Mom turned to face her adversary and drew herself up to her full five-foot-seven. "I beg your pardon?" she said in a carefully modulated voice.

Ike recognized a potential firefight. I was perfectly willing to let my mom tear a strip of verbal skin off Henrietta, but he was less bloodthirsty than me. "I'm sure Henrietta meant she was only surprised to hear it." He looked at Henrietta, who glared at my mom as though she was the anti-Christ.

Henrietta's frown turned to a simpering smile when she noticed Ike's attention. "I'm stunned. My uncle and I discussed his..." She paused as if searching for a suitable word, "...his odd idea about donating land for a wildlife sanctuary. He admitted he was swayed into considering the notion but he had very serious second thoughts." She shot Mom a malevolent look.

Mom rapped the brick sidewalk with her cane, reminding me of a battle general who tapped a map where X marked the target zone. "I spoke to Charlie the day before he died. He was adamant about donating the land."

"And I talked to him on the day he died and he told me would not donate the land," Henrietta countered.

"We had an agreement," I said, taking a step forward. "Your uncle was going to donate four hundred acres of land for a big cat animal sanctuary."

"A verbal agreement." Henrietta eyed Conan, who strained to reach her expensive leather boots. "Keep that animal away from me."

I loosened my grip on the leash and Conan surged ahead one doggy-baby-step. "It is not just a verbal agreement. I have his commitment in writing." I was chairwoman of the Wild Cat Freedom Committee, formed for the express purpose of using Charlie Baron's land to create a sanctuary for exotic animals who had lived their lives as someone's misguided idea of a pet.

"A commitment is not the same as a legal agreement. Once the will is probated, I'll have the opportunity to put the land to good use." Henrietta raised her chin in defiance. The way she turned brought her face into full sunlight, an unfortunate move because it revealed her poor makeup job. I was a connoisseur of cosmetics after my years in the industry and Henrietta's heavy-handed use of foundation was blotchy.

"How long will that take?" Mom asked.

Henrietta glanced at her then shrugged. "It's up to the court. I discussed it with Uncle Charles' lawyer and we've started the process. So nothing can be done with the land until the court has processed his will."

"It doesn't matter," I said, praying I was right. "We have his commitment in writing."

"And I told you that's irrelevant."

"I'm sorry to hear there might be an issue with the land," Ike said in a calming, conciliatory voice while he gently disentangled himself from Henrietta's grasp. "From what Acie has said, I thought your uncle was all for donating the land. Although if there is nothing legally committing the land, I suppose you can do as you like."

"Stay out of this, Ike," I snapped. "I had an agreement with your uncle," I said, taking another step forward. "We were going to set up the legal trust next week."

Henrietta's well-mascaraed eyes widened at the sight of my puppy straining at his lead, his tongue lolling. "A developer is interested in buying it and putting up a very nice subdivision and the Beacon Golf Club wants part of the land for an extension to the golf course."

"That's stupid." I loosened my grip again, this time unintentionally, and Conan wiggled past Mom, just inches from Henrietta's boots. "Money isn't everything. We have the opportunity to make the land count for something besides McMansions and two-acre tracts of lawn. We can help fund an honest-to-God animal sanctuary, one that can change the lives of dozens of wild animals currently in abusive circumstances. That's worth more than any money."

"Over my dead body," Henrietta said in a wavering voice, edging away from the canine nose seeking her shoes. She grabbed Ike's arm, dragging him with her.

"Don't tempt me," I warned.

"Acie, calm down." Ike shook off Henrietta and interposed himself between Conan and her, tucking the woman behind the bulk of his body. "Henrietta, we need to talk about this later. Acie has class and I have an appointment with a student." He turned and started to usher Henrietta back to the building.

"You can't block this sale, Dr. Doyle," Henrietta said, allowing Ike to steer her away from Conan and me while talking over her shoulder. "It would cost you a fortune to try."

"Just watch," I snarled.

"It will never happen. Not after what happened to my uncle. You just wait and see. I'll make sure that land is never used for some animal sanctuary."

Mom leveled her cane at Henrietta like a weapon. "What are you saying? What are you talking about? What do you mean, after what happened to him?"

"He was killed by a dog," Henrietta said, her voice venomous. Her eyes welled with tears when she regarded Conan, whose tail was going full-tilt in a *hello, let's be friends,* rhythm. "They found paw prints near Uncle Charles' body."

Chapter 2

I laughed out loud at Henrietta's dramatic pronouncement. "Prove it." I pulled Conan back to me and turned to go to my class.

"I will," Henrietta said, her voice rising. "You haven't heard the end of this. I'll make sure those stray dogs running loose out there are rounded up and taken care of. You wait and see."

I glanced back at her, startled by her hateful tone. Ike was between me and her, holding his hands up in a placating gesture. "You're crazy," I said. "Those dogs have lived on that tract of land for years and never harmed anyone or anything."

"That's not what I heard." Henrietta was speaking so fast she stuttered. "The leader—he's vicious. That's what I was told. They're wild dogs and they should be captured and put down."

"Moriarty is just protective of the pack," I said, thinking of the grizzled pack leader who was mostly Rottweiler and part German Shepherd. He could be vicious if backed into a corner, but I wasn't going to admit it to Henrietta. "They're all abandoned pets. They've had all their vaccinations and they're neutered. The farmers out near the woods make sure they're fed and have shelter in the winter. They aren't harming anyone. Just let them live out their lives in peace. God knows humans haven't given them any breaks." I took a step forward. Mom put a restraining hand on my arm, but I barely noticed.

Henrietta leaned toward me, her face a mask of fury. "They're strays and they should be shot."

I threw caution to the wind and let my grip on the leash slacken. Conan bounded joyfully forward. Henrietta gave an ear-splitting shriek and whirled, but her fashionable boots weren't made for such quick footwork. She tripped on the uneven bricks of the sidewalk, landing on her butt in the grass.

Conan barked happily, liking nothing more than a romp on the lawn. Ike shot me a reproving look and hurried to help Henrietta, who cowered, whimpering. Her arms were crossed over her head like she expected an attack from a vicious pack of wild dogs instead of an enthusiastic puppy.

Mom burst out laughing and I almost joined in, but I was still so pissed off my laugh came out more like a strangled gurgle. I made a grab for Conan who was pushing past Ike, trying to give Henrietta a good licking.

"It's okay, Henrietta," Ike said, kneeling next to her on the grass, putting himself between Conan and her. "He's just a puppy."

"Get it away from me!" Her shrill voice seemed to echo off the buildings around us. Startled passersby paused to watch the melee. "Stop it! It's attacking me!"

"Oh, for heaven's sake, grow up." I grabbed Conan's collar and tugged him back. "He's just a puppy. He's not hurting you."

Henrietta was sobbing, curled into a fetal ball on the lawn, her hands over her face. Ike knelt next to her. "It's okay," he said, gently touching her shoulder. "The dog's gone."

Henrietta peeked over her hands at him and I repressed a laugh. Her eye makeup was starting to meld over her face, making her into a ghoulish clown, like something from a Stephen King movie. "I can't believe she's allowed to bring that dog to campus," she gasped.

Ike rubbed Conan's head. "He's a good dog, usually, although sometimes his owner is less than strict." I saw a hint of mischief in Ike's blue eyes. "You're late for class."

I pulled Conan away from the slobbering woman. "I'll talk to you later, Henrietta. You haven't heard the last of this." I turned right and stalked to Devon Hall, two buildings away.

"She can't do this," Mom fumed, keeping pace with me.

"She's doing it." I glanced back to see Henrietta clinging to Ike, her face against his sweater. Her eyes met mine and I thought I saw malicious glee in their cold gray depths. Then Ike said something, his face bent to hers and she changed magically into a woeful, lost soul.

"I'll testify in court," my mother said. "Charlie was dedicated to the idea of having a sanctuary."

"I know. He and I talked about it just last week." I was so mad I could barely articulate the words. I'm not sure which made me madder—the fact that Ike was duped by that witch, or that the witch was putting our animal sanctuary in jeopardy. "I can't believe she's considering selling the land. It's not good for houses. It's too near the flood plain. A builder would have to come in and bulldoze everything then build it all back up again. And add an extension to the golf course?" I almost sneered overtly. "It's so hilly only a goat could use it." I was starting to marshal my arguments, going over all the objections I could formulate. "I need to call the other committee members. I'll do it right after class."

"I can do it," Mom volunteered. "I have the roster. Do you want to have them over to your house tonight to discuss it?"

I paused at the walkway leading to Devon Hall. "No, that won't be necessary. We have the town meeting tomorrow and we already know what we're saying. Just let them know about this glitch Henrietta is trying to toss at us."

"Will do," Mom said, tapping the sidewalk again with her cane. "This is an emergency." She hurried off to the parking lot behind the building, surprisingly spry for an elderly woman. Of course, she was an elderly woman on a mission, propelled by anger.

Conan and I entered the five-story stucco and brick building in front of us. I tried to push my anger to the back of my mind. I had twelve graduate students waiting to discuss British Victorian Writers, with today's focus on Tennyson and Browning.

I was, luckily, not essential to today's class. The students, PhD candidates all, were happy to take the metaphorical ball and run with it, avidly positing assorted theories about themes and motifs. A spirited discussion ensued about the intersection of politics, religion, spirituality, literature, and Victorian repression, something that helped take my mind off my present-day woes.

When I emerged two hours later, the sun was setting behind the shadowed bulk of the Union. I was beginning to put Henrietta and her histrionics into perspective. I had several witnesses to Charlie's assertion that he would donate the land plus his written statement saying he wanted to use the land for the animal sanctuary. I was sure his statement would trump any claims Henrietta could make.

I unearthed my iPhone from my bag and turned it on. It immediately informed me I had received a text message while I had the device turned off during class.

Committee called S and me your house 7 Mom

I presumed it meant Mother had spoken to the Committee members and she and my aunt would be coming to my house at seven o'clock. Mom wasn't very good with texting and punctuation was usually beyond her grasp.

Conan and I strolled under dark red-brown oak trees to the parking lot adjacent to Baker Hall, savoring the tart autumn air. I wasn't in a hurry. I had one class tomorrow at eleven and although I had a stack of research waiting for me as well as the aforementioned papers to grade, I also knew I had enough free time to tackle the problem of Henrietta and her refusal to honor her dead uncle's request.

The campus was quiet because most classes wrapped up by five and night classes didn't start until seven. The startling red maples were a stark contrast to the green of the grass and the fading blue of the sky. They were graceful reminders of how pristine this campus really was.

Des Moines, Iowa's largest urban center, was just fifty miles to our west, but it may as well have been on another planet. I felt a rush of affection for this quiet, small corner of the world. Stoneyburst wasn't a big research campus or a bustling metro university, but was rather a quaint, timeless bit of Americana where you expected to see Jimmy Stewart in a bowtie talking to Claudette Colbert in bobby sox. It was unchanged and calm, a beautiful haven in a buzzing electronic world.

Despite the charm, we weren't antiquated, by any means. All students were issued iPads on their first day of class and the entire campus hummed with WiFi. But it was an addition, not a replacement, to our serene surroundings.

I strapped Conan into his doggy seat belt in the back seat of my Toyota sedan and we drove east then north on Plymouth Road, a pretty boulevard paralleling Main Street which ran north and south. A mile or so north of the college, I drove past the intersection to Briony Lane. Ike lived four blocks west on Briony, a quiet and short dead end street backing onto a cemetery.

Just to the north of Ike was an acre or two of empty land, some of it marshy and part of it a gravel quarry. By an odd quirk of fate, I lived north of that empty land, on Norwood Street, an equally quiet dead-end street. My house was on a hill, facing south over the gravel quarry. Ike and I were separated by a mile of hilly land. At night I could see the lights of his house in the distance.

I turned onto my street and drove past the Siblings Streets on my right: Kingsley, Percy, Adrian, and Annette, streets named after the children of the farmer who originally owned the land. The road ended at my small one-level house, painted a deep brown-red with lighter brown trim.

I adored my home, the plans for which I purchased from a sketch I saw in the newspaper, one of the

"Homes of the Week." I found a builder who was willing to position the home just-so on the lot to take advantage of the southern light, so I often was able to use passive solar heating because walls of windows faced the empty land between me and Ike. The house was bordered by trees with just a few flower beds near the foundation and a small patch of lawn in front and in back to mow. Unlike Ike, I had a black thumb, not a green one, and I didn't enjoy gardening. A few shrubs, a few pots of flowers, and I was satisfied.

I drove into the garage and Conan and I entered the house via the mud room/laundry room. He paused to check his food dish and I continued on, passing the door to the spare bedroom on my left and my bedroom on the right until I got to the living room and the small den positioned off to one side.

I left my briefcase there then started a fire in the fireplace shared by the living room and den. Houdini, my portly blond cat, looked up from his spot on the hassock, yawned then returned to dozing. He was getting on in years and very little stirred him from sleep any more.

Just when I had that thought, the 'very little which stirred him' entered the room from her perch in the window in my den. Sprite, a year-old female tabby kitten, bounced across the wood floor to me, mewing in her insistent treble voice.

Houdini watched her through slitted eyes, pretending to be asleep. She paused, put her paws up on the hassock to sniff him, licked his head then bounded away again, all in the blink of an eye. Houdini sighed and tucked his head under his paw.

Conan ambled out to join Sprite, sniffing carefully

at her to make sure no one had switched cats on him while he was gone. She wove in and out of his legs, and thus escorted, I entered my kitchen when my landline phone rang. I plucked the receiver from the handset on the wall. "Doyle residence."

"Annabelle Clarinda? Is that you? How are you?" a bantering voice inquired. "Are you still the prettiest girl in town?"

I straightened in surprise at the sound of someone I hadn't talked to in decades. "Paul? Is that you? Really?"

"How did you know? Did you recognize my voice?" he teased.

"No, you're the only person who ever called me Annabelle Clarinda," I said. "I discouraged everybody else who tried."

He laughed, a big belly laugh I remembered so well, the belly laugh matching his big belly. Paul Wardlock was my agent when I was a clothing model, lo those many years ago. We stayed in sporadic touch via Christmas cards and an occasional email, but I hadn't talked to him in years.

His voice lost its bantering edge and settled down to his business-as-usual tone. "Listen, I just wanted to touch base with you. Are you interested in a modeling gig?"

I opened the wine cooler and pulled out an opened bottle of Pinot. "Are you serious?" I wedged the phone between my shoulder and ear while I got a wine glass from the rack near the wine fridge. "What kind of gig?"

"Remember the pictures you sent me last year? When I asked you to update your portfolio?"

I managed a wary, "Sure. Why?"

"I shopped them around. You're a hot commodity, Acie. Everybody's looking for older models now. All those Baby Boomers are growing up and they want hot older babes to represent them. You didn't cut your hair since then, did you?" he asked. "It's still long, right?"

"No, I didn't cut my hair. You know as well as I do that I can't style my hair worth a damn. It's easier to have it long."

"Thank God. There is a huge demand for sexy older babes with long hair."

"Even long white hair?" I asked in disbelief. "Seriously?"

"Seriously. Are you ready to get back in the game? There's a shoot coming up that's perfect."

"Holy mackerel." I poured my wine with a slightly trembling hand. "A job?"

"Not just one job, honey," Paul said. "I can probably get you full-time work if you come back. What do you say?"

"I'm not sure," I said. "I have a full-time job here."

Paul snorted. "Making what—sixty thousand a year? I can get you more than that. Trust me."

I had no doubt he could. Paul negotiated several very lucrative contracts for me in the past. "I'll consider it, I guess. Can you email me the details?"

"How about I call you tomorrow and we'll talk? I'm serious, honey. You can make good money. They've been calling me. They want you for this shoot. A rep from Ford called and asked me if the Iowa Girl was still modeling." He laughed again. "You and your Iowa reputation for hard work and fair play."

I let his hyperbole roll past me. Paul was good at exaggeration, but he had to be because he was an agent.

"Why don't I give you a call next week?"

"Can you make it sooner? They really want you. Don't let this chance slip by."

I considered my schedule. I had class tomorrow and I had to make a speech at the town meeting late in the afternoon. I didn't have time to think about a modeling gig until after the meeting. "Call me on Saturday around noon." That would be mid-afternoon for me and should give me plenty of time to consider his proposal. I gave him my cell phone number and home email address. "Send me the details if you can ahead of time so I can read through it."

"Sure, sure. There's one thing, kid."

I swallowed my wine. "There always is with you, Paul. What is it?"

"They want to do the shoot at your campus there." He hurried on when I started to protest. "It's a back to school issue. You'll be the mom taking the kid to college. It's a big spread in a national magazine. I can't tell you which one until you sign."

"My campus? Why here?" I was already arranging my arguments against it. I couldn't do a modeling gig at my place of employment. The faculty would never let me live it down, and Lord knows what effect it would have my students. "Why not go to Notre Dame or someplace fancy like that?"

"It's a Midwest magazine," Paul said. "The model they have for the daughter character visited the campus a few years ago. She dated a guy from out that way and they went to a football game there or something. She talked about how it was perfect. And the Production Coordinator for the shoot noticed how this model they're using looks like a younger you. You know the

PC—it's Laurie Lyons. You worked with her a few times. So they called me. They really want you and the wholesome charm angle."

I almost groaned aloud. I had just been mentally lauding the "wholesome charm angle of my college" and here it was being used against me. "I doubt if the administration will want to have—"

"They've already approved it. Laurie got in touch with the Dean or CEO or whoever runs the place. It's all set for the weekend after this. They want to start shooting a week from now and work through the weekend if necessary."

"Next weekend? They're working fast."

"Actually, not. They've been planning it for a month or two. They just decided on the location this week and that's when I was called."

I swallowed more wine as my mind raced, considering my schedule. "I have to think about it. I'm out of town all next week at a conference, Paul. I don't know if I can do it."

"When do you get back?"

"I leave on Tuesday and get home on Friday."

"They want to start shooting on Friday afternoon. Can you get back by then?"

"I'm not sure. It's a three hour drive from Chicago and I had planned to have lunch with friends at the conference. There's also an event here on campus on that Friday night. I have to make an appearance and give a speech."

"We can work around it. It's a great chance to get back in the business. Try to make it work, okay?"

"We'll see," I said, but I already knew I'd have to turn him down. There was no way I could do a modeling job on campus.

"Talk to you later."

I hung up the phone, staring at the small LED screen thoughtfully. "I never figured to return to modeling," I said to Conan, who watched me curiously. "I figured those days were long behind me."

I thought about it while I microwaved leftover homemade soup for supper. It was certainly tempting to pick up a modeling job here and there. The pay was good, and the work was easy for me. I was one of the lucky ones. I never had to diet, my complexion was excellent, and I wore clothes well, with a minimum amount of fuss or adjustments. When I left the business two decades before, I left behind a lot of friends and no enemies that I knew of. It would probably be easy to slip back into my old life.

I finished my meal then went to my bedroom and took off my school clothes. I paused to examine myself in the mirror before grabbing my jeans. I was as slender as ever thanks to good genetics, a love of healthful food and a dislike of fast food, and a rigorous yoga and aerobic exercise program I followed faithfully. Gravity hadn't taken a great toll on me since I was small-breasted to start with and my butt was still where it should be.

Of course, I had the typical hail damage of age with dimpling on my thighs, but it wasn't too bad. And I had a few lines around my eyes and mouth, and my chin probably wasn't as tight as before, but all in all, I could probably step back into the spotlight again and be happy with the results.

I pulled on faded jeans and a red V-neck sweater, slipping my feet into my worn Sock Monkey slippers before going back to the living room. It faced south and was starting to get dark. I switched on a lamp, refilled my wine, then went to my den to watch the sunset and read email.

I skimmed through various messages from the four Sanctuary committee members, most of which reflected disbelief and/or outrage. I already had my miniscule speech prepared for the town meeting to be held on the following night, but a couple of members had interesting points. I jotted notes for consideration later.

I turned my attention to the email from Paul. *Photo Shoot, October, Grimper, Iowa*. The headline at the top of the contract page was bold, italic, and large, emphasizing how unusual it was to be doing a major shoot in Nowhere, Iowa. I had done jobs in cemeteries, subways, atop buildings, in fields, and on boats, but had never done one on a college campus.

I could already see it shaping up in my mind. The football stadium and the area around it teemed with tailgaters on football Saturdays. The gorgeous fall foliage, the haze of barbeque in the air, the bright-faced people all waiting for the game—it was a perfect representation of an American way of life.

"No way," I muttered. I could also easily imagine what my staid peers would say if they found out I was modeling in a fashion layout. Joel Harris, professor of American Southern fiction, would probably grin and make a droll comment about *the deathless beauty of our distinguished colleague*, spoken in a Faulkneresq voice. Edie Warden, the grande dame of Women's Fiction, would undoubtedly pull me aside and discuss, very seriously, the exploitation of the female form in today's society. Ted Dreyser, associate professor of early 20th century American fiction, would probably ask me to set him up with one of the other models, preferably one younger than me. Ted was notorious for his wandering eye.

Nope. I wasn't going to open myself up to potential problems with my faculty mates. I was just granted tenure two years earlier, and I wasn't going to jeopardize my position. If the shoot was held at a different campus, then, maybe. But here?

"Won't happen," I told Sprite, who sat on the window ledge staring at the back yard and the birds clustered around my feeder.

I clicked open the next email from Paul. This was a PDF file containing rough sketches of what the Production Coordinator and the Location Scout had in mind for the shoot, probably after discussing it with the photographer who was hired. I printed the file and carried it and the contract with me to the living room.

I curled up on my couch and skimmed through the shoot summary, making notes in the margin. Although the scout had done homework, some of the setups he suggested just wouldn't work given the way the ground sloped or given the colors of the buildings or the surroundings. A person could only glean so much information from a college catalog or Google maps. There was nothing like having first-hand experience with a site.

I heard a car pull into the drive and the telltale sound of a key in the front door lock, fumbled by an elderly woman. I was just getting to my feet when I heard my mother's breezy, "We're coming in!" from the entryway.

Conan bounded out to greet the new arrivals,

followed closely by Sprite, who moved like a streak of gray fur. "Beware the kitten!" I called as I hurried to the front door.

"Gotcha," I heard my Aunt Sherry say. I rounded the corner to my small entry hall in time to see my mother tussling with Conan, restraining him from dashing out the front door, and my Aunt Sherry clasping Sprite to her chest.

"I swear, these two act like they're in a prison and every time the door opens, there's a chance to escape," Mom said, relinquishing her hold on Conan's collar to me.

I closed the door behind the two old ladies and shooed Conan back to the living room. "Conan was fine until Sprite decided the Big Outdoors is exciting." I moved to Aunt Sherry to help her extract Sprite, but the old lady beat me to it, deftly dropping the kitten to the entryway rug. Sprite took off running and Conan burst after her, sliding on the wood floor in his haste. I laughed at the sight of his cartoon-like antics when he scrambled for footing.

Sherry straightened her red cardigan sweater, which now bore tell-tale snags of a kitten's claws. I didn't mention it because I knew if I apologized for my pets, she'd wave it away. We had such talks in the past and Sherry always dismissed my concerns without batting an eyelash.

She was my father's sister and like Dad she was slender and angular, with a long, oval face, sharp gray eyes, and wavy gray hair that frequently had a mind of its own. When Mom left Dad and me behind, Aunt Sherry stepped in and helped raised me until she, too, left town after marrying Jonathan Holms.

When Uncle Jon died, he left Aunt Sherry well-off and disinclined to marry again. She came back to Grimper and settled down to a very active social life of bridge clubs, golf league, and charitable works. "A woman needs a man like a fish needs a bicycle," she often said, and while I sometimes agreed, I often wondered if she ever rued her single life all those years. Of course, I had been single most of my life except for a brief six years of marriage, and I had nothing to rue, so I guess I didn't need to question her.

Despite my mother's desertion years before, she and my mother were good friends. I asked Sherry about it once and she said, "When you get old, dear, you tend to forgive a lot of things you would never have forgiven in your youth. I suppose it's because friends are hard to find in later years." I admired her ability to forgive, because it's a trait I've never mastered.

Aunt Sherry and my mother headed for the living room. "I can't believe Charlie's niece is raising such a fuss. I swear to God, the woman has the brains of a gnat. We have Charlie's signed intention to use the land for an animal sanctuary. What does that hoity-toity bitch think she's up to?" Mom gave me a perfunctory kiss on the cheek then regarded me with exasperation, as if I was responsible for Henrietta's idiocy.

"She wants the money," Sherry declared, heading for the liquor cabinet near the kitchen entrance.

The ornate old cabinet was one of the few pieces of furniture from my father, and I occasionally wondered if mother remembered it from the house she and Dad shared. If she did, she never commented on it. She pulled out the bottle of Maker's Mark and took a highball glass from the shelf above the liquor bottles.

Aunt Sherry shook her head slightly at Mom's choice of toddy. "She's had a bad day," she murmured to me in a low voice. "This thing with Charlie has come as a blow." She gave Houdini a rub on the head and my portly cat looked up, yawned then resumed napping.

"I heard that," Mom said, pouring a straight shot of whiskey.

"Then I guess your hearing is still good." Sherry elbowed Mom aside and pulled out a bottle of Argentinian port. "I think I'll have a little toddy," she said, which was the same thing she always said when she came over.

"It's come as a shock to everybody," I said.

"Yes, but your mother and Charlie had a special relationship." Sherry took a cordial glass and poured a healthy dollop of the dark ruby port. She took one long sip then filled the glass again. "That hits the spot. Charlie knew how important the sanctuary was to your mother."

I went to get my wine glass to cover my surprise. I had no idea the sanctuary was important to my mother. I always had the impression she was humoring me and just going along with Charlie. I was saved from further discussion when someone knocked on the door. I went to answer, keeping an eye out for Sprite, but she and Conan were nowhere to be seen.

I opened the door and Ike smiled at me. "What are you doing here?" I asked.

"Thank you for your warm welcome." He tried on a hurt expression but the mischievous look in his blue eyes told me he wasn't truly upset.

"You know what I mean," I said, closing the door behind him. "After today's altercation with—" I almost said *your girlfriend* but said instead, "Henrietta, I would think I'm *persona non gratis*."

"Henrietta and I talked after you left," he said, edging past me. He held up a bottle of wine. "A peace offering. I told her I'd come here and talk to you."

"About what? Her need to make a bunch of money by selling out to the highest bidder?" I ignored the wine and backed up to let him enter the house.

"From what she told me, it might be *a lot* of money," Ike said. "At least listen to what I have to say on her behalf. You don't want this to end up in court."

"We've spent a lot of time and effort on gathering the information we need to get a sanctuary built," I said, going back to the living room. "There's no way I'm going to let an outsider come in here and toss up a bunch of ticky-tacky houses on land perfectly suited to a sanctuary."

Ike followed me into the room. "Good evening, ladies." He paused to smile at my mother and my aunt, who were now ensconced in the two armchairs nearest the wall of windows.

Sherry regarded him with cool evaluation over the rim of her port glass. She had told me on previous occasions that she considered Ike too handsome and too good-natured for belief, and sometimes I agreed with her. "Good evening, Professor Adler." She inclined her head like a queen greeting a subject.

"Acie didn't mention you were coming," Mom said. "Are we intruding?"

"Ike came to give us Henrietta's side of the story," I grumbled, unaccountably irritated by the thought.

"Oh, what a pity," Mom murmured.

The doorbell rang. "Now what?" I went to answer

it and found a uniformed police officer on my stoop. He seemed about the same age as most of my graduate students. He frowned when he saw me and straightened his shoulders.

"Ms. Annabelle Doyle?" he demanded, glancing at a piece of paper in his hand.

"Dr. Doyle," I corrected. "Yes?"

"I'm Officer Edward George, with the Grimper P.D. A complaint was filed about your dog's behavior." His gaze shifted to Conan, who had meandered out to see who was at the door. "A citizen claims your dog attacked her. He has to be quarantined for examination." The officer put his hand on his holster to emphasize his point.

Conan lunged forward.

Chapter 3

"Come back here," I said, grabbing Conan's collar. I dragged the wagging puppy away from the officer, who had taken a step back, his hand still on his gun. "He's just a puppy."

"It's a bulldog," Officer George said. "They can be ferocious."

"That's ridiculous," I snapped. "What kind of complaint?" I knew who the instigator was, of course. That bitch.

"Miss Baron states your dog attacked her this afternoon. She said he's a vicious animal." Officer George stared at Conan, who was scratching vigorously at his left ear.

"He didn't attack anyone," I said with what I felt was admirable calm. "He was merely trying to make friends with that—" I took a deep breath. "That woman."

"What's going on?" Aunt Sherry came into the entryway, port glass in hand. "Why is a cop here, Acie?"

"He says a complaint was filed about Conan." I was seething but attempted to keep my voice level and calm. "He says Conan is vicious."

Sherry looked at my puppy who now sat patiently at my left side, restraining his puppy curiosity at the sight of this stranger on his doorstep.

"That's stupid." Sherry pushed past me to confront Officer George, who was considerably larger and taller than her. He took a step back from my five-foot-six, one-hundred-thirty pound aunt. "Why are you wasting time harassing a poor innocent dog? You should be investigating a murder."

"A murder? What? When?" The officer's hand tightened on his gun butt and I had visions of my aunt merrily leading one of Grimper's Finest to Charlie Baron's house to discuss her "clues."

"Charlie was murdered," Sherry said. "I'm sure of it."

"Why?" Ike had come up behind us and now crowded into the entryway with Sherry and me.

I plucked the paper from Officer George's hand. "Is this it? Is this the complaint?" I turned to Ike. "Your friend, Henrietta, is lodging a complaint about Conan."

"If there's been a murder, you need to report it." The officer tried to grab the paper from me, but I held it out behind me.

Ike took the paper and skimmed it. "There seems to be a misunderstanding, Officer. I was there. The puppy didn't bite anyone."

"He could have, though," the officer insisted.

"So could I, but I didn't," Ike said. "Miss Baron is just upset. Let me talk to her and I'm sure we can straighten all this out."

"This is my problem, Ike, not yours," I protested.

"It's my problem, too, Acie, if it's Henrietta's problem. She always brings her problems to me."

My protest died on my lips. I guess it confirmed what everyone was saying. Henrietta and Ike were a Real Item. *What a waste,* I thought. *Ike is too good for her*. But I kept my thoughts to myself. Ike was only a colleague, after all, and he probably wouldn't appreciate my opinions.

The young officer seemed unsure of himself, his gaze going from me, to Conan, then to Ike. "I'll wait until tomorrow and if Miss Baron hasn't pressed charges, then we'll forget this incident. For now," he said with warning look at me. Then his gaze shifted to Aunt Sherry. "You shouldn't be making accusations if you have no proof. If you know a murder was committed, then you—"

"Thank you," I said, stepping back to close the door. "Good night."

"Murder is a serious crime and if evide—"

The young officer's voice was cut off in mid-word when I closed the door. I turned to face my crowded foyer and found Sherry glaring at me. "What?"

"All the clues point to murder," she said.

"What clues?" Ike asked.

"That's not the most important thing on my agenda right now," I said, going back into the living room. Sherry and Ike followed me, Conan tagging after Aunt Sherry because she was the Giver of Treats whenever she was in charge of pup-sitting.

I refilled my wine glass from the bottle on the kitchen counter and sat on the couch. "Right now I need to find a way to prove the land was slated to be used for a sanctuary." I saw Ike standing near the liquor cabinet and I gestured toward the glasses. "Help yourself."

He took a wine glass and filled it from my bottle in the kitchen then came to sit next to me, dropping the legal paper from the police officer on the coffee table next to my printouts from Paul. Sherry resumed her seat, shooting little glares at me the whole time.

"Henrietta has gotten good offers from developers for the land," Ike said. "Another nine holes added to the golf course with houses surrounding it makes for a lucrative land deal. There's several hundred acres of Baron's land plus other homeowners have said they'll sell, too. Most of it is usable for a course. It takes about one hundred acres for nine holes on a course."

"How do you know that?" Mom asked.

Ike propped his right ankle on his left knee and leaned back. He appeared totally at home. "My cousin is a landscape architect and he helped design a course in Kansas City."

"None of it would be useful as an addition to our golf course." My righteous indignation was bubbling over. "This town can barely keep a nine-hole course in business."

"Ah, but an eighteen-hole course with a nice clubhouse might attract people from Des Moines. People are getting priced out of clubs there. We're less than an hour's drive away. Some city people might enjoy joining a small town club. And a nice home on a golf course is often the dream of many people. The city fathers are always looking for a way to make Grimper more attractive to people. Don't underestimate it."

We were all silent, considering what he said. Sprite chose that moment to sidle into the room, ostentatiously avoiding looking at Ike, who was one of her favorite people. On all of his previous visits to my house, Sprite ended up sprawled on his lap, purring madly. Of course, she was a shameless hussy of a cat and had no principles when it came to affection but I found her magnetic attraction to Ike unusual, even for her. She wandered over to Houdini, who regarded her warily, one eye slitted slightly open to keep tabs on her.

"What's your interest in this, Dr. Adler?" Sherry glanced at me when she said it. I shrugged slightly, telling her I had no idea where she was going with her line of questioning.

Ike shifted position, putting his left ankle on his right knee. "Like I told Acie, when Henrietta has a problem, it often becomes my problem." He smiled but it seemed forced to me. Sprite jumped up on the back of the couch and paused near Ike to sniff his hair. He turned to look at her and our eyes met. Then Sprite oozed onto his shoulder and his face was hidden by a tabby kitten's stripes.

"I was checking Facebook just this afternoon," Sherry said. "Henrietta Baron posted she's going to Switzerland this winter, to ski."

I almost dropped my wine glass. "You're Facebook friends with Henrietta?"

"You have a Facebook account?" Ike asked.

"Of course I do," Sherry said, sipping her port. "I doubt Henrietta knew who she was friending when she sent me a friend request. I think she sent friend requests to everyone who listed Grimper as their home town."

"I didn't get a friend request." I wasn't sure whether to be relieved or miffed. I decided to be relieved. I was finding Facebook to be a depressing exercise when I stacked my life against the lives of others who posted there. My life inevitably came up short by comparison.

"You have a rather obvious name, dear," Sherry said. "I'm sure Henrietta avoided you. I doubt she knew who I was."

"I know about Acie's Facebook account," Ike said. "It's DoyleDoesBooks. What's yours?" Sprite was now on his lap, stretched on his leg like a small limpet attached at the knee.

"Game Afoot," she said smugly.

I groaned at the pun. Ike looked puzzled. "It's her name," I said. "Sherry Holms. Sherlock Holmes." I shot my aunt a quelling stare. "And the fact she's quite the detective."

"Which brings us back to Charlie Baron's murder," Sherry said promptly.

"I'm curious about Henrietta's trip to Switzerland," my mother said, eyes focused on Ike. "You're going to Europe during the Christmas holiday break, aren't you, Dr. Adler?"

My stomach did a little flip-flop. I forgot about Ike's upcoming research trip to Italy and France.

Ike fidgeted again, re-propping his right ankle on his left knee and rearranging Sprite in the process. She took exception to his handling and bounded into the kitchen. "Yes, I am. Henrietta and I may meet up if our travels coincide." He took a swallow of wine, a dark blush on his cheeks.

Coincide? That sounded pretty lame. "Maybe we'll get lucky and Henrietta will fall off an Alp," I muttered.

Ike's eyes widened. "That's sort of harsh."

"She's a harsh sort of woman," I noted.

My mother quirked one eyebrow at me, something she did when I was guilty of violating a social rule of hers. I ignored it and picked up the document from the police officer. "Look at this. Lies, damn lies, and more lies." I skimmed through the legal jargon, all of which added up to *Your dog is a vicious mongrel and must be restrained.*

"Henrietta frequently over-reacts," Ike said. "I'm sure by tomorrow she'll be calmer."

"Not if I have my way." I tossed the paper back to the coffee table, but it fluttered to the floor. "Tomorrow's the town meeting and I plan to do everything I can to dissuade the voters from allowing her to put in a subdivision on the land."

Ike retrieved the damning legal paper, sliding it back on the coffee table. "What's this?" He picked up Paul's document. "You're going back in the modeling business?"

I tried to grab it away from him but he was too fast, turning so all I encountered was his right shoulder. I ended up pressed against his back, reaching for the email. I was somewhat surprised by how broad his shoulders were and how warm he was. "That's private," I said, pushing away from him. His aftershave was a faint and tantalizing fragrance, vaguely spicy.

"It was lying on the table," Mom said. "So it's not too private. You're going back into modeling?"

"No, I'm not. My agent has an offer I'm considering, that's all." I sipped my wine, cursing my stupidity in leaving such damning evidence lying around.

"They want to do a photo session here, on campus?" Ike asked, skimming the email.

"Yes, they do, and I told them absolutely not."

"Why not?" Sherry asked.

"Because I don't think it would be good for me to be modeling on campus."

Three sets of eyes regarded me with perplexed curiosity. Even Sprite peeked around the kitchen doorway at me.

"Why?" Ike asked.

"For heaven's sake," I said. "Can you imagine the reaction of my students if they find out I'm a model?"

Ike started to smile. "You'll probably get even more male students in your class than you usually get."

I turned to regard him, my back rigid. "I beg your pardon?"

"You mean you didn't know? You're a hottie, Dr. Doyle. Graduate guys just love your classes."

I opened my mouth to form a scathing retort, but my mother's giggles made me stop. "It's not funny, Mother," I said. "It's tough enough for a woman to gain respect. I don't need it being implied I'm getting by on my looks."

"No one is saying that," Ike said.

"It's what you said." I reached for my wine glass.

"It's not what he said," my mother said. "He said young men find you attractive."

"Men have always found you attractive, dear," Aunt Sherry said. "You're really quite beautiful. That's not important. What is important is Charlie Baron's death. I've been thinking about what happened today. Perhaps Henrietta was right. Perhaps those dogs were responsible for Charlie's death."

I took a swallow of wine. "I'm sure if Charlie was attacked by dogs we would have heard about it by now."

"I didn't say they attacked him. Maybe they scared him to death. Moriarty is a devil."

I held on to my frayed temper. Aunt Sherry had named the leader of the pack of feral dogs Moriarty, after the villain in the Holmes stories. This villain was a big dog who was sleek, muscular, and fearless.

"Charlie wasn't afraid of Moriarty," my mother said confidently. "He scared those dogs away more than once. In fact, he told me he bought one of those taser things, a stun gun. He said if a dog got near him, he'd give Moriarty a zap. No, something else killed Charlie."

"There's no evidence a dog had anything to do with Charlie Baron's death." I got up to refill my wine glass. "He probably had a heart attack."

The doorbell rang while I was returning to the living room. I set my glass on the coffee table. "Who could that be?" I grabbed Sprite when she made a mad dash for the door and thrust her into Ike's arms. "Be useful. Hold on to her." I stepped over his legs and hurried to the front door, peering through the glass side panel to check outside.

I sighed when I saw who was there and I considered not answering. But then a face peered back at me and I knew I was seen. I pulled open the door. "Good evening, Mr. Staples."

John Staples was a neighbor of Charlie Baron's and a self-professed neighborhood activist, who devoted his considerable free time to opposing the idea of an animal sanctuary. He reminded me of Mr. Rogers in blue jeans topped by a sagging navy blue sweater because he was tall, slender and bookish with thinning blond hair and an air of perpetual surprise. I think he was retired, though he appeared to be only in his forties or maybe fifties. He didn't work that I knew of, but he and his sister owned a house down the road from Charlie's farm.

He launched right into his arguments without so much as a *Sorry if I'm interrupting you.* "I wanted to see if you were going to drop your support for this ridiculous proposal because Miss Baron refuses to go along with your plan."

I slipped outside, partially closing the door so it wouldn't lock behind me just in case Ike didn't have a good grip on my kitten. "Her support is irrelevant."

"Think of the liability. Think of the insurance. Think of the publicity." He regarded me with an expression I think was supposed to appear desperate, but really looked cunning. "It would be devastating."

"Devastating? It would be great." I held up my hands, framing an imaginary news headline. "Town steps in to save animals, providing them with a new lease on life. Film at eleven."

"It's insane," he insisted. "Who would put wild animals so near a town?"

"Wild animals used to live there once," I pointed out. "Why not again? We'll be the town that gave abused and homeless animals a new chance at—"

"It's ridiculous. It's time we found a good use for the land. There are acres of woodland and meadow that could make a profit."

I crossed my arms and leaned against my screen door. It would make him a profit as well as Henrietta, since he had a home near there. If the property values went up near him, especially if the golf course was extended, then presumably his values would go up as well. "We should be preserving it, not parceling it out. We don't need more McMansions and swimming pools. We need more wild spaces and places where people can see nature, where people can know wild creatures have a chance to—"

"Miss Baron has assured me she has irrefutable

proof that her uncle did not agree to such a use for his land."

Miss Baron is full of shit. I restrained my immediate response. "And I have irrefutable proof he did agree. So I suppose it may require a legal solution. From what she said, nothing can be acted upon until the will is probated, and it won't happen immediately."

"It will all take time and money. You can't imagine that—"

I tuned him out and focused on a large dark blue sedan pulling up to the curb, parking behind Ike's sleek sports car. When I saw the woman who emerged from the front seat, I groaned. "Now what?" I muttered.

Staples turned. "Who's that?" he asked suspiciously.

"It's Dr. Bell. She's the President of the University, and thus my boss." I brushed by Staples. "You need to excuse me, Mr. Staples. I'm busy and I don't have time to talk now."

I ignored whatever he said in response. I met the middle-aged woman at the middle of my front walk. Her steel-gray hair, cut in an uncompromising bob, accented the sharp angles of her face and matched the dark gray dress she wore under a black cape. She was considerably shorter than me, probably only five-foot-three, but she exuded an air of confidence and calm when she took my outstretched hand.

"I hope I'm not intruding, Dr. Doyle." Dr. Bell gave my hand a brisk shake. "I'm on my way to an alumni fundraiser and I wanted to stop in and chat." She smiled perfunctorily at Staples.

"You're not intruding at all, Dr. Bell." I led the way to my front door, edging Staples aside as I did so.

"Mr. Staples was just leaving."

"I'm not done discussing this with you—" Staples said hotly.

"You'll have a chance to discuss everything tomorrow night at the town meeting. There's no use talking about it now and rehashing the same thing tomorrow." I opened the front door and ushered Dr. Bell into my house. I turned before closing the door to regard my unwanted visitor. "Good night, Mr. Staples."

I intercepted a look of such animosity I took an involuntary step back, distancing myself from him and almost treading on Dr. Bell. I hurriedly closed the door. "Can I take your coat?" I asked. "Would you care for a glass of wine?"

"A glass of wine would be lovely if it's no trouble." She slipped the black wool cape off her shoulders and handed it to me. "I'm not due at the fundraiser for a few minutes, and I'd welcome a chance to relax beforehand."

I hung up her outerwear in the hall closet then led the way out of the foyer and into the living room. "You know Dr. Adler, from my department, and I'd like to introduce my mother, Janelle Watson, and my aunt, Sherry Holms. Ladies, this is Dr. Josephine Bell, President of Stoneyburst College." I gestured to each of the old ladies in turn then went to the kitchen. "White wine, Dr. Bell? Red?"

"Whatever you have opened," she said, crossing the room to shake hands with my mother and my aunt. Then she turned and regarded Ike, who had risen to his feet, Sprite balanced precariously on his shoulder. "You appear to have a friend, Dr. Adler."

"She's rather clingy." He turned to me, imploring.

"I can't remove her without tearing my sweater apart."

I could understand his dilemma. I grabbed a treats can and rattled it. Sprite's ears swiveled at the sound and Houdini, still sacked out on the hassock, raised his head. "Come on, guys." I rattled the can again. "Let's go." I walked down the hall leading to the mud room. "Ike, can you get Dr. Bell a drink, please?"

"I will if the little hellion will—Whoa!"

I glanced back to see Sprite catapult herself off Ike's shoulder, bounce once on the back of the couch, ricochet off the couch arm then tangle with Houdini, who thumped off the hassock to waddle after me. Conan emerged from my den and padded after the felines, alert to the possibility of canine treats.

I doled out goodies near the food dishes then diverted Sprite with one of her favorite catnip toys, tossing it into the spare bedroom. She and Conan raced off to play and Houdini settled down for serious kibble eating. I returned to my guests to find Dr. Bell next to Ike on the couch, examining the papers Paul sent me.

"I see you know about the magazine that requested an opportunity to do a layout at the college," Dr. Bell said.

I retrieved my glass of wine and sat in the easy chair matching Houdini's hassock. "Yes, my agent contacted me earlier today. He said you agreed to the project."

Dr. Bell regarded me with calm impassivity, her pale gray eyes framed by rimless eyeglasses. She had been Stoneyburst's President for five years and in that time she ruthlessly evaluated then slashed programs, secured large endowments from three major donors, and worked with the Business Department to secure a large grant. She was tough, shrewd, and charismatic and was definitely a force to be reckoned with.

"Yes, I discussed it with the head of the magazine fashion department. She gave me the phone number of the photographer and I talked to him, too. I made it plain this was to be a tasteful project and I expected the campus to be shown in a positive light. He seemed to understand what was needed."

I wondered how the photographer reacted to being treated like a hired hand. Photographers often considered themselves as important, if not more so, than the clothes or the theme being presented. I had worked with the photographer they hired for this job before and he was relatively easy to work with, but I saw him pitch a fit a time or two in the past when he didn't get exactly what he wanted.

"It might be great publicity for the school," Ike said.

"They want to do a photo shoot here?" Mom asked. "At the school?"

I nodded. "Paul called me and said the modeling agency requested me for the shoot." I eyed Dr. Bell enquiringly. "I'm not sure what magazine it is. It's customary for it to be kept under wraps until all contracts are signed."

"I wouldn't even consider the idea until I was told what magazine it was." Dr. Bell sipped her wine. "It's what convinced me it was a fine idea." I noticed Ike had poured her a glass of the red wine he brought, not the white wine I was drinking. Knowing Ike's taste in wines, it was probably far superior to the bottle I opened.

I smiled uncertainly, silently encouraging her to

share the magazine's identity. "I beg your pardon?"

"It must be a good magazine," my mother said. "One that's tasteful."

"And obviously you wouldn't be involved in anything tacky or vulgar, my dear," Aunt Sherry said.

Dr. Bell gave both old ladies an approving nod. "Exactly. It's important that Stoneyburst be shown in the best light possible. This magazine has national circulation and it could give us well-deserved publicity."

"I haven't agreed to do it yet," I said. "I told Paul I needed to consider the proposal."

Dr. Bell's shoulders straightened and her chin raised slightly. "I wasn't aware you would have concerns about it. Are you not interested in doing this job?" Before I could answer, she said, "I don't want to influence your decision, of course. I was under impression you were interested."

I fumed inwardly while keeping a bland expression on my face. *Damn you, Paul. This has all the earmarks of one of your tricks.* I could well imagine him implying I would be happy to take the job, doing it in such a way so his words could easily be misconstrued. He was a master at the art of double-talk.

"I haven't thought about modeling for years. I'm not sure I'm right for the part. And I'm not sure it would be—" I hesitated, searching for the right word. "I'm not sure it would be appropriate for me."

"Appropriate?" Dr. Bell looked at my mother and Aunt Sherry, as if they could interpret my odd vocabulary.

"I mean, what would the students think if they found out a professor was modeling in a magazine?"

"They'd probably think it was cool," Aunt Sherry said.

"I think they say hip now," my mother said. "They'd think it was hip."

I opened my mouth to argue, but Dr. Bell beat me to it. "The magazine editor thought you were right for the part." She took another sip of her wine. "The woman was quite enthusiastic about your talent. I admit I was intrigued. I was unaware you were a model before you entered academe."

She made it sound like I had taken the veil and become a nun when all I had done was become a college professor. I forced a smile. "I modeled for a decade or so, right out of high school while I went to college to get my degrees. It's been a long time since I've been in front of a camera."

Dr. Bell set her glass on the coffee table and stood. I scrambled to my feet, as did Ike. "I hope you'll consider it, Dr. Doyle. I think it would be nothing but positive publicity for the school. Just imagine, photos taken at Homecoming, the Harvest Dance, on campus. It's all very good for our image."

"The Harvest Dance? The information I received didn't mention it."

"I mentioned it to the fashion editor today," Dr. Bell said, stepping around the coffee table. "She was very interested in the idea of using the dance in the layout. I think that's what she said."

I grasped at whatever straw I could find. "I'm scheduled to speak at the dance for the endowment ceremony."

"The editor assured me they wouldn't need to start their work until you were done." She regarded me with sharp curiosity. "It sounded like they wanted to do evening pictures, as well."

"I need to get the entire schedule to know what they have in mind," I said.

"She said they were finalizing the schedule soon." Dr. Bell glanced at her watch. "I'm sorry, but I need to go. I hate to keep the alumni waiting." Dr. Bell smiled at me, her plain face suffused with good cheer. "I do hope you'll consider it. The editor was very enthused about the whole idea."

Dr. Bell sounded enthused, too, probably by the fact she had hobnobbed with an editor at a national magazine. "I doubt if they'll want to do anything at the dance," I said. "Photographers tend to like very tightly controlled settings."

"Really?" Dr. Bell turned to my mother and Aunt Sherry. "It was nice to meet you."

"It's nice to meet you, too," Mother said. "It's good to meet my daughter's boss."

Dr. Bell smiled genially. "I suppose I am, although her department chairman is technically her real boss." She went to the doorway and I fell into step with her, Ike trailing behind us. "Yes, the editor thought the Harvest Dance might be a very nice venue, especially for the more dressy parts of this fashion layout. But I'm sure we'll find out for sure when or if they decide to do it here."

I took her cape from the closet, my head spinning from the direction this conversation had taken. Ike took the cape from me and held it for Dr. Bell. "Thank you, Dr. Adler," she murmured when he settled the fabric around her shoulders. "I hope you'll consider this project, Dr. Doyle," she said when I opened the door for her.

Ike moved behind me, keeping an eye on the hallway lest Sprite or Conan appear. I smiled gratefully at him. "I am considering it," I said. "Very seriously."

She turned to me. "Good." Her gaze went beyond me, to Ike. "Perhaps you can influence her, Dr. Adler." Then she turned and, with a swirl of her cape, she left.

I stared after her, dumbfounded. Ike leaned around me and closed the door. "Looks like your modeling career is back on track," he said with a smug smile.

Chapter 4

Ike left shortly after Dr. Bell and it wasn't until I poured myself another glass of wine that I realized he didn't give us Henrietta's side of the story, like he promised. I said as much to my mother.

"He probably forgot about it in the fuss about your modeling again," she said. "Besides, he can't truly give you her side of the story because he doesn't know it." She said this with the air of a woman who is the recipient of a deep confidence from a bosom friend. Since she and Henrietta knew each other only enough to snarl at one another, I doubted this.

"That's true," my aunt said.

I looked from her to my mother. "What do you mean? Is there a secret here I'm missing?"

"It's not much of a secret, of course." Mom sipped her whiskey. "Dr. Adler probably doesn't realize Henrietta has a peeve with you." She smiled brightly. "You're Henrietta's vendetta, I guess you could say."

"About what? The sanctuary?"

My mother waved an airy hand. It was an overly dramatic gesture, even for her, and I suspect the whiskey was making itself felt. "Not just that. She's jealous about your past life as a model. It seems so glamorous."

I snorted. "Long days in uncomfortable positions waiting for a photographer to get just the right shot." I framed an imaginary picture with my hands. "If she only knew."

"I suppose she still remembers you from high school, too," Aunt Sherry said quietly.

I shot her a quelling look but it wasn't fast enough. "What?" Mom demanded. "What about high school?"

"I think what Aunt Sherry is saying is that Henrietta may still regard me as the girl she used to know in high school." I kept my tone neutral, but it was hard. "After all, I was the daughter of the town drunk. It must be hard for Henrietta to reconcile that memory with who I am today."

Mom regarded me with her glass upraised and two bright spots of color on her cheeks. I seldom talked about what my life was like after she left and she had never asked for details. I suspect neither of us was anxious to open an old wound.

Aunt Sherry rushed to fill the silence. "And of course, there's how Dr. Adler feels about you, too. She's jealous. Although if you ask me, she should be equally worried about Meryl Staples. That woman has her eye on Dr. Adler."

I took a big slug of wine, which I needed after my evening visitors. The cops, an irate townsperson and my boss. I had more company tonight than I had in a week and…Aunt Sherry's words registered and I almost choked. "He? Ike? Feel about me?"

"Of course. You know, I'll bet Henrietta made her plans about traveling to Europe once she knew what his plans were." Sherry eyed me. "I could tell how upset you were that he's going to Europe at the same time as Henrietta. After all, you and he have been seeing each other."

I managed a credible incredulous look. "What?"

"You and Ike. You're seeing each other."

"We are not."

"Of course you are," Mom said. "You go out together, don't you?"

I shook my head. "Just because we go to a movie occasionally, it doesn't mean we're dating. I'm just surprised. I didn't know they'd be traveling together."

"He didn't say they were," Sherry pointed out.

"I assumed—"

"Never assume anything," my mother said. "Things aren't always what they seem."

"Exactly," I said. "Just because Ike and I go out now and again, it doesn't mean we're seeing each other."

"Right," my aunt said in the tone of voice older people reserve for elementary age children. "I still think it's low of her to involve Conan. I mean, really—to call the police."

"A vendetta," my mother said firmly. "That's what it is." She gestured to the modeling information on the coffee table. "You're going to do it, aren't you?"

"I don't know if I have much choice."

"I think you're worrying about nothing," Aunt Sherry said. "Students will probably shrug it off. They're far more blasé about those kinds of things nowadays."

I took another healthy swallow of wine while I gloomily considered her words. If this shoot went the same way others had gone in my past, there would be some work for me ahead of time but most of it wouldn't involve me. If they were going with the kid-at-college theme, then there might be a male model or two involved, plus the girl Paul mentioned who would act the part of my daughter, and maybe others as well. I started forming a checklist in my mind of things to do.

"…ready for your speech tomorrow?"

I realized my mother was speaking to me. "I'm sorry, what?"

"I said, are you ready for your speech tomorrow?"

"It's not much. I just have to say a few words in support of the sanctuary along with the other committee members." I leaned back on the couch and tucked my feet under Conan, who took over Ike's spot as soon as Ike left. "Do you think Henrietta will speak?"

"Probably. And Staples will probably want to talk, too. I heard you talking to him earlier." My mother shook her head. "That man is a pain in the butt."

"I'm not as worried about him as I am about the possibility of a legal fight. That could be costly." I considered tomorrow's town meeting, at which I and several others would speak about the need for the sanctuary. A special election was being held in ten days so the citizens could vote on the proposal, a necessity because zoning laws would need to be changed.

"It's a pity you have to leave town for the conference," Mom said. "I'm sure people will have questions about setting up a sanctuary."

"Well, that's why we have a Freedom Committee. Other people can answer questions, too." I leaned over to grab the shooting summary Paul sent me. "I'll have to meet with the fashion editor and set designer sometime next week. I'll bet the production scout will want to talk to me, too."

"I can't wait to see you model." My mother finished her whiskey with one neat tilt of her head and a ladylike gulp.

"You won't see me model," I said, skimming through the summary.

"Why not?"

I looked up at her indignant tone of voice. Both she and Aunt Sherry appeared to be offended. "It's not a public event. I'll be modeling clothes which won't be seen in stores until next year. Designers like to have a closed set."

"Closed? To your mother?" Mom and Sherry exchanged a look. "And your aunt?"

Lord, give me patience, I prayed silently. "I can talk to the Production Coordinator and see if she will let visitors on the set. But it's not my call, Mom. Someone else runs the show."

"They want you to be their model, don't they? Then you have a say in what goes on. Put your foot down, Annabelle. Stand up for yourself."

Actually, I'll be standing up for you. I didn't voice my thought but just nodded. "I'll try."

Mom leveled a gaze at me that said, *Try hard.* I returned to studying the shooting summary before examining the contract. "Looks like they'll need me next Friday on campus locations and Saturday in the afternoon." I thought about my conversation with Paul. "I guess this means I'll have to cut my conference short."

"I'm sure by then you'll be ready to come home anyway," Mom said. "After all, how exciting can a conference about Victorian literature be?"

"Friday is the Harvest Dance and the endowment ceremony," Aunt Sherry said. "They're going to take pictures there?"

I nodded, taking a sip of wine. My eyes widened when I saw the amount of money Paul was asking for me in the contract. If he got the price he asked for, I'd have a nice chunk of money for a few days of work.

"And Saturday's Homecoming and the football game," Mom said.

I nodded again, already daydreaming about the money Paul was asking.

"Then it's obviously not a closed set because there will be hundreds of people at the dance and at the game," Mom said triumphantly. She stood and helped my aunt to her feet. "Right?"

I fell back on my standard reply. "We'll see."

As usual, Mom had the last word. "Yes, we will, won't we?"

****

I emailed my acceptance to Paul the next morning and within minutes my phone rang. We discussed the details of the contract and I insisted he add a clause that I would not begin my modeling duties on Friday until after the endowment ceremony. He agreed then he told me Laurie Lyon's assistant would be in town this weekend and was hoping I could take the time to be a tour guide.

"You don't know this guy," Paul said. "He's only been working with Laurie for a few years. His name is…hold on, it's here somewhere…yeah, George Budd. He's coming there on Saturday to scout locations. Do you have time to show him around? You'll get paid for it, of course, your usual hourly rate."

My objections died on my tongue. "I suppose I have time. Where do I meet him?"

"I'll have him email you. Is there a hotel there?"

"Sure. There are several. This is a college town, after all. We need someplace for parents to stay when they come to visit."

My deadpan humor was lost on Paul, whose acquaintance with small towns was limited to suburbs of Los Angeles or New York City. "Okay, good. He'll probably stay right there if he decides to do an overnighter. I'll send the final contract to you this afternoon and Laurie will be in touch next week with the schedule. This is just like old times, Annabelle. Have fun!"

I hung up and mentally rearranged my weekend plans. Ike and I had talked about going to a movie, but now I could cancel it and have a valid excuse. I was uneasy with the thought people assumed Ike and I were dating. We were professional colleagues and that was all. Heaven knows, there was enough gossip on campus without adding the fuel of a supposed romance.

I fed the animals and settled Conan in the mud room, his home away from home when I was at school. We were still in the training phase of his puppyhood and I didn't trust him to have the run of the house. For that matter, I didn't trust Sprite, but corralling her was far more difficult than Conan, who usually obeyed me.

As though giving action to the thought, Sprite romped past me, chased by Houdini, who lumbered after the petite kitten like a blimp chasing a bubble. They had these chase sessions each morning and late afternoon, and Houdini would retire after fifteen minutes and sleep for the rest of the day or night. He wasn't as young or as lithe as he used to be, and Sprite always gave him a run for his money.

I left the house and drove through a sparkling

autumn day to campus. The scent of crumbling leaves was in the air and the sun filtered through the gorgeous colors on the trees, making me feel like I was in the middle of an Impressionist painting. I was buoyed by the world around me and my charming little town in the middle of Iowa, one of the prettiest states in the Union. I was lucky to be here and to be going to a job I loved.

My mood lasted through the day, giving me energy for my one class, my appointments with students, and my dash home to check on Conan at noon. My afternoon was spent grading papers and working on dissertations because my weekend was now booked with modeling chores. I lost track of time and didn't look up until my iPhone rang.

"Dr. Doyle, this is Maggie Lippincott. Can we meet before the town meeting tonight? Some of the committee members thought we should get together and talk beforehand."

I checked the clock on my wall and winced. It was close to 6:00 and I was due at the town meeting at 7:00. "Possibly," I said doubtfully. "But I'm running late. I'll get there as soon as I can."

"Oh, good. We just thought given what Henrietta Baron is up to, we should meet."

"I'm not too worried," I assured her. Maggie was one of the veterinarians in town and she was a key figure in helping us map out plans for the sanctuary. In fact, she was the one who got me involved in the first place. Maggie knew the vet who helped at The Wildcat Sanctuary in Minnesota. The vet mentioned to Maggie that TWS knew of a similar sanctuary group who was looking for land in Iowa.

Maggie mentioned it to me when I had Houdini in

for a checkup. I mentioned it to Mother. Mother mentioned it to Charlie Baron. And the Wild Cat Freedom Committee was born. Now I tried to inject all the confidence I could into my voice. "We have Mr. Baron's wishes in writing."

"But she's hired the Franks to represent her interests," Maggie said worriedly.

I sighed. The Franks law firm was composed of Old Mr. Frankland Franklin or "Frank Two," and his "young" son, Frank the Third or Frank Three, aged fifty. Both lawyers loved litigation and were often involved in convoluted lawsuits that dragged on for months in court. "Let's meet at the Club in a few minutes," I said with as much reassurance as I could muster.

"Good. Thank you." Maggie hung up and her abrupt sign-off told me she was still worried. Maggie was normally very effusive in her thanks and her good-byes.

I tidied my desk, wondering how I was going to get home, feed and walk Conan, and get to the pre-meeting meeting, all in forty-five minutes. I didn't have to change clothes, at least, or primp. My hair was dressed into a serviceable and sedate braid and I wore dark blue jeans, and a red-and-white sweater set matching my red low-heeled pumps. It would all suffice for a town meeting.

As I was hurrying to my car, my iPhone rang again. This time it was Aunt Sherry. "Just thought I'd check in with you and see if you need anything before the meeting. Are you all set?"

I had a brilliant idea. "Could you or Mom run over to the house and let Conan out for a potty break? I need to get to the meeting early so I can chat with other committee members."

"Sure, no problem. Your mom and I will stop on our way. Anything else?"

I breathed a sigh of relief. "Nope, that's it. Thanks, Aunt Sherry."

"Glad to help, dear."

I drove north on Main Street but instead of going left and west at Norwood, I took a right and went east, driving two blocks to the Beacon Golf Club where the town meeting would be held. The sun was an indistinct glow in a cloudy sky behind me, huge and bloody-looking where it shone through rain clouds piling up on the horizon.

I pulled into the paved lot on the west side of the building, surprised to find it almost full. The east parking lot on the far side of the building also held quite a few cars, but that lot was shared with the city park, so perhaps people were still there despite the late hour.

The Beacon clubhouse was an older two-story stucco building with a meeting room and banquet hall on the upper level and a walk-out lower level housing the bar and the locker rooms. The pool was drained and the tennis courts were covered by tarps, but the golf course was still an expanse of pale green with flags marking the holes. The course wouldn't close until Thanksgiving, weather permitting. The upper floor of the clubhouse was used throughout the winter by various groups who held meetings there and for the thrice-weekly bridge clubs who met for cut-throat matches.

I walked to the concrete porch that spanned the

width of the upper story. Two large picture windows showed me people inside, many already seated in the banquet room, which had rows of chairs lined up and waiting.

I had my hand on the door handle, preparing to enter, when Henrietta shoved the door open. I jumped out of the way, narrowly avoiding a black eye. Her normally smooth complexion was blotchy, as though her makeup wasn't up to the task of covering the bright splotches of red on her cheeks and forehead.

Henrietta is way pissed off, I thought, and I considered beating a retreat rather than add to her anger inferno. But a little devil took hold of me, and I smiled prettily at her, one of my best Model efforts. "Just the person I wanted to see," I said with a happy lilt to my voice.

"Why?" Her chic Burberry plaid skirt and red loose-collared, cashmere sweater were too lightweight for the cold air starting to whip along the porch from the west side of the building. She tugged her short black leather jacket tighter. "What do we have to talk about?"

I was no good at subterfuge, so I decided to try blunt honesty. "Henrietta, why are you doing this? Why are you blocking the Sanctuary?"

"Why? Because it's not in the best interests of the town, that's why." She said it in that carefully enunciated tone of voice which people reserved for idiots or fools.

"Since when have you cared about the best interests of the town?" I used the same tone of voice on her, but it bounced right off her shield of righteous indignation.

"I plan to move back here and I have an interest in

seeing this town thrive." Henrietta jerked her chin, causing her hair to bounce artfully over one leather-clad shoulder. Her eyes went to the doorway behind her then she turned her attention back to me, crossing her arms.

"I suppose you think a ticky-tacky suburb will be a good thing." I struggled to control my temper, but it was a failing cause.

"I have it on good authority these will be high-end homes, suitable for a golf course setting." Her voice rose and the blotchiness on her face deepened. "Don't forget, too, there might be another nine holes added to our golf course." She smiled smugly. "If we do that, it's considered community improvement. You need to convince the townspeople that a sanctuary which will bring in no money will help the town. Nothing can happen unless the town votes to allow the sanctuary. So no matter who—I mean, no matter how the land is—no matter what my uncle wanted to do with the land, it doesn't matter unless the town agrees."

I fought to keep my anger in check. She was right, damn it, and I knew it. "If we add the nine holes, then it still has to come up for a vote. It's not a slam-dunk acceptance, you know."

"Indeed." Henrietta's voice was as cold as the darkness settling around us. "I think we know how a vote would go, don't we?"

"Who's going to pay for a golf course design?" I challenged. "Where is the money coming from? You can't just slap in another nine holes. What would another nine holes give us? It's not a fantastic golf course, not by any stretch of the imagination. For that matter, what would a dozen or so homes give us? Just one more suburban neighborhood. An animal sanctuary would be such a benefit. It would give us a reputation as a caring, responsible community. It would make us seem—"

"Make us seem deranged." Her voice was rising and her blotchiness was suffusing her neck as well. "Honestly—"

I managed a credible mocking laugh. "Look who's talking about honesty."

She leaned closer to me and for an instant she reminded me of Cruella DeVille—an arch-villainess with murder on her mind. "Just what do you mean?"

I stared her down. "Since when did you decide to move to town?"

"I've been considering it for a quite a long time. I enjoyed living here when I was growing up and when I came back to college, I fell in love with the place. I enjoy my visits here to visit Uncle Charlie." She regarded me with haughty superiority. "I have reason to move here."

My mother's words came back to me. "For Ike?" I managed a credible laugh. "Don't count on it, Henrietta."

Her face slackened and the blood drained away, leaving her complexion bone white with funny little Raggedy Anne patches of red on her cheeks. Her dark gray eyes were enormous, her lids open so wide I could clearly see the underside of her eyelashes. "Just what are you saying?" she said in an odd whispery tone.

"Acie."

We both turned at Ike's calm voice. He emerged from the door behind me. Tonight he wore a dark gray tweed jacket over a black sweater and black jeans, making him appear to materialize out of shadows of the foyer into the light overhead on the porch. "I think you should save your arguments for the meeting, Acie."

"I'm just trying to understand what Henrietta is getting out of this." I looked beyond Ike to the doorway where members of the Wild Cat Freedom Committee peered anxiously at me. "Part of the land is in the flood plain. We shouldn't even be considering selling it for a profit."

"There are conflicting evaluations about that." Ike touched Henrietta's arm and she jumped as though scalded. "Let's go inside and sit down."

Henrietta glared from him to me, her eyes wide. She dug a hand into her jacket pocket, her mouth open and her shoulders shifting in her jacket.

"Are you okay?" I suddenly realized she looked like a fish out of water.

"Asthma," she gasped, her breath coming out in choked wheezes.

I started forward, but Ike held me back. "She has an inhaler. Don't interfere. She knows what she's doing."

He sounded quite calm, so I suppose he had seen this before, but it was new to me and it was actually somewhat frightening. I watched Henrietta pull out a small tube-like thing and put it to her lips. She squirted then inhaled deeply, shoulders rising again and staying near her ears while she held her breath. When she finally released it, she sagged then began to take in small sips of air, like an athlete getting pumped before an event. "This time of year it's bad," she gasped shakily, hand still clutching the inhaler.

I looked out at the trees encircling the club house, all of them in their autumn glory, the mums in the flower beds like small mounds of jewels. What a shame to not be able to enjoy such things. Henrietta must have seen my pity, because she straightened, color returning to her cheeks. "You haven't heard the last of this. I'm not going to let the land go to waste. You'll be hearing from my lawyer soon." She still wheezed slightly, but she didn't appear any the worse for her attack. "Are you coming in?" This was directed to Ike.

He moved slightly nearer to me. "I'll be there in a minute," he said softly.

Henrietta's mouth tightened into a flat, hard line. "I think I'll take a walk, then. I'd like to get some air before I speak."

"I vant to be alone," I intoned softly in my best Garbo voice.

She leveled a glare at me which could have pierced my eyeball then she stalked away, heading for the stairs leading from the parking lot to the lower level. From there she could walk out to the golf course or to nearby city park to the northeast of the club property. Of course, given the fact she was wearing high-heeled boots and she had asthma, I doubted she'd go far.

Ike moved in front of me, blocking my view of the onlookers in the doorway. "That was a low blow," he murmured.

I considered evading his gaze then I decided to confront him. What the heck. What did I have to lose? "Why? Is she right? Is there something between the two of you?"

He shook his head. "I don't know if it matters to you. Does it?" He met my eyes, his searching mine for—what? An answer?

I didn't have any answers. I glared at the lurkers

who had hung on every word. "Back inside," I said, making a shooing motion. "The entertainment's over."

Ike stood to one side to let me enter. I was painfully aware of his nearness when I sidled past. The Committee members surrounded me as soon as I entered the foyer and I was borne away by their anxious questions to an alcove on the left where we could talk privately. Ike shot me an angry look then he strode off in the direction where Henrietta had disappeared.

The committee and I discussed Henrietta's legal move and our potential counter-moves for twenty minutes or so while people continued to enter. When we finished our discussion, I peered around the large banquet space. "Where did all these people come from? There aren't many cars in the lot."

"The Junior League had dinner scheduled for tonight but they canceled it. Most of them parked in the lower lot so they could have their business meeting ahead of time." Maggie smiled, her tanned face creasing. She was a sturdy lady in her early thirties with cropped blonde hair and muscular arms. Maggie and her husband had a vet practice in town. Her specialty was pets, both 'regular' and exotic, and her husband specialized in farm animal care. "I think they had their meeting in the bar."

The Leaguers were a great-hearted bunch of ladies, all of whom enjoyed a cocktail now and then. I'm sure they would love an opportunity to have a drink before dinner. "What time are we supposed to speak?"

"We?" Maggie appeared confused.

I nodded. "I thought we were all going to take turns."

"Uh, no." They exchanged anxious looks. "You're

doing most of the talking. Then I think Henrietta will talk and a few others." Maggie held up a notecard. "I'm going to mention the medical aspects of the sanctuary, but you're the one making the argument for us."

This was not what I had planned. I considered the brief little speech I prepared. If I was the lead speaker for the Sanctuary, I needed more than what I had. I listened with half an ear while Maggie and the others exchanged worried comments about Henrietta and her plans. The other half of my brain was occupied with my upcoming speech and quelling my incipient panic.

"And we have this, of course." Maggie handed me the brochure she helped design.

Our emcee, Marge Crandon, bustled toward us. "We're getting ready for speakers," she said, brandishing her clipboard at me. "Come along." She was a short, skinny woman with spikey bleached blonde hair, a year or two younger than me. Marge was one of those women who married often and divorced well, leaving her with ample income and the time and inclination to handle just about any social activity in town. She probably could have managed a presidential campaign without breaking a sweat.

Marge continued speaking, ushering us to the front of the room with occasional pauses to talk with people. Like Henrietta, she was dressed in the height of fashion in designer jeans that made her legs appear even longer and a loosely draped green sweater emphasizing her sizeable chest. She strode to the podium while I trailed in her wake.

"I'm so glad you're speaking," she murmured, bestowing a faint aroma of bourbon around me. "You're far more cooperative than Henrietta." Her sweater shifted and I had a glimpse of cleavage before she straightened, laughing happily. Since Marge was the chairwoman of the Junior League's Fundraising Committee, I suspected at least one drink had passed her pretty pink lips that evening. "The surveyor will speak first then I think Henrietta wanted to speak next then I want you to talk about the pro-animal point of view."

I eyed the room. I was no judge of numbers, but it seemed like a few hundred people were there. Through the windows I saw more people coming in then I glimpsed Ike with Meryl Staples, his head bent to hers and her face upturned to his as they stood on the outside porch.

My heart lurched at the sight. Meryl was a beautiful woman in her late thirties with a voluptuous body, raven-black hair and the most amazing pair of blue eyes I had ever seen except for a model I knew who wore contact lenses. Meryl and her obnoxious brother frequently attended college events, and I often saw her and Ike in conversation. I watched him put an arm around her shoulders and lead her away from the doorway and the light illuminating them.

I remembered my mother's comment, that Meryl had her eye on Ike. If any woman could snag Ike's heart, it would be Meryl Staples with her sweet personality, gorgeous looks, and her air of wistful mystery. For some reason, the idea made me angry. "I think Henrietta is outside," I said, interrupting Marge in the middle of whatever it was she was saying. "I saw her and Dr. Adler earlier."

"Outside?" Marge examined her clipboard. "Well, that's just wrong. I'll have to send someone to find her.

Now the rules are we're limiting you all to a ten-minute speech. Mr. Staples has said he wants to talk, too." Marge looked around the room. "Where is he? He was just here a minute ago. Heavens, what is it with these people? Anyway, I think a few other townspeople want to make comments, too. We're trying to keep this to a one-hour meeting, just a presentation of the merits of each side of the discussion."

Any previous disquiet I felt regarding Meryl Staples was replaced by shock. Good Lord, I was supposed to come up with ten minutes of convincing arguments? I hadn't planned on more than two or three minutes.

"You go have a seat in the front. I'll send someone out to find Henrietta and any others who want to talk." Marge gestured to the first row, which was marked off with red crepe paper streamers draped over the chairs.

"But—"

My words fell on empty space. I headed for a seat but as I did, someone grabbed me by the arm. I turned to find Aunt Sherry, cheeks red with cold and her dark brown hand-knit cape at a crazy angle on her shoulders.

"He's gone," she said breathlessly. "I'm so sorry, he just slipped past me."

"What?"

"Conan. He got loose."

Chapter 5

I stared at her, speechless. Damn. That was all I needed. More stress on top of the stress I already had. "What do you mean, he got out?"

"He wasn't in the mud room when I arrived. The door was open." Aunt Sherry looked at my mother, who joined us while I was trying to gather my wits.

Mom nodded, tapping the floor with her cane for emphasis. "The mud room door was wide open. We walked in the front door and before we knew what was happening, that hellion cat of yours was racing straight for us. We got her corralled but your dog was gone like a bolt of lightning."

"How did he get out? I was there at noon and—" I stopped. No use worrying about it now. I had a lost puppy and a speech to make. "When did it happen?" I started to leave, but Maggie took hold of my arm.

"We're on," she said. "Marge is having a fit. She can't find Henrietta, so I think we're talking first, right after the County surveyor gives his report."

"Conan is loose," I said. "I have to go find him."

"Oh, no." Maggie released me immediately, her vet's appreciation for my dilemma evident. "I'll tell you what, you go first. I'll talk to a few of the committee members. They can go out and look for him while you're talking." Her head turned from me to Mom and Aunt Sherry, who appeared doubtful about this plan.

"She has to talk."

"I'll go out and drive around," Mom volunteered.

"And I'll be home base for the volunteers," Aunt Sherry said. "They can call me if they see anything of him."

"But—" I turned to the doorway, fully intending to search for my puppy. Maggie dashed away, heading for our committee members who watched our agitated discussion with puzzled expressions. My mother and Sherry followed her, talking urgently.

"Okay, folks, can I have your attention please?" Marge tapped on the microphone, which responded with a startled shriek. She fiddled with knobs and it subsided.

I sank into a folding chair and struggled to put my thoughts into a semblance of order. Where was Conan? Through the windows, I could see trees whipping in the wind. Why did I always get roped into stuff like this? I had to learn to say no. People would ask me to help and without thinking, I just said, 'sure' when I would really like to say, 'are you insane?' Why did I always let this happen to me?

"…and Dr. Annabelle Doyle will speak for the Sanctuary point of view. Then each proponent will summarize the arguments for inclusion in the newspaper. The pro-Sanctuary group will prepare an article for Tuesday's paper and the pro-development group will prepare an article for Thursday." Marge smiled at me. "They'll need your draft by Monday morning. That won't be a problem, will it?" She turned back to the audience. "It will give you plenty of time to review the issues before the vote, ten days from now. We thought it would be…"

What? I was supposed to summarize the arguments? That plus babysitting a location scout meant my weekend would be shot to hell.

"…introduce the county surveyor, who will give us a summary of…"

I tuned out Marge while I reviewed my plans for the weekend. I had to prepare for my presentation at next week's conference, grade papers, and now I had to write a newspaper article? I could imagine my few free hours on Saturday night and Sunday spent closeted with Maggie and others, trying to come up with the requisite words.

"…and I'll be discussing both of the, um, so-called, uh, human alternatives to the, um, land use. Since I advised the, um, Board, and the um, developers who are interested in the land, I think I am uniquely qualified to, um, discuss the um, merits of, um, the proposals to…"

I forced myself to appear interested while the surveyor droned on, unnecessarily introducing himself and his qualifications. If it came to that, why the hell was I qualified to talk? Just because somebody asked me and I said I would?

"…surveying reports are in conflict, but as we all know, um, the floods we experienced several years ago were an anomaly and…"

I almost laughed out loud. We were lucky the entire town didn't get washed away, like what happened in Cedar Rapids and Des Moines and Iowa City. The catastrophic floods inundated the low ground along the river, but Maggie assured us if it was used as a Sanctuary and it flooded again, the animals were capable of finding their own higher ground and would be in no danger. There was ample space for them to get out of the way, and the flood plain was broad enough it would take another more-than-catastrophic flood to cause concerns.

That led my thoughts to my errant dog. Where was Conan? Maggie sat a few seats away from me, near the side. Aunt Sherry stood behind me at the doorway with a phone in her hand. She saw me eyeing her and she waved the phone, mouthing something I couldn't interpret.

Where could he be? The two other times Conan escaped from me, he ended up in the gravel quarry between my house and Ike. In fact, once Ike found Conan when I called in a panic. He hiked to my house through the intervening space, rounded up my puppy and both of them appeared on my doorstep, muddy and disheveled.

That reminded me. Where was Ike? I scanned the crowd. I didn't see either Ike or Henrietta or Meryl. Was something going on between Ike and Henrietta? Ike and Meryl? Ike never gave me any indication he had any, well, any feelings for me. He was a tenured professor when I joined the faculty, having joined the college in his mid-thirties. We were the only single people in the English Department, so naturally we often chatted with each other at various events.

It would really be too bad if Ike and Henrietta ended up together. She just wasn't the right sort of person to be a Faculty Spouse. Most of the spouses were easy-going, non-competitive kinds of people who endured our eccentric academic humor with good grace. I couldn't visualize Henrietta at a faculty picnic, chatting with retired professors and watching the Philosophy Department and Engineering Department engage in chess tournaments or cheer us on while the Business Department and the English Department each struggled to make a hit in softball.

Ike and Meryl, though…She was quiet and enjoyed reading and was…I struggled for the right word. *Compliant,* I thought. *Demure.* I scowled at the speaker and I must have flustered him because he stuttered even more and his face reddened. He was starting to sound like the voice of the parents in the Peanuts movie— *wha-wha-wha-wha.* I gave up listening when he starting talking about elevation, soil types, and river currents.

I turned my attention to the brochure Maggie handed me. It was actually a folded poster which when unfolded was eleven-by-seventeen. On the front of the folded poster was an enormous lion's face staring into the camera, the eyes implacable and wise.

I envisioned myself as one of those poor creatures, forced to live in a cage or a cramped apartment or forced to perform on command. Why should it happen to them just because they were animals? Why did anyone think they could own a wild creature? Why would anyone try to control a creature like that? They should be allowed to run wild, to roam free, to be unrestrained. It was their breeding, in their DNA. They were born to be themselves, not a tame house pet or zoo curiosity.

House pet…where was Conan? I tried to find the committee members, but those whom Maggie sent out hadn't returned yet. Conan was a sweet puppy and wouldn't cause a fuss if someone tried to catch him, but knowing him, he'd see it as more of a game and would evade capture if he could, just to keep the silly humans running after him. I didn't hold out much hope they'd find him. I tried not to think of the streets he might be crossing or the obstacles he might be encountering. He had little knowledge of cars and traffic. What if something happened to him? How did he get out?

I tried to push my worry to one side. I raised my head and regarded the human faces, most of them politely focused on the surveyor. I needed to target this audience and figure out a way to make them empathize with a bunch of wild animals. This was a chance for us—these humans, these residents of Grimper—to make amends. We could prove to ourselves and others that there were compassionate, caring humans in the world.

We were more than fancy homes and a view of a golf course. We were more than just sand traps and ponds and a chance to relax on a Sunday afternoon. By God, we could draw line in the dirt—good Iowa farm dirt—and say, "no more." I began to form arguments, phrases, and ideas in my brain.

Ten minutes later, polite applause told me the city surveyor was mercifully finished. Marge leaned over and tapped my knee lightly. "Your turn."

I sprang to my feet and strode to the podium. I unhooked the microphone from the stand and took a relaxing breath. As I did, a rumble in the distance told me a thunderstorm was moving in. I thought briefly of Conan out there, alone in the cold and the damp then I channeled my worry and my fear into my voice. I peered into the crowd, many of whom were regarding the windows with apprehension. Early snow wasn't unheard of it, and the temperature was dropping. It gave me the opening I needed.

"Try to imagine being cold, with no food, no water,

and someone tormenting you. Imagine living in a cage."

I paused for a minute, letting the thought soak in. "Now imagine having to do it just because you're you. Just because someone can do it to you. It wasn't something you did. It wasn't a punishment. It's because you are who you are. Imagine it for a minute." I held up the brochure in my hand and waggled it, shaking my head in mock disbelief. "Look at this. Read it. Can you imagine it? What kind of idiot would buy a lion cub and think he could raise it in a damn New York apartment?"

A chuckle ran through the crowd, the combined humor of solid Midwesterners who heard all kinds of stories about city folks and the crazy things they did.

"I know all about the so-called benefits of having a new subdivision put in, or having new golf holes added. And I suppose there are good aspects to that." I made sure the audience could hear the doubt in my voice. "Now let me tell you about the real benefits of having an animal sanctuary in our back yard." I paced to the other side of the room, thinking furiously. Then I stopped and stared out at my neighbors.

"We have a chance to prove to the world—to prove to ourselves, and to our kids—that we know what's important. It's not about short term gains. It's not about tax enhancements and green fees. We're Iowans. We know the land."

I eyed several men in the middle of the room, most of them wearing seed company caps and gray overalls. They regarded me stoically, arms crossed on their ample chests. "This is Iowa. This is the best land in the world. Why the hell would we want to tear it up and put down a house and have sod brought in to make a lawn? Why would we want to reshape it so it conformed to somebody's idea of what's pretty, and put in ponds and some hills and a few bushes to make it look challenging to golfers?"

I wheeled and paced back again to the other end, glancing now and again at my audience. "Iowans are not big city people. Never have been, never will be, and I say, thank you, God, for that." Another chuckle, louder this time, rumbled through the hall. "We hold on to certain traditions and to certain values whether they're popular or not. We live in Flyover Land, and you know what?"

I stopped in the center of the room and smiled. "We're lucky we live here, because we don't have a lot of the problems plaguing the world. Oh, yeah, we have problems. We have unemployment and there are drug problems in spots, and all the other crap that goes along with modern living. But we haven't lost track of who we are, the way a lot of people in cities have. We know what is right and we try to do what's right. We don't necessarily do what everybody else says we should do. We do what we know is right, here." I splayed my hand out over my heart.

"We have a chance to right a wrong for a handful of creatures who did nothing bad. All they did was be born and be sold to someone who thought they wanted an exotic pet. Or be sold to someone who threw together a traveling animal show then found out they couldn't handle it. We have a chance to take land which really can't be used for much of anything, given the floods we get now and again, and we can use the land for something good."

Heads were nodding in the audience now, and a rustling of paper told me many people were going through the brochure.

"There isn't anything tangible in this for us," I continued. "We won't get a big tax break, and we can't be a tourist destination because it's a sanctuary, not a zoo, so visitors won't be welcomed." I paused and said thoughtfully, "But I suppose there will be jobs for people here in town." I glanced at Maggie, who nodded vigorously. "Can you imagine it?" I asked the audience. "How cool would it be, to work at a place alongside tigers and lions?"

"Way cool!" someone called out, and the audience laughed.

I set down the microphone and opened the brochure, holding up the large sheet. I kept holding it, picking up the mike again to resume talking, reading off the information about "a day in a life of a wildcat resident" and commenting on the various pictures. Medication, food, shelter, cleaning—I chatted about it and at the end of five minutes, I said, "Do you see what's missing from these pictures?" I shook the paper slightly then let it drop to the floor.

"Cages. There aren't any cages. There is grass, and sunshine, and places for animals to roam. There are fences, yes, but there aren't any cages. For most of these animals, this is as close as they'll ever get to normal. They were denied their chance to roam free in their natural habitat. But we can give them a chance to at least have a measure of freedom in a place where they'll be protected. And it's all because someone donated the land needed for these animals to have a second chance."

Movement on my right caught my eye. John Staples entered by the side door, his pale face white with cold and his dark jacket shining damply. I had a brief thought for poor Conan, out in this weather, shivering and lost. Staples leaned against the wall with his arms crossed on his chest and stared at me with unnerving intensity. For just an instant I stared back then I returned my attention to my audience and continued.

"The land is only the first step, of course. There are a lot of other things that need to fall into place to make this happen. Once we get the land, we can start fund-raising. We'll need to consider habitats, and shelters, and people to run it all. We'll need volunteers and equipment. I've been in touch with the director of a similar sanctuary in Minnesota, and they've pledged their time and experience to help us. Us—this town. Because a lot of the work will come from us. A few outsiders will be needed, those people with the necessary experience and talents. But we're going to be calling on all of you to be advocates for this sanctuary, to be our good will ambassadors. We'll be asking you for help, too."

I paced again across the front of the room then stopped in the center to regard my fellow townspeople. "Land, sunshine, and freedom. It's all they're asking for. We have it. There isn't anything in it for us except the knowledge that we did the right thing. We did what we could to right a wrong in the world. And we did it because, by God, it was the right thing to do. It's what we do. We're in Flyover Land. We know what's right. We're Iowans. Thank you."

Applause broke out, with a scattered "yeah!" and "you bet!" included. I waved my brochure at the crowd and set the microphone on the podium before covertly checking my watch. I had done my spiel in a little under ten minutes. *Good work,* I silently congratulated myself.

Marge took up the mike. "Does anyone else have any comments they want to make?"

Staples hurried forward while I went to Maggie, who sat in the front row. "I'm going to look for Conan," I whispered.

She nodded. "I'll try to do a summary sort of speech on top of the medical stuff I was going to say. Should we plan to talk tonight about the write-up they need?"

"Send me an email. I'm going to be busy with other things this weekend, but I'll make time."

"Good luck finding him," she murmured then she turned her attention to Staples, who was expounding on the glory of a new subdivision.

I skirted the perimeter of the room, nodding to people who offered me congratulations on my impromptu speech. I hurried to the coat rack and grabbed my denim jacket then headed for the door.

Aunt Sherry leaned close to whisper to me. "I'm keeping track of the search party," she said, brandishing her phone. "They've been sending me text messages. No sign of Conan anywhere near your house or the quarry. Your mother is back at the house, keeping watch."

I nodded my understanding. "I'll go to the house and start there. Maybe he's hiding nearby and will come if he hears my voice."

She patted my arm. "I'm so sorry about this. It's my fault."

I wished I could blame her, but honesty forced me

to say, "It isn't, Aunt Sherry. I should have known this would happen. From now on, when you come over to check on the critters, just use the garage door. You have the keypad combination."

Sherry nodded vigorously. "I remember you showing me how it works. I'm so sorry. I should have thought of that."

"No, I should have thought of it." I put my arm around her and gave her a quick hug. "It's too easy for Conan or Sprite to get out of the front door."

She appeared slightly mollified by my words. "He'll be fine, dear. I'm sure of it."

I wasn't so sure. I emerged into bone-chilling cold, but at least the rain had stopped. The temperature was dropping fast and I could imagine Conan, shivering and hiding under a bush. I started to the parking lot and my car but stopped when someone called my name.

"Acie!"

I turned to find Ike striding toward me from the far end of the porch. Like before, he seemed to materialize from thin air, his clothing blending in with the darkness behind him. Light sparkled on the dampness on his thick hair. "Where have you been?" I snapped, more harshly than I meant.

He paused in mid-step. "I was at the park. I talked to Henrietta."

"The last time I saw you, you were with Meryl Staples." I was appalled I let those words slip out of my mouth. I turned to walk to the parking lot. "Conan got out. I have to go find him."

"Meryl was looking for her brother. Henrietta's going to donate the land."

I whirled. "What?"

"I convinced her to donate the land." Ike approached cautiously, his gaze intent on me. "Once her uncle's will is probated, she won't object to having the land used for the sanctuary. We talked about it and she—"

"What could you possibly tell her that would make her change her mind?" I demanded.

Ike looked away from me. His gaze went to the window on his right where I saw people inside, listening to John Staples. "Did you talk already?"

"Yes, I did. I went first because like I said, Conan is lost." I hesitated, anxious to go to my car but also anxious about Ike. Anxious? Well, maybe not *anxious* but certainly curious. "Where's Henrietta?"

Ike shrugged. "She said she was going home. I followed her when she left earlier and we talked at the park. When did Conan get out?"

"Right before I got here. What did you and Henrietta talk about, Ike?" I approached him and now that I was closer, I thought he seemed embarrassed, his gaze flitting to the window, the porch behind me, the parking lot—anywhere but to me. "What happened?"

He drew in a long sigh then he finally met my gaze. "I told her I didn't love her and I would never love her. I told her you were right."

I shook my head slightly, puzzled. "Right about what?"

He put his hands on my shoulders. "When you said not to count on me caring for her."

"I never said that," I protested. "I just said—" My words were cut off when Ike bent his head to mine and kissed me.

I'll admit, I'm out of practice with kissing, but

even given the fact I was rusty at it, this was still one damn fine kiss. He pulled me into his arms and I felt his long body, warm and solid, pressing on me. Then he drew back his head, his pale blue eyes intent on me. "Damn it, Acie, I love you. Didn't you know?"

A long, drawn-out howl echoed around us. I was thankful for the excuse to break away from Ike. The kiss was marvelous but this was neither the time nor the place for it. "What is it?" I gasped, pulling away from Ike so quickly I almost fell. "Conan—he's gotten out. What if he—"

Excited barking broke out, faint in the distance. Ike turned, his arm still around me, and I turned with him, slipping out from under his arm when I took a step away. He stared at the city park in the distance. "I saw a pack of dogs earlier. They were outside the park."

"Did you see Conan?"

Ike shook his head. "I'm not sure. They were pretty far away. I did see Moriarty, but he's easy to spot. There were four or five other dogs, too. There was a small one with the pack, but I only caught a glimpse of them." His mouth straightened into a harsh line. "Henrietta just finished yelling at me and I was distracted."

"Where were you?" I was torn. If I went home and Conan was here, I'd lose precious time looking for him. But if I wasted my time looking for him here, blocks from my house, I might not find him for hours.

"Henrietta and I went to the park shelter, the one near the gate." Ike gestured at the park in the distance. The sky had cleared and the moon was rising, making it relatively easy to see the tennis courts and the entrance sign illuminated by overhead lights.

"The park's closed, isn't it? How'd you get in?" My gaze alternated between the park and the parking lot where my car sat. Which way to go?

"The gates are closed but you can walk in. There's a path near the entrance. The shelter was unlocked." Ike jammed his hands into his jacket pockets and hunched his shoulders against the cold wind whipping along the porch. "There's nothing there to steal, so I suppose they leave it open. We argued and I started back here. That's when I saw the dogs, over by the country club side of the park. I went back and got Henrietta. You know how she is about dogs. I told her I'd walk her to her car, but she—" He shook his head. "She didn't want my help."

I visualized the scene. The park was slightly northeast of the club, sandwiched between the country club and Charlie Baron's land and surrounded by dense trees marking its boundaries. The club and the park were on a bluff that overlooked the Dart River, which flowed north-south on the east edge of town. The park was only a few acres in size and below it and the country club was a gravel road leading to the water treatment plant directly below the park.

I hesitated. "Conan wouldn't be with them. My house is blocks from here. He couldn't have gotten wind of them." I turned to the parking lot and my car. "I'm going home to start looking for him there."

"Check the park first. I'll help you." Ike moved to the stairs leading to the parking lot then he noticed my shoes. "You can't go out there in those shoes. They're in the woods."

"I have sneakers in the car. I'll change shoes." When I turned to go to my car, I caught a glimpse of shadowy figures near the park entrance. For an instant they paused under the light then they vanished into the darkness. "There they are!" I took off running.

"Acie! Wait!"

I heard Ike behind me, but I didn't pause until I saw the glistening parking lot, realizing it was just damp, not icy. *Thank God I don't wear high heels,* I thought while I ran. *I'd be flat out and face down on the pavement if I did.* I was halfway to the park before Ike caught up to me.

"Be careful," he panted, keeping pace beside me. "It's slippery out here."

"Will do," I gasped, which was all I had breath for.

We reached the park entrance, nothing more than a dense row of trees flanking a largely decorative metal gate attached to two limestone pillars like sentinels on either side of the drive into the park. Ike led the way, going to the left and taking a narrow path, disappearing from sight. I followed after him and joined him on the graveled roadway leading into the park.

I fumbled in my purse hanging over my shoulder and extracted my key chain. "I have a mini-flashlight thing," I muttered, turning it on. The high-intensity light was startling blue in the semi-darkness. "Which way?" I turned slowly.

"The shelter's right there." Ike gestured to the right and ahead of us. I peered through the gloom and saw a brown structure, faintly illuminated by low-wattage exterior lights. "I saw the dogs on the other side, over by the golf course." He headed to his left and I followed, but he stopped immediately. "There," he whispered, pointing ahead. "On the Tor."

I looked to where he gestured and saw shapes milling around on the rocky promontory over the river road. They were clearly outlined against the sky, tails wagging as they moved. "Conan!" I shouted.

One smaller figure broke away from the others and started toward me then the pack dispersed. The smaller shape disappeared into the darkness around Bloody Vixen Tor, so-called because on the left side was a tall, narrow pinnacle of rock that was vaguely like a fox at its top, tail upraised and one paw in the air. The reddish stains in the rock only added to the appearance, making it look like bloodstains trailing across the surface to the ground below.

I remembered scrambling up the steep pinnacle when I was a child, balancing on top and gazing over the river, totally fearless. I used to think it was enchanted and if I wished hard enough, my wishes would come true. The thought of doing it now made my palms sweat.

The main look-out was a narrow wedge jutting out over two lower out-jutting promontories, one about thirty or forty feet below and another fifty or sixty feet below the first one. A classmate of mine died here, slipping over the edge and landing on the ledge before crashing through trees and underbrush to land on the river road hundreds of feet below.

"Conan? Are you out here?" I started forward, flashlight bobbing in my hand. There were lights along the path leading to the Tor, but they were solar-powered and very dim, serving only to outline the way, not really provide illumination. "Conan?"

Ike strode ahead of me and I followed, keeping the light on the ground to help me pick my way over the uneven surface. Even so, I tripped over a root poking up through the hard-packed earth and the rock that composed the lower edge of the promontory. I went down hard, bruising my knee and scraping my hands. I picked myself up and hurried ahead, skidding into Ike where he stood at the top of the promontory, the Tor on his left.

He peered over the drop-off. "My God."

"What is it?" I asked, fear making my stomach heave. Would I see a small puppy? I inched forward, taking baby steps, to peek over the edge. I moved the flashlight in a slow arc. At first I saw nothing, just darkness and branches. Then the moon broke through the clouds and moonlight, combined with my light, illuminated a bright red pile of something.

That's when I realized the pile of something was Henrietta.

Chapter 6

Ike moved to the side of the promontory and I grabbed his arm. "You can't go. It's too steep. There's not enough light."

He stopped, poised at the top of the path that seemed to drop off into nothingness. "I have a flashlight app on my phone." Ike pulled out his cell phone and stared at the screen, flicking through pages on the display.

A phone. I grabbed my purse and yanked it open, jerking out my mobile phone. "I'll call the fire department." My purse hit the ground with a soft thud when I fumbled open my phone. "They'll send a rescue unit and—"

Ike was gone, his phone held ahead of him and shining brightly on the dark, steep path. I thought about grabbing him again, but was afraid if I did I'd unbalance him. I managed to get the phone app started, tapping in 9-1-1 with trembling fingers. I didn't dare go near the edge again. I didn't want to see Ike make his way down the treacherous slope.

The 9-1-1 dispatcher came on the phone. "I'm at the city park in Grimper," I said in a rush. "There's been an accident. Someone fell. She's on a ledge at the bottom of the Tor. You need to get an ambulance and maybe the fire and rescue people because—"

"Calm down," the man said in what was probably

supposed to be a reassuring way. "Tell me who this is and where you are."

I took a deep breath and tried to curb my impatience. "I'm Dr. Annabelle Doyle and I'm at the park in Grimper, out near the Beacon Country Club. Someone has fallen and—"

"The park is closed, ma'am. How did you get in?"

"Oh, for heaven's sake—I walked here. Get an ambulance and the police out here." I edged close to the drop-off and peered over. Ike's phone was bobbing down the hillside. "You need lights and ropes and medical personnel. I don't know if she's still alive or—"

"When did this happen, ma'am?"

The man was maddeningly calm. "I have no idea." I used my best *you're an undergraduate idiot and you are wasting my time* tone of voice. "We just found the body. She can't have been here long because—"

"We?" he interrupted.

"Yes, we! Get the police out here, the fire and rescue, and an ambulance. Now!" I gave up on politeness and stuffed the phone into my jacket pocket, effectively silencing any more questions. "Ike?" I called. "Are you okay?"

The light from below wavered. "I'm almost there. Don't try to come down, Acie. It's too steep."

I had no intention of going anywhere near the hillside. "I called 9-1-1." He didn't reply then a crashing sound made me jump back. I slipped on the rocky surface, this time landing on my butt.

I cursed softly when a new bruise was added to the ones I already had. I didn't trust myself to get to my feet this close to the edge, so I crept on my hands and knees to drop-off. I peered over. "Ike? Are you okay?"

The light below me shone upward then swung downward again, illuminating the scene. "I knocked a rock off the bluff. I'm fine." Ike sounded breathless and I think the light trembled. I glimpsed an arm and then I clearly saw Henrietta. She lay on her stomach, her skirt twisted around her legs and her right arm twisted back, next to her body. The right side of her face was pressed into the small rocks and dust of the ledge.

The light moved again when Ike shifted position. Henrietta's unblinking gaze seemed to swim up to meet me. "Is she—" I swallowed in a suddenly dry throat.

The light below me swept over the body lying on the rocky ledge. "She's dead."

I sat and scrabbled away from the edge, digging my heels into the earth to push myself as far as I could go from the drop-off. An urgent voice was yammering at me from the phone in my pocket and I heard, in the distance, the faint sound of sirens.

****

The police arrived first then the fire department. I met them at the park gates and led them to the promontory. Large portable searchlights were brought in and Ike was helped up from where he stood on the precarious ledge, near Henrietta's body. When I saw how little space he had and how shear the drop-off was, I almost had heart failure. Thank God I hadn't seen it earlier. If I had, I might have fainted.

Ike and I told our story to the officer on the scene, who listened, then asked us to move aside so they could work. We went to stand near the shelter house. "We need to find Conan," Ike said softly.

Something in his voice made me draw nearer to

him. "Why?"

"Those dogs were out here." His face has half in shadow but I could see he was looking beyond me, to the garishly lit scene. "I should have made sure she was okay. I shouldn't have left her."

"It's not your fault, Ike," I said in a low voice.

"The dogs were out here and she was afraid of them." Ike's face was haggard, his mouth narrowed in a taut frown. "This might be all that's needed to get rid of the pack of dogs. If Conan was with them—" He touched my face gently. "You need to find him."

That was all the privacy we had. The officer came back and told us to leave but warned us we would be needed the next day to give a statement at the police station. We were escorted off the park grounds, stopping first by Ike's car, which sat next to Henrietta's BMW.

"I'll call you in the morning." Ike's glance flickered to the police officer then he grabbed my hand and squeezed it before sliding into the car.

The officer escorted me to my car in the far parking lot and I drove home like a robot, my mind in a fog. When I arrived at my house, my mother was waiting for me by the mud room door when I left the garage to enter the house.

"He's home!" she shouted triumphantly. "Sherry saw him when she was leaving the country club and she grabbed him. The little pooper was muddy, but we got him!" She gestured to the doggie bed next to the clothes dryer.

Conan looked up at me and yawned, acting as though nothing had happened. He appeared none the worse for wear, although I saw the remains of his adventure on the muddy towels in the nearby laundry basket. I bent to pet him and my bruised knee made itself felt. "Damn it," I whispered, clinging to the wall for support.

"What happened?" Mom asked anxiously. "Your clothes are all dirty and—Annabelle, is that dirt on your face?"

"What happened?" Aunt Sherry asked from the doorway into the house.

I looked longingly at the glass of wine in my aunt's hand. "Get me one of those and I'll tell you."

****

I didn't get rid of my guests until midnight, after we thoroughly discussed the night's events. When I lay down to sleep, I tossed and turned, finally dozing off at around four o'clock. Then I remembered the kiss and I woke up, sitting bolt upright in bed.

Ike said he loved me. Ike kissed me.

I sank back on my pillow and Sprite, who was sleeping next to me in my full-sized bed, settled back, too. She regarded me sleepily, her paws working hypnotically on pounding the pillow into shape. Her throaty purr helped me drift back into sleep, or something like it, while my mind hashed over everything that had happened.

It was a decade since my last love affair with a Des Moines businessman whom I met at a school fundraiser. Lou was a fun guy to be with, but we just didn't have enough interest to sustain a long-distance relationship.

I stared at my ceiling and tried to imagine a relationship with Ike—funny, handsome, easy-going Ike. Oddly enough, I could easily envision it. But it didn't matter. There was no way he and I could embark on a romantic entanglement. After all, we were colleagues. What if we had, well, what if we had an affair and then broke it off? It could get ugly. We had to work together, see each other at meetings. It could be a disaster.

Well, it wasn't going to happen. There was simply too much risk involved. I got out of bed and showered, taking my time and shampooing my hair, something I did only once or twice a week because it took so long to dry. I felt the need to rinse away the residue of the previous night's fear and the memory of Henrietta, staring up at me with those dead eyes.

By the time I dried and plaited my hair into an upswept crown-braid, it was after seven o'clock. I dressed in my Saturday jeans and an old blue striped turtleneck sweater then made coffee and wandered out to the living room, staring south to the quarry and, beyond it, to Ike. I saw lights in the distance. One of them was probably his house. Then Conan nudged my leg and I turned away from the windows to let my puppy out for his morning break in my back yard.

I gave him a thorough check when we came back in, but he seemed fine after his adventure the night before. I wish I could say the same. My hip and knee were bruised and my right hand was scraped. Then I remembered Henrietta and my injuries didn't hurt so badly anymore.

A few minutes later my phone rang. I checked the caller ID on the set in the kitchen then picked up the receiver with a trembling hand. "Good morning, Ike," I managed.

"I wondered if you'd be awake."

"I had a hard time sleeping last night," I admitted, taking my coffee and going back to the living room to stare out the windows. Houdini lumbered past me, chased by Sprite and I smiled at the sight. "I suppose we need to talk to the police today."

"That's one reason I called. I heard from them already. They want me to come in and make a statement." There was a brief pause and I wondered if he was standing at his kitchen window, looking beyond the quarry, to me. "I was the last one to see Henrietta alive."

It took a second for the import of his words to sink in. "So? Why should it matter?"

"The police have to reconstruct what happened to her. So they'll need to talk to me."

"I talked to her, too," I pointed out. "At the country club."

"I know. Don't forget to tell them." He hesitated then said, "Did I surprise you last night?"

I took a sip of coffee, not sure how to reply. I decided on honesty. "You stunned me."

He laughed. "You're so blind sometimes, Acie. How could you not know how I felt?"

"Well, you haven't exactly showed me," I said defensively. "I mean, how was I to know?"

"Don't let it worry you. I know how you are. You're already thinking of reasons why we shouldn't get involved, aren't you?"

"Well, of course I was thinking—"

"Don't think. Just let yourself feel for a change."

"But what if we—"

"Don't. Don't go down the what-if path. Let's just see where this goes for now, okay?" He lowered his voice. "I know where I'd like this to go."

I shivered at the undercurrent of sensuality in his voice. Ike? In bed? Oh, my. "We'll see."

He laughed again. "I'm going to hold you to that. For once, 'we'll see' won't mean 'no'. I'll talk to you later, okay?"

"Okay." I hung up the phone smiling. How did he do it? Just a few minutes ago I was gloom and doom and now I was feeling positively, well, positive about him. I began to map out a schedule for my day. I should call Maggie and have Conan checked, just in case. I didn't see any wounds or bites on his body, but I wanted to be sure. Despite what I said to Henrietta, I wasn't completely sure all those stray dogs were disease-free.

Henrietta. I leaned against the kitchen counter while sunlight streamed into the east-facing room. Poor Henrietta was dead. True, I didn't like her but to have her life snuffed out like that. I shivered again, but it wasn't from sexual tension. I remembered her dead eyes, staring up at me, and her twisted body. I remembered Ike bending over her, his face half in shadow.

Ike. Life was short. I should take a chance. Who knew what might happen? Look at Henrietta. In just a few short minutes, everything changed. Life was short.

And my free time was short, too. I had a lot to do and very little time to do it in. I would have to go the police station this morning. I also needed to hone the presentation I was giving on Thursday at the Chicago conference. I wanted to get laundry done, do a bit of cleaning, and get groceries.

Conan flopped at my feet, tired from his morning

romp with the felines. "But first I need to check your door," I said, heading for the mud room. "How did you get out last night?"

I inspected the mud room door, pulling it closed and leaning on it. It didn't budge. All my doors had levers rather than doorknobs, so perhaps he grabbed it with his paw. I checked from the mud room side but there was no telltale sign of paw prints or scratches to show Conan had lunged upward and pressed on the lever.

I turned to Conan, who followed me into the mud room. "How did you do it?"

He didn't answer. I ushered him out of the room and pulled the door closed behind me then went to the kitchen to work on my grocery list. Conan joined Sprite in another romp, this one wending its way through the living room, my den, and ending in the spare bedroom. Houdini wisely stayed on his hassock, dozing.

I had just grabbed my purse to make a start on my day when the doorbell rang. I looked at the wall clock. It was only seven-forty-five. Who could be at my house so early? Neither Mom nor Sherry were early risers and if they were up, they'd call, not come for a visit.

I peeked through the spyhole and saw a pudgy young man in a brown sweater with brown slacks and brown hair standing on my doorstep. He had that bland, confident air I associated with Mormons and other proselytizers. I opened the door. "Yes?"

"Miss Doyle? George Budd. Shall we get started?" He held up a clipboard.

Ever conscious of the escape artists in my house, I sidled outside, pulling the door almost-closed behind me. "I beg your pardon?"

"George Budd." He held out a business card.

I scanned it. *George Budd, Assistant, Laurie Lyons Productions.* Oh, damn. It was the location scout. I forgot all about him. "I didn't realize you would be coming to my house," I said, my Saturday schedule evaporating in my mind.

"I sent you an email. Didn't you receive it?"

I thought guiltily of my computer, sitting dark in my den, and my cell phone, with messages unread. "I've been busy. Can you come in for a minute? I need to change clothes and perhaps we can discuss what you want to—-"

"Excellent." He started forward and I pushed open the door to let him pass by me. "Here's the list of appointments I made. As you can see, we're meeting the Mayor at eight o'clock at the town square, so we don't have much time." He paused inside my foyer, pale green eyes sweeping around the space. My impression of a Mormon was fading, replaced by the epitome of *Assistant:* organized, tidy, on-time, and inconspicuous.

His eyes widened slightly when Sprite wandered into the area, intent on checking out the stranger. "Stay there," he muttered, glaring at her.

I glanced at my tiny cat, who eyed Budd with a stare I recognized: *why is he ignoring me? I'm pretty.* "Sprite," I said warningly.

Sprite stretched elaborately, displaying razor sharp claws.

"Good God, didn't you have her fixed?" Budd took a step closer to me.

"Of course. Oh, you mean her claws? Of course not. That's inhumane." I stepped over Conan when he entered, eyes focused on the newcomer.

Budd sidled even closer, worry etched on his face. "That's a dog," he said, his voice rising slightly.

I changed my mind about changing my clothes. I doubted if Budd would let me out of his sight that long. I grabbed my purse from the kitchen counter and pulled a jacket from the wall closet, stumbling over Budd as I did so. "Yes. He's a bulldog."

"What?" His voice was definitely getting higher.

"He's quite harmless." I took the clipboard from Budd's unresisting fingers, scanning the list of entries. "Good heavens. You have a full day planned."

Budd tore his gaze from my two pets, who watched him with equal intensity. "I'm only here for one day so I need to take advantage of every opportunity."

"Are you driving or am I?" I asked.

"I'll drive. It will help acclimate me to the town." He whirled and raced for the front door.

"How long do you anticipate this will take?" I asked, following him outside.

"I have a plane flight out of Des Moines at six tonight, so I hope to be done by mid-afternoon."

I hastily re-drew my Saturday schedule in my mind while Budd unlocked the doors of a dark blue sedan at the curb. I slipped into the passenger side. Maggie's office didn't open until nine, so perhaps I could get Conan scheduled for the afternoon. Maybe the day wouldn't be a bust after all.

I reviewed the list on Budd's clipboard while he drove us to the town center. "There's a home football game today," I said, noting his afternoon notation of *Check stadium and other outdoor venues.* "There will probably be a crowd of tailgaters."

"Is there a home game next week?" He drove with fierce concentration along our nearly empty boulevard.

"Yes. It's Homecoming."

"Excellent. Perhaps we can use it in our shoot. We want the authentic Midwestern college look. It should fit in nicely." He stopped at the four-way stop a few blocks from town and checked carefully for non-existent traffic. His defensive driving skills, honed in a big city, were impressive.

"Perhaps for crowd shots," I said doubtfully. "Or background."

"Of course." He looked at me, his eyes thoughtful. "You have a good look for this project. It's been a while since you did this, hasn't it?"

"Yes, but I doubt it's changed much." I flipped through the sheets on his clipboard. "This location at the library won't work if you do it in the afternoon. There's too much shade."

His thin lips got even thinner as he frowned. "We'll see about that."

I smiled. "Yes. We'll see."

Budd parked on the north side of the town square and we emerged into a sunny October day. The park was full of maples, all in their red and gold glory. The mayor stood near the gazebo in the center, drinking a cup of coffee from a paper cup.

I introduced Budd to him then I stepped back, listening with half an ear while they talked about security for the shoot. I took a seat on one of the benches in the eight-sided gazebo, leaning into the sunlight filtering through the trees. The sky was a deep, almost pulsating blue with large white fluffy clouds meandering across it. All in all, it was a perfect fall day and despite the inconvenience, I was looking forward to my morning of campus sightseeing.

I had a clear view of the police station across First Avenue on the south as well as the Dart-and-Drink Coffee Shop on Main Street to the east next to the grocery store. It was a game day and downtown was busier than on non-game Saturdays. We were only a mile or so from the stadium where the hard-core tailgating would take place, so people were going in and out of the grocery store, probably stocking up on booze and food. The six bars in town would undoubtedly be busy at night. I made a mental note to postpone my grocery shopping until Sunday.

I pulled out my phone and called Maggie. We made arrangements for her to come by my house at five. We'd order in a pizza for supper. She would give Conan a quick check then we'd work on the summary for the newspaper article. Maybe while we worked I could get my laundry done. Two more checklist items handled.

My iPhone chimed while I sat, basking in the sunlight. I checked the display. "Hello, Mom."

"What are you up to this morning?" my mother asked.

"I'm with the location scout." I eyed Budd, walking and talking with the mayor. "We're going to locations in town so he can look them over before next week's project."

"Really? Why do you have to be there?"

"I'm a local, Mom. It sort of makes sense I'd show him around town." A gentle breeze wafted over me, bringing the smell of burning leaves. Someone had a bonfire going. Memories of hot dog roasts and marshmallow s'mores were suddenly vivid.

"How long will it take?"

"Why? Do you need something?"

"No, I don't—well, maybe. Hold on." Her voice became muffled but I heard something that sounded like "…can't find their ass in a closet…"

"Mom, what's going on?"

"I was talking with Sherry and Mrs. Hudson about Charlie's death. We all think there's something wrong about it."

I sighed, my enjoyment of the pristine autumn day dampened. I could imagine Mom and her cronies all chatting over coffee about the latest doings in town. "We've had this talk before, Mom. There's nothing to suggest foul play or—"

"And there's nothing to suggest natural causes. Now that his heir has died, I would think the police would take more interest in Charlie's death."

"Henrietta's death was an accident."

"How do you know?" she demanded fiercely.

I straightened, surprised by her snappish tone. "I don't know, of course. But there's no reason to believe it was anything else."

"That's the problem with you young people. You have no imagination. I have half a mind to go out to Charlie's house and poke around for myself."

"I'm not sure it would be such a good idea, Mom." I looked around for my companion and finally found him on the far side of the square. He had a small camera and was taking pictures of the park.

"I'm sure you're busy," she said. "I'll let you go."

"No, that's fine, I'm—" I was speaking to empty air. She had hung up.

I considered calling her back. Knowing Mom, she and Sherry and some of their buddies might embark on a detective mission. Of course, what harm would it do? Charlie Baron's house was probably locked.

As I tucked the phone back in my purse I saw Meryl Staples emerge from the coffee shop and turn the corner at First Avenue, making a beeline for the police station. Even from a block away I could tell she was intent on something or someone, although her frown of concentration didn't detract from her good looks. Today her dark hair was loose on her shoulders, catching the breeze and gently twining around her neck while she walked. Her pale blue jeans matched her slightly darker blue sweater, which highlighted her curvaceous figure very well.

I twisted slightly in my seat to see what had her hurrying so fast. As I did, I saw Budd take pictures of the town square, including one of me in the gazebo. He and the mayor continued to talk while they walked around the gazebo, Budd snapping pictures all the while.

My gaze went back to Meryl Staples, who by now was near the police station entrance. That's when I saw Ike, emerging from the side entrance near the parking lot. He was very casual yet chic in his dark denim jacket, dark blue T-shirt and pale blue jeans. Trust Ike to look sartorially correct even when making a visit to the police.

John Staples was also emerging from the station, but he was coming from the front entrance facing the park. Unlike Ike, Staples was like a rumpled little librarian with his baggy black pants, lopsided blue sweater, and his unruly pale blond hair. I compared him to Meryl, who was almost running now, heading straight to the parking lot. *How the hell could they be related?* I wondered. *She must have gotten all the looks in the family.*

Meryl slowed when she neared the lot, casting an anxious look over her shoulder when she finally reached Ike. He stopped when she said something.

She didn't pause but threw herself into his arms and wrapped her arms around his neck, pulling his head to hers in a passionate kiss.

Chapter 7

"Well, poop," I muttered.

"I beg your pardon?" Budd asked.

I jumped in surprise. He had somehow come into the gazebo and now stood in front of me, watching me while I watched Ike and Meryl in a passionate embrace.

"Nothing." I stood. "Nothing at all. Are you done here?"

"Yes. Our next stop is the college library, I believe. Are you ready?"

I was already out of the gazebo and moving. I said over my shoulder, "Of course I'm ready. Let's go."

"Acie!"

I hunched my shoulders as if that would prevent me from being seen. "This is a charming park, isn't it?" I strode away, careful to stay on the north side of the park, away from the police station side. "It might be nice to use it for one of the location studies, don't you think?"

"Acie!"

"I believe that man is calling you," Budd said, stopping in his tracks.

I turned slowly. Ike was running across First Avenue while John and Meryl Staples argued in the police station parking lot. Meryl seemed sick, her face pale. She clutched her brother while he struggled to get away. Ike dodged a slow moving car and came to a halt in front of me, barely giving Budd a glance. "It's not what it looks like," he said breathlessly.

I managed a credible smile. "I'm sure it isn't. I'm sorry, Ike, but I'm busy at the moment. Maybe we can talk later."

"Don't let me interrupt. I'll just take a few pictures." Budd walked off, camera in hand.

"Asshole," I muttered under my breath. I regarded Ike with what I hoped was haughty calmness. "He's a location scout for the modeling project. I have to show him around town."

"I don't know why she did that." Ike stood close to me, his pale blue eyes intent and beseeching. I tried to avoid his gaze so I turned to the right. John Staples was heading for us, his fists clenched and his face murderous. Meryl was at his side, tugging on his arm.

"I believe Mr. Staples is upset with you," I said.

Ike didn't remove his attention from me. "She's frightened of him and she begged me to help her. I told her to talk to the police. I told her the same thing last night when she asked me for help."

"Why is she asking you?" I tried to keep my voice calm and not accusatory, but I'm not sure I succeeded.

Ike threw his hands in the air. "I have no idea. I think Henrietta told her I would help. That's what Meryl said, anyway. I get the feeling Meryl is the kind of woman who has to have a man to help her. She and Henrietta were kindred spirits. Not like you."

Good heavens, it was hard to stay mad at the man. "You did seem a bit shocked when she grabbed you," I admitted.

His smile broadened into a grin with little laugh lines crinkling around his eyes. "I was hoping you'd rescue me." He put an arm around my shoulder and pulled me to him in a hug.

Our brief embrace lasted about three seconds. Then Ike was dragged from me when John Staples put a hand on Ike's shoulder and yanked. Ike released me and turned, putting out his left arm and shoving Staples away. "Don't," he said in a low voice.

Staples started after Ike, but Meryl tugged his arm. "Leave it alone," she whispered, tears streaming down her face.

"I told the police I saw you with Miss Baron last night," Staples said, his face pale except for two bright red spots of color on his pale cheeks.

Ike regarded him steadily. "I told them, too."

"They were screaming at each other so loud I'm surprised you didn't hear." He directed this at me. "After all, they were screaming about you."

Meryl's quiet crying punctuated the silence that met those words. "What?" I asked, looking from Staples to Ike.

Ike nodded. "I told Henrietta how I felt about you and that there could never be anything between her and me."

Staples gave a harsh laugh. "She was furious. And now she's dead. I'm sure the police are interested in the fact you were the last person to see her alive."

"I discussed it with them." Ike's voice didn't waver, but his hands clenched. I took his right hand in my left hand, easing open the tense fingers. "I told them I had no idea what happened to her after I left her."

"I suppose you'll say you don't know anything about her will, either," Staples sneered.

"Her will?" I stared at him, dumbfounded. "Why?"

"It's critically important. Now she's dead, who gets the land?"

"Good Lord," I said. "Who cares?"

"Don't you? Good. That means it can be sold."

"I didn't say that. I just meant there are other, more important things to care about."

Staples' scrawny neck straightened, making him look like a self-important chicken. "Really? Like what?"

"Like who killed Henrietta," I snapped.

His eyes widened comically. "What do you mean? It was an accident. Those dogs chased her and she fell."

"No one said anything about dogs chasing her," I said. "Why do you say that?"

"Everyone knows those dogs are out there every night. That's what we can expect if an animal sanctuary goes in. Wild animals, chasing people."

I laughed. "People won't be allowed anywhere near those animals. It's a completely different thing."

"Miss Doyle?"

I turned. George Budd was behind me, camera in hand. There he was—my built-in excuse. "I'm sorry, Mr. Budd. Are you ready to go? I know you're on a tight schedule."

"I have all the pictures I need from here." He regarded Ike thoughtfully. "Are you a friend of Miss Doyle's? Perhaps I could ask you to stand in for our model in our shots. It won't take long, just an hour or two. It helps a great deal to have another person in the frame so I can give our production chief a good idea of the location, as well as perspective."

"Ike doesn't have time to go around town and—"

"I'd be happy to," Ike said, smoothly interrupting

111

me. "Just let me know what I have to do." He looked at Meryl, who stood miserably behind her brother, wiping her tears. "I'm sorry I can't help you," he said gently. "If you have concerns, you need to talk to the police."

Her eyes opened wide and she cringed when her brother turned, his anger now directed away from Ike.

"I mentioned to them you talked to me," Ike continued. "So you don't have anything to worry about." He turned to Budd expectantly, putting his left arm around my shoulders. "You said you're on a schedule?"

Budd nodded. "I'm so pleased you could help us, Mr.—?"

"Dr. Adler." Ike extended his hand for a shake while walking away from Meryl and her brother, pulling me with him. "Ike Adler. Dr. Doyle and I are co-workers."

"Doctor?" Budd regarded me with comical surprise, his eyebrows lifting to his hairline.

I nodded and slipped from Ike's embrace to walk beside him, both of us herding Budd ahead of us. "Yes, I'm a professor at Stoneyburst College." I glanced back to see Meryl following after her brother, who was striding to the parking lot like a man on a mission. When I resumed facing forward, I intercepted an angry look from Ike, which made me pause.

"Really? I thought—" Budd's voice stammered to a halt.

I resumed walking but now Ike was ahead of me, level with Budd. I frowned at his back, not sure what to make of his behavior. "I used my modeling career to pay for my college education," I said. "By the time I was done modeling, I had my Ph.D. It took me longer than most students, but I wasn't in any hurry."

"We're lucky to have her at Stoneyburst," Ike said. "Her articles on Victorian feminism are considered required reading for anyone in the field." He sounded like a stodgy college professor, something so not like him I stared, wondering where that comment came from.

"Very impressive. I had no idea." Budd fumbled with the car door locks while Ike and I watched. I kept my face impassive at this lack of trust in our small town, but Ike didn't bother trying to hide his humor. "Sorry," Budd muttered, finally getting the doors open. "It's just force of habit."

"I'm sure," Ike said gravely. He started for the back seat but I forestalled him by opening the rear door and slipping inside.

"You sit in front," I said. "You have longer legs."

"Thanks." He dropped into the seat and Budd settled himself behind the wheel. "Where to?" Ike asked, picking up the clipboard Budd left on the front seat.

"The college library, I think." I slid over so I sat in the middle of the rear seat, letting me peer into the front. "Go left at the stop light then right at the next light." I turned to Ike. "Did you make a statement at the police station?"

"Police station?" Budd asked, following my directions.

Ike answered for me. "Dr. Doyle and I found a mutual acquaintance of ours last night. The woman had an unfortunate accident. The police wanted us to give our statements." He turned in his seat, craning his neck over the headrest to regard me. "You need to stop there this afternoon and give your statement, too."

"I'm sure I don't have anything to add to what you had to say, but I'll stop. Did John Staples really go to the police and tell them he heard you arguing with Henrietta last night?"

"Make a right turn here," Ike said, gesturing ahead. Budd made a slightly late turn, surprising the car behind us. Ike turned back to me. "I suppose he did. Henrietta was very upset." He frowned then he turned completely in the cramped seat. "And yes, your name did come up. She accused me of leading her on. I suppose it seemed like that to her, but I didn't make any promises to her. She made a lot of assumptions."

He sounded so sincere, but did I dare believe him? After all, he and Henrietta dated every time she came to town.

Budd cleared his throat. "I, um, I don't mean to intrude, but it appears the campus is quite busy today. Do you have any idea where we can park?"

I looked through the front window. Traffic had slowed as we neared campus, and cars were angling away, heading for parking spots. I reached for my purse. "I have my faculty parking permit," I said. "We can park in the lot near my office then walk to the library."

"I always leave mine in my car," Ike said, turning away from me and facing the front of the car again. "You come prepared."

His words sounded like an accusation. "I suppose I am."

"Your mother mentioned you dislike being disorganized. Of course, I knew that already. I mean, your lectures are the model of organization."

What was he getting at? "I don't like being surprised," I said.

"There can be pleasant surprises, you know." Ike's shoulders were rigid while he glared straight ahead, his gaze focused on the street crowded with football fans heading toward the stadium a half-mile north of us.

"I'm sure. And there can be unpleasant ones."

"Should I turn here?" Budd asked.

I turned my attention back to the road. "Go straight ahead then pull into the lot on the left," I directed. "There's a gate. Just use this." I handed Budd my key card then peered around the seat at Ike. "I like to be prepared, that's all."

Ike nodded once, a short jerk of his chin. "Spontaneity isn't your strong suit, is it?"

I leaned back. "What's the problem, Ike? What's got you in a snit all of a sudden?"

"Why don't you trust me, Acie? We've known each other for a lot of years, but you act like—" His turned, his pale blue eyes wary. "You act like I'm guilty."

"Guilty of what?" I was happy to use Budd as an excuse so I didn't have to look at Ike. "The card reader is tricky. Jiggle it."

Budd did as I directed and the pole arm swung upward. We proceeded into the parking lot, which was about three-quarters full to its two hundred car capacity. "Park anywhere," I said. "It's not a long walk from here."

"I'm not sure what you think I'm guilty about," Ike said. "But you act like I've offended you or something."

"When did I do that?" I demanded.

Budd pulled the car into a spot near Baker Hall. "Which way now?" He snatched the clipboard out of Ike's hand and threw open his car door.

I followed his lead, getting out and coming around the car before Ike barely had his door open. "This way." I headed for the sidewalk between the buildings.

Budd fell into step beside me. "I won't lock the car," he murmured. "Apparently you don't feel it's necessary."

"It's not a bad habit to cultivate," I said apologetically. "But I don't think it's essential. This is my office building here." I gestured to the left. "Class buildings are there," and I gestured right. I peeked over my shoulder. Ike followed us, hands dug into his jacket pockets and frowning at the sidewalk in concentration.

I managed a credible dialog with Budd about the campus while we walked, emerging into the central circle where the Student Union sat, the hub of campus. As I expected, there were dozens of people milling around. "It's a football weekend." I dodged groups of students in purple and gold attire. "I'm sure it will be busy everywhere."

"Excellent," Budd said. "It will give me local color for my shots." He pulled out his small camera and sighted through the viewer.

"Do you want to do interior shots at the library or do you want exteriors?"

"Both, I hope," Budd said when we approached the glass-and-steel structure dominating the southwest side of the campus. "Dr. Adler, could you join Dr. Doyle in front of the building? I'd like to get a sense of scale." He walked off without waiting to see if we would follow his instructions, camera hanging from his wrist

116

by a strap while he scribbled a note on his clipboard.

I went up the slight incline to the front entrance. The steps had long ago been removed at this building and all others to make the campus totally handicap-accessible. Thus the campus had wide sweeping sidewalks around us interspersed with flowers, trees, and shrubs. I moved to one side of the ramp to the library, out of the way of anyone entering or leaving the building.

Ike leaned back on the railing overlooking a pretty seating area to the left of the entrance under the shade of two beautiful oak trees with dark red foliage. I touched his arm tentatively. "I don't think you're guilty, Ike."

"Really?" His head was lowered and he stared at the pavement so I couldn't see his eyes. "You're not exactly giving me the idea you welcome my affection, Acie. Every time I try to touch you, you jump away. And last night I had the feeling you didn't really welcome my kiss."

I blew out an exasperated sigh. "It was hardly the place for a kiss, Ike."

"You worry too much about what people will think."

I started to object, but honesty forced me to say, "Perhaps. I suppose I'm over-sensitive. I just didn't imagine you would care for me that way. I—I'm just surprised, that's all."

"And you don't like surprises, right?" He raised his head then and looked at me. We were so close I saw little flecks of dark gray in the pale blue of his eyes. His gaze was hypnotic, so direct and unwavering.

"Some surprises aren't happy ones, Ike." I forced

myself to maintain eye contact when all I wanted to do was hide from his penetrating stare. A chaotic swirl of memories bubbled up from my subconscious. "My mother ran off and left me and father when I was little. That's when I found out he was an alcoholic. It was one of my first bad surprises in my life."

He took my hand from his arm and held it in his left hand, his right hand gently stroking it like he was soothing a frightened kitten. "I know," he said softly.

"How did you know?" I had to duck my head closer to his to hear his answer.

"Your mother told me." His face was inches from mine. "I don't remember when it was. We were at a faculty gathering, I think. She was watching you. I said how proud she must be of you. That's when she said she had nothing to do with your success. You earned it all on your own. She sounded so sad I asked her what she meant, and she told me how she left you." His fingers rubbed over the fine bones on the back of my hand. "So I asked a few people in town about what happened and I learned about it all."

"Then you can understand why I'm not very good at handling surprises. And why I'm anxious about what other people might think. When I was growing up, I was always—" I stopped, appalled I was baring my heart to him. Good heavens, I barely knew the man.

Of course, that wasn't the truth. I did know Ike. We had spent countless hours together, going to movies, chatting about books, going to faculty parties together. The knowledge settled over me like a well-worn and comfortable sweater. *I know him. I can trust him.*

Sunlight filtering through the trees highlighted the white and gray strands in Ike's thick hair when he tilted his head to regard me. "All I'm asking is for you to give the idea some thought."

"Oh, I have," I said. "Believe me."

He smiled, little dimples showing at the corners of his mouth. "Good. That sounds promising."

"I'm just nervous about, well, about rules and regulations and what people might think. We have positions to consider at the college. I don't want to jeopardize my career."

"I'm not worried at all. We're both adults and whatever we do won't affect anyone else. I'm sure there's nothing to stop us from seeing each other." He moved my hand so it rested on his left shoulder, holding it there by pressing his left hand on it. "No one cares about us, Acie. Believe me."

I stared into his intense blue eyes, seeing seduction and promise there.

"Excellent!" Budd called out.

I pulled my gaze away from Ike, bewildered. I had totally forgotten anyone else was nearby. On my left, Budd and a dozen other people were watching us with rapt attention while Budd snapped pictures. To my mortified shock, I recognized two of the onlookers as students of mine. "Oh, for heaven's sake—" I started to pull away from Ike, but he kept me firmly next to him by slipping his arm around my waist.

He straightened. "Shall we go inside?" he asked with a broad smile.

Budd nodded eagerly. "You and Dr. Doyle are perfect subjects." The little man said, bounding up the ramp to us. "I can't wait to show these to Laurie."

Ike shifted his arm to around my shoulders so I couldn't escape without making it obvious. I looked behind me, startled to see two students give me grins along with big thumbs-up gestures. Then Ike led me into the library, following the bobbing shape of George Budd.

****

We did a cursory inspection of the library interior then we went into Baker Hall, where Budd inspected my office, but decided it just wouldn't do for the type of scenes they were envisioning.

Next we went to the Student Union. Budd had arranged to meet the custodian so we could check the ballroom where the dance would be held the following Friday. An elderly janitor obligingly turned on lights for Budd while he walked around the space, muttering to himself.

"Is it always like this?" Ike asked. He and I sat in chairs near one of the doors leading to an outside patio. "Walking around and looking at things and taking pictures?"

"I'm not sure. I've never gone with a scout before. They always did it all before I started on the project."

Ike leaned forward, forearms resting on his thighs and his hands clasped between his knees. "Modeling isn't what I thought it would be."

I laughed. "It's more work than you thought, right?"

He nodded ruefully. "I thought you just stood around, somebody took pictures then you went home and collected the money."

"It's like writing a book. Everybody thinks they can do it, but not many people really can. You haven't seen half of it, either." I gestured toward Budd. "There's makeup, and lighting, and clothing changes.

There're temperamental photographers, rain-outs, and co-workers who are a pain." I frowned. "I wonder who the male lead will be. I didn't see any names." I shrugged. "Maybe they'll decide to just have it be me and the daughter."

Budd approached us, clipboard in hand. "I have what I need here. Where's the stadium?"

Ike stood and extended his hand, helping me to my feet. "There's a game today," I reminded Budd. "It will be busy."

He beamed. "Perfect."

It was a short walk across campus to the stadium, where we joined the tailgaters in the parking lot. Ike and I were greeted raucously by several students, who insisted we stop for bratwurst and beer.

I hesitated, not sure it would be appropriate, but I was swept along on a tide of good will and finally acquiesced. Ike joined in an impromptu game of football catch while I sat on a lawn chair and watched, surrounded by students and their families. I was bemused to find my quieter students appeared to be partying most heartily. Still waters did indeed run deep.

During a lull in conversation I was suddenly struck by the shocking disparity between my life and Henrietta's shortened life. I was sitting here in a parking lot, beer in one hand, while a man who professed to love me was cavorting nearby. People around me were talking, laughing, and anticipating even more good times later this afternoon and into the evening.

Henrietta was—where would they take her body? Would they do an autopsy? I struggled to remember what little I knew of her circumstances. Her family moved away from Grimper after Henrietta graduated, and her parents were dead. She lived in Chicago for years, and presumably had friends there. Who could claim her body and make arrangements for burial? What if it was me lying dead in a morgue somewhere? Who would mourn for me?

I thought of my mother and Aunt Sherry, my extended circle of friends from the faculty, Maggie, and others. Life was so fleeting, so brief. At any moment it could be snuffed out. For just an instant I had a sense of what my mother must have experienced when she fled Grimper, leaving me and my father behind. Had she felt the same way? Was she afraid life was speeding past her and if she didn't grab for something else, she would regret it?

"This is perfect," Budd said, clutching his clipboard in one hand and a hamburger in the other. He was dancing from foot to foot with excitement. "This is exactly the kind of atmosphere we need. Maybe we could have your daughter in the shoot be dating a football player. That would be great. Do you know the football coach? I'd like to get in and see the locker room."

I pointed out the coach was probably busy because the game was starting in an hour or so. One of the tailgaters overheard our conversation and dragged over a very large young man who was introduced as an alumnus of the football team, having graduated the year previously. Budd was ecstatic and he peppered the man with questions and took photographs. When we left an hour later, Budd's now grease-stained clipboard was bristling with several scraps of papers adorned with phone numbers, ideas, and notes.

"I have everything I need for the shoot," Budd said when we drove away from the campus and back to town. "Several locations we can use. Of course, we don't know what the dance will be like until we see the venue when the decorations are in place, but I think I have an idea of what we can do." He smiled, tapping a merry little tune on the steering wheel. "Laurie will be very pleased." He looked at Ike, sitting in the passenger seat. "Shall I drop you at your car, Dr. Adler?"

"Sure. It's at the police station, near the city square." Ike looked over his shoulder at me. "Do you want me to give you a ride home?"

I checked my watch. It was a little after two o'clock. I had to give a statement to the police, let Conan out for his break, and be ready to meet Maggie in just a few hours. "I'd better get home and get work done," I said, hoping Ike wouldn't read my reluctance the wrong way. "Maggie is coming for us to work on the article for the paper."

Ike nodded and I breathed a sigh of relief. I wasn't sure *where* I wanted this relationship to go, but I didn't want it to be nipped in the bud until I knew. Budd followed Ike's directions to the police station, pulling into the lot next to Ike's car. I got out of the car when Ike did.

"Thanks for being such a good sport about today," I murmured while I prepared to take Ike's place in the front seat. "I'm sure it's not how you planned to spend your Saturday."

Ike smiled, those intriguing dimples making a showing again. "It wasn't what I planned but I had fun." He leaned forward and our lips met in a quick kiss. "I'll call you later, okay?"

I nodded and turned to slide into the car.

"Acie?"

I paused.

"Give it a thought, okay?"

I smiled at him. "Will do." I settled into the seat and pulled the seat belt tight around me. Budd started the car and while we drove away I turned to wave to Ike.

"I emailed Laurie the photos I took," Budd said, turning onto Main Street. "She's very excited. I think this will be an excellent shoot. I appreciate you taking so much time to help me today."

"I'm glad to do it," I said. "I've found that having a good sense of location can make a shoot go so much better."

"Exactly," Budd agreed. "Many models don't have that appreciation." He once again tapped the steering wheel in time to a song only he could hear. "Yes. A good day indeed."

I reviewed the tumultuous day, starting with a phone call from Ike and ending with his kiss. "A good day indeed," I agreed.

Chapter 8

I invited Mr. Budd inside for coffee when we arrived at my house, but he was anxious to get to the airport. "My flight leaves at five, so I better get going."

"Are you sure? There's plenty of time. There shouldn't be a lot of traffic, so it'll probably only take you an hour or so to get there."

"I need to return the car and clear security. No, I'd better get on the road."

Clear security? I almost laughed out loud. He appeared anxious so I didn't bother arguing but instead just left the car. If he wanted to sit in the Des Moines airport for two hours that was fine with me. I leaned over to speak to him, hanging on to the car door. "You have my email address, so if you need anything, just let me know. I suppose Laurie will send us the schedule next week?"

"She and I will coordinate the project and get information to you and the others ASAP." He waggled his small camera at me. "Thank you so much for the help. This will be a fabulous shoot."

"My pleasure." I closed the door and watched him pull away then I headed for the front door. I had a puppy to walk, a house to tidy, and a conference to prep for. I went inside where Conan greeted me, sitting on the foyer rug with an eager expression. I recognized his expression. It was potty time.

I clipped his leash to his collar and we were off for a brisk fifteen minute walk around the neighborhood and into what I called Conan's Latrine in the scrub woods to the west of my house. If he did his business here, I didn't bother to clean up after him since he and I were usually the only ones who roamed around these trees. I was careful to move any offending offerings off the beaten path.

We returned to the house and I fed the resident feline critters their afternoon canned food then I settled down with the mail, which arrived while I was out. When I sat at my desk, I saw the flashing light indicating a message was waiting on my answering machine. I tapped the play button and an authoritative male voice boomed into my den.

"Miss Doyle, I'm calling from the Grimper Police Department. You need to make a statement regarding last night's events when you found Miss Baron at the park. Please come to the station as soon as possible and report to Detective Inspector Lee Street. Thank you."

I sat back, glaring at the unoffending piece of machinery. I had forgotten all about making a statement, but I suppose it was required. If I hurried, I could go to the station, make my statement then get back here to tidy up the house in preparation for Maggie's visit. Conan, seated at my feet, looked eagerly at me. "Sorry, honey," I said, giving his ears a good rub. "I need to go out again. Let's put you in your bed while I'm gone." He did well while I was out during the morning, but I didn't feel like pushing my luck.

He followed me into the mud room, curling up on his bed. I made sure the door was securely closed behind me then I exited by the garage door, keys jingling in my hand. Traffic near town was heavier now. The game was almost over and people were already vacating the stadium and heading for the bars.

I parked in the police department parking lot and went inside, where I introduced myself to the gloomy looking man at the front desk. After a short wait I was ushered into an office with a view of the park across the street. Another man sat behind a gray metal desk. He rose to shake my hand when I entered and gestured me to a hard wooden chair in front of the desk.

Detective Lee Street was a slender man with slicked-back thinning dark hair, a very narrow face, and dark brown eyes set slightly too close together. His hunched shoulders reminded me of a cartoon ferret or gangster, lurking and peering at people from under heavy dark eyebrows. This look was enhanced by his habit of pursing his lips, making his already thin face appear even more pinched. He wore a wrinkled pale blue shirt with a striped blue necktie tied unevenly, with one end far longer than the other.

My few previous conversations with him were mostly civil and occurred when my mother and aunt insisted on involving the Grimper PD with their investigative efforts. He always struck me as a man with a rigid sense of right and wrong and without much sense of humor, but I suppose that was to be expected of a police officer.

I crossed my legs, left over right, and regarded him with polite curiosity. "I was told I needed to give you a statement regarding what happened last night."

He nodded and held up a small digital recorder, similar to the ones I've seen my students use in my class. "Do you object to being recorded?"

"No, I don't."

"Will you please state your name and today's date and time, for the record?"

I did as he asked then I answered with a clear "Yes" to his question: "Are you aware you are being recorded?" and "No" to "Do you object having your statement recorded in this manner?"

"Would you please tell me, in your own words, what happened last night that led you to discover Miss Baron's body?" He sat back in his mesh office chair, apparently relaxed. This pose was offset by his right hand fingers, which tapped a slow rhythm on the arm of his chair.

I paused to order my thoughts then I gave a brief summary of my time at the Country Club and my talk, how I ran into Ike, our trek to the park and finding Henrietta. When I finished, Street continued watching me, his expression thoughtful. "Is that all?" I prompted when he seemed disinclined to speak.

He leaned forward and clasped his hands on his desk, centering them over the top of a manila file folder. "I have just a few questions. Did you go down the path to the ledge below?"

"No," I said. "I wasn't that brave."

"But Dr. Adler went down."

I nodded then remembered the recorder. "Yes, he did."

"Weren't you worried he might fall?"

"He didn't ask for my opinion," I said.

"That's not what I asked. I asked if you were worried he might fall." Street's eyes didn't waver while he gazed at me.

I was accustomed to such scrutiny. I had perfected my deadpan expression after innumerable visits from Child Welfare Service workers, investigating my home life with my father when I was younger. I had fooled them. A mere police officer didn't worry me. "Of course I was worried," I said in an even tone. "It's very steep there."

"You've been there before last night?"

"I grew up in Grimper. I've been there before."

Street sat back in his chair. "That's right. You grew up here."

"Yes, I did."

"You called 9-1-1 from the park," Street said.

"Yes, I did."

"Why didn't Dr. Adler call?"

"He was using his cell phone as a flashlight," I said.

Street's gaze dropped to the file folder then back to me. "Were you aware Miss Baron had asthma?"

"Yes. She had an asthma attack earlier in the evening."

"When you and she argued." It wasn't a question.

"We had a disagreement before I was due to speak." I resisted the urge to uncross and re-cross my legs. His emotionless questions made me want to counteract his monotony with movement. I suppose that was his method.

"People said you argued."

"Who?" I regarded him with one upraised eyebrow.

He didn't rise to my bait. "Eyewitnesses."

"We disagreed about the use of the land Miss Baron was inheriting from her uncle."

"You claim her uncle agreed to donate the land for this animal sanctuary you're trying to get started."

"I'm not the only person involved. Several townspeople are anxious to see a sanctuary near town. I'm on the committee that was formed to investigate the idea."

"What would you do if you couldn't get the land?"

"We had Mr. Baron's express wishes, in writing, as to the disposition of the land."

Street leaned forward, his clasped once again sliding over the folder. I wondered if he kept his hands together so he wouldn't fidget. "From what I've been told, Miss Baron claimed she also had a document that asserted she could sell the land."

"As I understood it, Mr. Baron's will hasn't even been probated yet. So perhaps this discussion is moot. Maybe Miss Baron isn't even his heir."

He straightened. "Who told you that?"

I kept my face smooth but inside I was frowning in surprise. "No one told me anything about his will."

Street stared at me, his cold eyes evaluating me. "You're right. Mr. Baron's will has not been officially probated. But you seem to assume Miss Baron was his heir."

Officially probated? What did that mean? "Miss Baron led me to believe that she was."

"And she claimed she had a document from her uncle saying she could sell the land?"

I nodded. "I'm sure her heirs will be anxious to produce the document so this issue can be laid to rest. Do you know who is named in her will?" I mustered my best innocent expression, but it appeared to bounce off Street's laconic facade.

"It hasn't been made public yet." He opened the manila folder with the flick of one finger. "Miss Baron made a complaint about your dog."

I forced myself to remain still in my chair. "Yes, she did," I said levelly.

"She said your dog attacked her."

I paused before answering, giving myself time to find the right wording. "Miss Baron misconstrued a puppy's friendly advances as an attack. It was a misunderstanding and I'm sure, had she lived, we would have straightened it out."

Street continued reading the page in front of him. "Officer George said Dr. Adler was at your house and he indicated he would talk to Miss Baron about the attack."

"Alleged attack," I said quickly. "Yes, he was there."

"Are you and Dr. Adler romantically involved?" Street looked up at me.

I considered and discarded several replies. "Why do you want to know?"

He made a small notation on the paper. "You prefer not to answer?"

"I prefer to know why you would like to know." I smiled when he stared coldly at me.

"You're sure you didn't go down the hillside or touch Miss Baron in any way?"

"I'm sure." I experienced a faint prickle of concern. What was he getting at? Why did he have this insistence about me being near her body?

"Were you at the park earlier in the evening?"

I shook my head. "No, I wasn't."

"But your dog was there." He shifted his gaze from

my face to my hands then back again.

I recognized this tactic, meant to throw me off balance. I countered it with calmness. "Why do you think my dog was there?"

He kept his gaze fixed on my face. "There are dog prints all around the area where Miss Baron's body was found."

"There's a pack of dogs living in the area," I said.

He nodded. "You're familiar with them?"

"I know of them," I corrected. "No one is friends with them, although Dr. Lippincott and her husband have managed to trap most of the dogs and give them their vaccinations."

"Which you paid for."

"Yes, I did. I felt sorry for them and—" I stopped. I didn't owe him an explanation for my charitable work.

He was silent for a moment then he said, "I'm trying to get a sense of the timing. When did you finish your speech and meet Dr. Adler?"

I crossed my legs, right over left, and straightened the crease in my jeans. "You're implying I went to meet Dr. Adler. That isn't true. I ran into Dr. Adler after I spoke. I believe the meeting started at seven o'clock, but you should check with Marge Crandon because she was in charge of running the meeting. The surveyor spoke first then I followed. I believe he spoke for fifteen minutes, and I spoke for about ten minutes. So it was probably seven-thirty or so when I saw Dr. Adler."

"So Dr. Adler was gone for a half hour?"

My hands twitched with the need to clench them. I forced myself to stillness. "I'm not sure. He may have been on the porch or in the back of the room. It was quite full."

"He's a tall man. You probably would notice him if he was in the room."

"As I said, the room was full. I may have missed seeing him when I was giving my speech."

"Were you surprised he wasn't there while you were talking?"

"As I said, I'm not sure if he was or wasn't there."

"But he must not have been there," Staples said. "Because he was outside when you left."

"I don't know where he was," I repeated. "He may have stepped out to the porch, gone to his car, or he may have been in the back of the hall then left. I'm not sure."

"Why did you run into him?" Street asked.

"Because he was on the porch and I was leaving."

"Why were you leaving?"

"I had finished my speech and I wanted to go home." I was not about to reveal I wanted to search for my lost dog.

"Why?"

"Why what?" I asked politely.

"Why didn't you stay and hear the remainder of the speeches?"

I clasped my hands and balanced them on my right knee, praying I was the picture of patience. "I had no need to hear them. I have talked with Mr. Staples before about his opinions, Dr. Lippincott and I have discussed the medical aspects of the sanctuary, and I had a long day at work and I was tired."

"I see. What did you and Dr. Adler talk about while you were outside?"

"He asked how my speech went."

"Is that all?"

"I don't really remember details. We weren't on the porch for long." *Not a lie,* I reasoned. The only detail I remembered vividly was the kiss, and I damn sure wasn't going to share that with this cold-hearted jerk. I uncrossed my legs. "Is that all?"

"No." Street looked at the piece of paper on his desk. "You and Miss Baron knew each other for a long time."

I eyed him warily. "We were acquaintances when we were younger."

"You went to school together."

"I went to school with many people from Grimper. Some of whom are still in town and many who moved away."

"But you came back." It was a statement with a question in it.

"An opening became available at the college here."

Street regarded me without any expression in his flat, dark eyes. "I'm surprised you would want to return here. From what I've heard, you had an unpleasant childhood in Grimper."

I returned his gaze with what I hoped were equally expressionless eyes. "I had an uncomfortable childhood," I corrected. "I was embarrassed by my father and his inability to hold a job. Those kinds of things are important to a young person. Once I was older I was able to appreciate the town without the memories it invoked."

"That's a good skill," Street said. "Were you able to do the same about Henrietta Baron?"

I frowned. "I beg your pardon?"

"I've been told you and she had quite a feud, going back many years."

I considered his words. "I don't think that's true."

"Didn't she steal away a boyfriend of yours back in high school?"

My puzzled expression changed to an incredulous one. "Mr. Street, it was thirty-five or forty years ago. If it happened, I don't even remember the name of the boy involved."

"Really? So you're saying you and Henrietta Baron were on good terms?"

"I didn't say that. I said she and I disagreed about the use of her uncle's land."

"Did you like Miss Baron?"

"I don't believe that is relevant to any discussion here." I decided this fishing expedition of his had gone on long enough, so I stood and picked up my purse, slinging it over my shoulder. "Are we done?"

He didn't stand, but just regarded me from behind his desk. "For now. I'll have your statement typed up and ready for your signature on Monday, if you'll stop in then."

I nodded my assent and turned to leave.

"Dr. Doyle?"

I turned back to him. "Yes?"

"Why did you and Dr. Adler go to the park?"

I was, thankfully, able to answer honestly. Not *completely* honestly, but honestly nonetheless. "We saw movement near the front gate and weren't sure what it was. Dr. Adler wasn't sure if Miss Baron might need his assistance, so we thought we'd go there and check."

"So Dr. Adler knew Miss Baron was there?"

I met his flinty gaze with one of my own. "I'm sure he's already told you that he and Miss Baron were at the picnic shelter earlier."

"Did he know she was still there?"

I stared thoughtfully at his desk then said, "I believe he said she said she was going home. I'm sorry, I don't remember for sure." I raised my eyes and encountered his gaze fixed on me.

"Did Dr. Adler tell you what he and Miss Baron talked about?"

"He didn't tell me any details. We were distracted by the movement we saw."

Street nodded, a slow, ponderous movement of his head. "I see. Thank you for coming."

I escaped the claustrophobic confines of his office, emerging from the police station to a town bustling with after-football activity. While I drove carefully through the congested streets I reviewed my conversation with the intrepid detective. I concluded it went as well as I could have hoped for.

Maggie arrived an hour later, bringing with her a take-and-bake pizza. While I got it into the oven, she gave Conan a brief exam then washed her hands and rejoined me in the living room near the little dining nook off the kitchen. "He appears fine," she said, taking the glass of wine I handed her. "None the worse for his adventure."

"It makes my skin crawl to think he was with that pack of dogs." I placed the pizza on the table and gestured to Maggie to sit. "I'm still surprised he went that far afield. The last time he escaped, he only went a block or so. But the Country Club is five blocks from here." I thought of the busy streets Conan had to cross to get to the woods around the club. "I'm lucky he didn't get hit by a car or bit by one of the strays."

"At least there's little traffic this far north of

town." Maggie shook out her napkin and slid onto the window seat which made up half of the dining seating. "He probably cut through back yards along the little stream which runs east-west."

"Maybe." I was relieved at the thought of Conan ducking under the little roadway bridge spanning the meandering creek.

"I'll bet he caught the scent of those dogs." Maggie took a slice of pizza, setting it on her plate to cool. "Someone has been taking care of them. The last time we went out to check on them, there was a pile of bones. Somebody set out meat for them."

"Why would someone do that? I thought everyone out in the neighborhood didn't care for them. In fact, didn't Mr. Staples threaten to poison them?" I took a slice of pizza and bit into the cheesy goodness.

"He threatened, but I made sure he knew if he did anything, he'd be in trouble." Maggie followed my lead and for a minute we focused on eating. "It's against the law to set out poison bait for anything larger than a rat. That stuff is inhumane and dangerous unless it's closely monitored." She looked at the floor. "Where are your animals? Nobody is bugging me for food."

"None of my critters cares about human food. They're probably all in the den or the bedroom, snoozing."

"Lucky you. We have two basset hounds. If there's food, there's a hound right on your foot, waiting to help you eat." She took another bite of pizza. "We have to lock them out of the room, otherwise they'll manage to get up on the table and snatch the food off."

"Where did you find the food left for the strays?"

"Not far from Charlie Baron's house. Do you think

he was feeding them?"

I considered the question while I continued eating. "I don't think so," I finally said. "I was under the impression he didn't care about the dogs enough to feed them. I think he mainly ignored them."

"Maybe ask your mother," Maggie suggested. "She might know. She and Mr. Baron were so close. He might have said something to her about it."

"Close?"

Maggie nodded. "I thought it was kind of sweet. They always had tea together in the afternoon and dinner twice a week. And I heard about the casino outing, when they went over to Des Moines and spent the day."

I almost choked on my pizza. Tea in the afternoon? Dinner? Casino?

"I'm sure his death has hit her hard." Maggie looked enquiringly at me, but I dodged her gaze by taking a lengthy swallow of wine.

"It has," I said when I lowered the glass. "But she's coping very well." I picked up the brochure Maggie created for the town meeting. "Do you know what's needed for this article we're writing?"

"I got an outline from the newspaper editor and I talked to one of the teachers in the Journalism department at the college." Maggie dabbed her lips with her napkin then opened the voluminous tote bag she set on the floor at her feet. "I have a few ideas and the professor said he'd work with us on the text."

"That's a relief. I have no idea how to write a news story, or whatever is needed." I was also relieved we changed the subject from my mother and Charlie. I resolved to call Aunt Sherry and pump her for details about my mother's so-called relationship with the dead man.

Maggie drew out a notebook and several sheets of paper from the bag. "Here's the outline and here are the notes I put together."

I leaned back and started reading while I nibbled pizza. Ideas began to percolate in my mind about how to formulate our arguments. "Let's get started," I said, pulling over the notepad and pen.

****

Three hours later, I bid Maggie good-bye. We had accomplished an excellent first draft of the news article, jotting ideas on paper first then moving to my den and my desktop computer. I printed the article for her and we decided we'd both review it and I would forward any comments to her. Then Maggie would take the draft to the journalism teacher for a final review before turning it in to the newspaper on Monday.

I tided up our dishes and went back to my den, determined to accomplish my other assignments for the weekend. I didn't have the energy to focus on grading papers, so I turned my attention to my presentation for the upcoming conference. It was mainly finished so all I had to do were little tweaks and a mental walk-through to make sure my timing was acceptable. I ran through it a few times then shut down my computer for the night and went into the living room, curling up on the couch with a glass of wine in front of the fireplace.

What a crazy twenty-four hours! The town meeting, the kiss with Ike, finding Henrietta, Conan lost and found, the location scout. I had jammed a week's worth of activities into one brief day.

Ike.

I sipped my wine and stared at the windows, the crackling of the logs and Houdini's snoring the only sounds in the room. What was I going to do about Ike?

I had been single for more than twenty years. My ill-fated marriage ended when I was thirty and I was now settled in my ways, not anxious to share my home or my life with anyone. I was happy. Of course I was.

But Ike was so easy to be with. We had so many of the same interests and the ones we didn't have in common were fun to explore. *Just give us a chance,* he said, but did he really know what he was asking?

I was super-sensitive to what others would think but it wasn't only that. I got up and refilled my wine glass and stood at the window, peering into the darkness. I had to be honest. I was afraid of intimacy. I was just rounding the final phases of menopause and I no longer cared about sex, or lust, or love. I relegated those emotions to my past and closed the door on a part of my life with no regret. "A woman needs a man like a fish needs a bicycle," I murmured.

But Ike…I could imagine what kind of lover he'd be. He was so attentive, so alert to small changes in my mood. He would be the same in bed, I was sure. I could visualize his body. I'd seen him often in a T-shirt and shorts, the shirt clinging damply to him while he worked in his garden with me watching from the shade of the porch. His body was still taut and lean, his arms brown from working in the sun.

I took another swallow of wine, surprised by the flush of excitement the thought of Ike gave me. Maybe I wasn't totally past those feelings. I turned from the window and when I did I saw movement outside, near the trees at the edge of my yard. I stepped back, my stomach lurching with fear. Although other houses weren't far away, my house had a great deal of privacy because of the trees around it. I had a sharp sense of isolation, a feeling I used to enjoy but which now made me nervous.

A memory of Henrietta's face swam in front of me and I stepped back again, setting my wine on the end table and reaching for the lamp. I turned it off then went into my den, edging around the doorway wall and sidling up to the window to stare out into the darkness beyond the patio.

Movement again. It was a shadow moving among other shadows, something quick and sinuous. Many of the trees and underbrush had already lost their foliage, leaving skeletal silhouettes stark against the moonlit horizon. I couldn't tell if the movement was animal or human, although it seemed tall enough to be human. I glanced at the phone on my desk. Should I call the police?

As soon as I thought it, I dismissed the idea. I wasn't threatened and I had no idea what was out there. It might be a deer.

It might be a murderer.

The thought made me take a step toward the phone. Just as I did, it rang. I jumped so quickly I slammed into the desk, re-bruising my hip. I snatched up the receiver. "Doyle residence," I said breathlessly.

"Are you busy?" Ike's warm voice eased my rattled senses with just those three little words.

I laughed softly. "No, I'm just jumping at shadows. I thought I saw something outside."

"Do you want me to come over?" he asked immediately.

"No, it's probably nothing. I'm just nervous, I think, because of what happened to Henrietta. Thanks for offering, though."

"I'd enjoy coming over there and soothing your nerves," he said in a teasing voice.

I went into the living room, the dancing light from the fireplace showing me the way. I picked up my wine glass. "It's okay. It's probably just a deer."

"Are you at your window?"

"Yes. That's where I saw it, near the hill."

"Look in the distance. Do you see it?"

I leaned forward, staring through the glass and blocking out the fireplace glow behind me. "What am I supposed to see?"

"Look."

I stared more and gradually my eyes adapted to the darkness. I peered beyond the property line into the distance and saw a faint glimmer that flared then vanished. "The light?"

"That's me. I'm like a lightning bug, flashing my glow."

I laughed out loud, my shaken spirits lifting. "Wiggling your butt at me?"

He laughed, too. "You can say so, I guess." There was a pause. "Give me a chance, Acie. I won't let you down."

I put my hand on the glass. "I'm not sure about it, Ike."

"I know you aren't. Let me convince you."

I smiled at the flashing light in the distance. "I have to go to the conference next week. Let me think about it all while I'm gone."

"That's all I'm asking. Are you sure you don't

want me to come over?"

I stepped back from the glass. "No, it's fine."

"Okay. Good night, Acie."

"Good night, Ike." I turned off the phone and lay the receiver on the coffee table. Then I finished my wine and resolutely went to bed, not looking back at the window.

Whatever was there, I wasn't going to let it spoil my sweet dreams.

Chapter 9

Sunday dawned cold with a coating of white frost on everything, reminding me that winter was just a few weeks away. It prompted me to rearrange my closet to give me easier access to warmer clothing. While I was at it, I chose what I would take for my upcoming four day conference which led me to the mud room where my washer and dryer were located. I started a load of laundry and pulled the door closed behind me.

I indulged in my usual Sunday morning breakfast of waffles while I read the Sunday paper, sipping coffee sitting at my dining table and gazing southward, where Ike's house was located. What was he doing on this Sunday morning? He was probably out golfing, getting in a last few rounds before winter set in. Or maybe he was gardening, trimming and pruning and getting his beautiful flower beds ready for hibernation.

I shook myself out of a daydream and put away my dirty dishes then I started another load of laundry while Sprite supervised, fascinated by the water swirling in the utility basin. I shooed her out and closed the door again then I took Conan for a brisk walk around the neighborhood. We went near the woods where I saw my intruder the night before, but there was nothing to indicate anyone, neither man nor beast, had been there. I dismissed my concerns from my mind and hurried home.

When Conan and I came in the front door, I found the mud room door open. Sprite sat on the washing machine, watching the water slosh into the drain in the utility sink. "How did you get in here?" I asked her, scooping her up and taking her out of the room. I closed the door again and started back to the living room.

I had gone just a couple of steps when Sprite dodged around me and jumped on the small end table outside the mud room door. Then she flung herself at the door handle, clinging for an instant before pushing away with her back feet against the jamb. The door swung inward and she let go, landing with a thump on the rug before springing up onto the utility sink to peer in fascination at the disappearing water.

I laughed. "That explains one mystery," I said to Conan, who stared anxiously at the kitten balanced on the side of the sink. I left her to the mysteries of laundry and went to my den where I focused for several hours on getting caught up on schoolwork and to review the article Maggie and I drafted.

Paul called me late in the afternoon. "I heard the location scout was very happy," he said by way of greeting.

"Glad to hear it." A happy location scout meant we'd have an easy shoot, or at least I hoped. "Did they have any problem with starting the shoot after I'm done at the dance?"

"Nope. Laurie said you go to the dance, do your thing, then they'll grab you as soon as the ceremony is over and you'll start doing your part of the work. They'll come into town earlier and do a few shots with the kid they have who's playing your daughter."

I breathed a sigh of relief. I was somewhat worried

I'd be forced to give my acceptance speech while in full makeup and clothing for the layout. At least I'd be able to face the audience as myself, not Myself the Model.

"Listen, about the guy who was with you."

I went on immediate alert. Anytime Paul started a sentence with *Listen,* something I might object to was coming. "Dr. Adler?"

"Yeah, him. According to the scout, he was good."

"Good in what way?" I looked outside, eyeing the dark clouds piling up. Another rain storm was coming.

"Photogenic. You and he looked good together. The scout—who was he? Yeah, Budd. He took pictures and showed them to Laurie. She was interested."

"Interested in what?"

"Using him in the shoot."

"What?" I sank next to Houdini on the couch. The big blond cat mumbled an objection then resumed snoring. "Ike's not a model. You can't use him."

"It's not like he's the primary. You and the girl are the primaries. He'll just be window dressing. Laurie thought he was perfect for it. So I need you to give me his contact information and I'm going to call him, see if I can get him signed to a contract."

I opened my mouth to object but words failed me. I finally managed, "Paul, he's a college professor, he's not a model. Why do you think he'd want to participate in something like a photo shoot? For heaven's sake, he's a busy man. He—"

"Why don't you let him speak for himself, Annabelle? Maybe he'd get a kick out of it. Who knows, maybe he's always wanted to have a second career." When I didn't answer, Paul said, "I can get his information without your help, you know. I just called you because I didn't want you to be surprised when your boyfriend showed up at the shoot."

"He's not my boyfriend. Women my age don't have boyfriends." My mind was racing, going over the shooting summary. It called for a male model in one or two of the pictures in addition to the crowd scenes. It probably wouldn't be a big imposition for Ike to do it.

"From what I saw in those pictures, you're boyfriend-girlfriend."

"You saw the pictures? Why haven't I seen the pictures?" I demanded. "That's not fair and you know it, Paul. If the scout is setting up the shoot and he's using me in the setup, I should get a chance to evaluate the pictures."

"Okay, hold on." There was a pause and a faint dinging noise. "Done. I just emailed 'em to you. You and he look good together, Annabelle. It would really help the shoot. You know it's always good to be cooperative."

I sighed. He was right. I cultivated an easy-going persona during my modeling days, staying flexible when schedules were shifted or sets were rearranged. Other models got a reputation for being difficult to work with while I was often sought out after a diva was fired.

"Hold on, and I'll get you Dr. Adler's contact information," I said, going to the den. I picked up my mobile phone and checked my contact list then I rattled off phone numbers and email information to Paul. "Have you seen the shooting schedule yet?"

"Laurie said she'd send a copy tonight. I'll forward it to you as soon as I get it."

"Good. I need to know when to be back in town." I

pulled out the conference schedule and consulted it. "There's one panel discussion on Friday morning I would really like to attend, but I suppose I can change my plans to get here if I'm needed."

"What kind of conference is it?"

"It focuses on literature at the turn of last century. There's been fascinating research about the influence of Frank Norris on Dreiser and other contemporaries. I'm anticipating some excellent discussions with colleagues about—"

"Sounds like a blast," Paul interrupted. "I'll give you a call on your cell phone later in the week and we'll talk about the schedule. Gotta go. Talk to you later."

I hung up and the phone rang again immediately. It was my mother. "How did it go yesterday with the scout person?"

"Fine," I said. "It didn't take long. He was only here for the morning then had to leave by mid-afternoon."

"Where did you go?"

"The library, around campus, to the stadium. After that I worked with Maggie on the article we had to prepare for the newspaper. That reminds me. I know how Conan got out of the mud room." I described Sprite's trick with the door lever. "So that explains that."

"Thank God Sprite doesn't have opposable thumbs," Mom said. "If she did, she'd probably be raiding your larder and selling the food to animals on the street. Speaking of mammals with thumbs, I suppose you heard the latest news."

"About what?"

"Henrietta Baron's will."

I pulled over my desk chair and sat. "What about her will?"

"She left everything to the college."

"What? Where did you hear that?"

"Martha Hudson's granddaughter is a secretary for young Frank Franklin. They're going to file the will with the court tomorrow."

"Isn't that illegal?" I checked my email queue on my computer screen and saw Paul's email with the little paper clip attachment icon. "I mean, she's not supposed to share information if it hasn't been made public yet, is she?"

"It's her grandmother. What harm is there?"

I clicked the attachment icon and thumbnail pictures opened on my screen. I chose the slideshow option and the pictures began to scroll. "I wonder why Henrietta left her estate to the school."

"Who else would she leave it to? Her parents are dead, she has no brothers or sisters, and I don't think she was close to any cousins. In a lot of ways, she's like you, Annabelle."

A picture of Ike popped up on the screen from the previous day. He was partially turned toward the camera, a football in his right hand. He'd shed his denim jacket and his dark blue T-shirt strained across his chest when he pivoted with the ball. I was near him, laughing at something one of the onlookers said. Ike grinned at me, his blue eyes startling in his tanned face. We were the picture of healthy all-American fun, albeit middle-aged Americans with our gray-and-white hair.

I stared at the picture, mesmerized. Ike was so handsome, so self-possessed. I struggled to find the right word, then my mother's words registered.

"Henrietta and I are nothing alike."

"Of course you are. You're both professional women, you both committed yourselves to your careers, and you are—and she was—in love with Isaac Adler."

"I'm not in love with Ike," I said automatically.

"I won't argue with you." Not said but implied was *I won't argue with you now about it, but we'll revisit this later.* I started to protest but she continued before I could get a word in edgewise. "It's rather awkward, isn't it? I mean, the school is inheriting Henrietta's estate but they're also receiving an endowment from Charlie, who left his estate to Henrietta, who left the estate to the school. So in essence the school is giving itself an endowment."

She had a point. "It is rather odd," I admitted. The picture on my screen now was a shot of the football stadium, taken from a distance. "Have they processed Charlie's will?"

"I don't think so. Martha's granddaughter said there was something odd with it."

"Odd?"

"Apparently Frank Two talked to Henrietta about it and Henrietta was filing a protest or something."

"A protest? What does that mean?"

"I don't know. But I suppose it's all messed up since Henrietta is dead, too. Anyway, about the endowment. Martha's granddaughter said she thought one of the Franks would take Henrietta's place and present the endowment check to you. That way it at least appears that the Baron family had something to do with it. I suppose you'll go to the dance with Dr. Adler?"

"We haven't talked about it." I made a mental note

to chat with Ike. It might make sense for us to go together to the dance if he would work with me on the shoot. And, I had to admit, it might be nice to go to the dance with him just because, well, it might be nice to be at the dance with him.

"That reminds me. I heard he went with you yesterday when you were out and about with the scout."

The pictures scrolled again on my screen and this time it was a shot of Ike and me in front of the library. I was leaned near him, straining to hear what he said. Ike watched me from under his eyelashes like a little boy peeking up at a window full of candy. "How did you know Ike was with us yesterday?"

"Sherry was at the police station and she saw you leave together. She also mentioned Meryl Staples almost threw Ike down in the parking lot and had her way with him."

"I didn't see Sherry there."

"You were busy."

"What was she doing there?" The picture scrolled again, this time showing an image of the campus, with beautiful autumn trees highlighted against a blue sky.

"She wanted to find out if we can go out to Charlie's house. Sherry had to do some shopping in town so she stopped at the police department to find out. Are you busy tomorrow?"

Of course I'm busy. I have a job. "Just the usual," I said. "Why?"

"I was wondering. Charlie Baron's funeral is tomorrow. I was wondering if you'd go."

"I didn't know him very well." *And I hate funerals,* I thought but didn't say. "Will you go?"

There was a pause. "I plan to. I thought if you were

going then I'd go with you."

"When is it?" My face popped up on my screen. I was in silhouette and Budd caught a wistful expression on my face. The gazebo from the town park was on my right, so I suppose I was watching Ike and Meryl Staple kiss at that moment. My stomach flip-flopped at the memory.

"The service is at eleven and there's luncheon afterward."

I breathed a sigh of relief. "I have class at eleven, Mom. I'm sorry."

"Oh."

I belatedly remembered what Maggie said about Charlie and Mom dating. *Dating? They're in their 80s. Nobody dates when they're 80.* "I'm sure Sherry and others from the home will go. Can you go with them?"

"Oh, of course. It's just that all the fuss about Henrietta has pushed Charlie out of mind. I don't think the police are even investigating his death."

"They're not investigating because it was an accident, Mom." The pictures on my screen scrolled again and I regarded my image critically. My casual clothing wasn't the most flattering, but all in all, I wasn't unhappy with my look. Once the hair and makeup people were done with me, I would be very presentable.

"I don't think so. I have a bad feeling about it."

Mom's bad feelings seldom rang true, but if I said so, I'd be treated to a list of the times when, according to Mom, they did indeed ring true. I decided to try a different tactic. "Why do you think he was murdered?"

"I told you. He was waiting to talk to someone that night but no one ever came forward and said they were visiting him."

"No, that's not what I meant. Why would someone want to kill him?" The image changed on my screen and once again Ike was there, this time with me by his side when he argued with John Staples in the town park.

"Oh. I'm not sure."

"Did he have any enemies?" Something about the picture of Staples bothered me. What was it? I had a nagging feeling I should remember something he said or did.

"I'm sure he didn't have any enemies," Mom said, more assured now. "He really was the sweetest man. I'm sorry you didn't get to know him better."

"I'm sure he was very nice," I said automatically, trying to decipher why the picture of John Staples bothered me. Then the picture changed again, this time showing the campus with football fans hurrying to and fro.

A rumble of thunder sounded in the distance, diverting my attention from the computer to the window. I was startled to find it was getting dark outside. I glanced at my desk clock. It was after five o'clock. Where had the afternoon gone? "Mom, I need to go. I have to get ready for my conference."

"I just wish—I wish I knew what to do about Charlie's death."

"There's nothing you can do." I queued Paul's pictures to print then I turned my attention to the conference schedule sitting on the side of my desk. "If there was any doubt about his death, the police would be investigating it."

"I'm not so sure about that," Mom said stubbornly.

"It's much easier to the police to just let things go. Just because Charlie was old, it doesn't mean there wasn't foul play."

"Mom, why do you insist it was murder?" I said it more sharply than I meant to, but her dogged persistence grated on my nerves. "He had a heart attack and he died. End of story."

There was a silence that seemed to stretch a long time. "Of course," she finally said briskly. "You're right. Have a good trip if I don't see you before you go. Sherry and I will check in on the house while you're gone. You're taking Conan to the vet for boarding, right?"

"Yes, I'll take him on Tuesday morning. He loves it there. Make sure to come in through the garage when you stop. I talked to Sherry about it at the town meeting."

"Will do. 'Bye." She hung up before I could reply.

I felt vaguely guilty as I replaced the receiver, but that wasn't unusual with my mother. She had an uncanny ability to take even the simplest statements from me and make them seem like criticisms of her, leaving me feeling like an ungrateful daughter. Which I was, really, but I hated to be reminded of it. Why did she want me to go to the funeral with her? For heaven's sake, I didn't know Charlie Baron.

I took the pictures from my printer and leafed through them. Ike was incredibly photogenic and Paul was right, I had to admit. Ike and I did have a certain chemistry together. It would certainly make for an interesting shoot if he was involved.

I put the pictures and thoughts about my upcoming modeling gig to one side and focused on the conference listings. I was scheduled to participate in a panel discussion on Tuesday late in the afternoon and to speak and then lead a discussion on Thursday morning. I loaded my conference notes onto my iPad and started to review them.

I took a break for a quick sandwich for supper and a brief walk with Conan, cut short when it started to rain. When we passed a neighbor's house, I heard laughing voices drift out to us from an opened kitchen window. They sounded loud in the night air and I suddenly remembered why the picture of John Staples had jogged a memory.

He said he heard Henrietta argue with Ike. I rubbed the mud off Conan's paws when we entered the front door then he raced off to check his kibble dish, as if it had magically refilled while we were gone. I shrugged out of my jacket and hung it up, thinking furiously.

Staples said he heard Ike and Henrietta arguing about me. That meant that he was at the picnic shelter in the park, too. He claimed they were screaming, but I doubted it. They may have raised their voices, but screaming? I shook my head and went in to the living room to get the fire going. Even if Ike and Henrietta hollered at the top of their lungs, a person would still need to be relatively close to hear what they were saying.

And Staples did know what they were saying. He told me they were yelling about me. Did the police know he was at the park, too? I went into the den and sank into my desk chair, staring at the mesmerizing flames surrounding the logs in the grate. The events of Friday night were all blurred together in my brain.

I pulled over a notepad and jotted the sequence of

events as I remembered them:

Arrive at meeting
Argue with Henrietta and Ike
Talk to Maggie
Make speech
Ike and Meryl?

I stared at my list. When did I see Ike talking to Meryl on the country club porch? Was it during my speech or after? I couldn't remember.

I added *Find out Conan gone* above *Make speech* then continued the list.

Leave meeting
Run into Ike
Kiss
Dogs howl
Go to park

I frowned. When did Staples go to the park? He was in the Country Club waiting to speak while Ike was gone with Henrietta. For that matter, when did Ike and Henrietta go to the park? I glared at the words on the page, tore off the paper, and started afresh.

Arrive at meeting
Argue with Henrietta and Ike
Talk to Maggie
Ike and Meryl?
Find out Conan gone
Ike and Henrietta to park?
Make speech
Leave meeting
Run into Ike
Kiss
Dogs howl
Go to park

I closed my eyes, trying to remember the scene at the town meeting. I made my speech, walking around the front of the room. Was that when I saw Ike and Meryl? No, I wasn't speaking yet. I was talking to Marge Crandon when I saw Meryl.

Where was Meryl while I was speaking? My eyes popped open. I saw her with Ike before I started speaking but I'm pretty sure I didn't see her in the audience. Of course, it was a full house and I didn't take the time to note everyone but I think I would have noticed Meryl and her brother.

That's right. Staples came in by the side door while I was talking. He'd been outside. I added it to my list, under *Make speech* then I leaned back to regard what I wrote before I added *Henrietta killed* right under my *Staples enters room* entry.

Ike had no alibi for the time when Henrietta was killed.

I replayed my conversation with Lee Street in my mind. There was at least thirty minutes of time when I didn't see Ike. Did anyone else see him? Could someone else give him an alibi?

I shivered, a ghostly chill turning me cold. There was no alibi. That was why Street was so insistent on finding out if I had seen Ike in the room. He either wanted corroboration Ike was gone or he wanted to see if I would lie to give Ike an alibi.

What a damn mess. I pushed the paper away from me and started for the living room but the phone rang.

I checked the caller ID. *Think of him and there he is.* "Hi, Ike," I said.

"I just talked to your agent. It sounds like I may need some modeling tips."

I took the phone with me to the living room and sank onto the couch. "I told you, there's nothing to do it. Just stand where you're told to stand and smile when you're supposed to. You can do it, can't you?"

"It can't be that easy. They're paying me to do it, and paying me rather well, I might add. Although I'm sure I'm not getting paid as well as you are."

"Tell me how good you think the salary is after hours of standing around, doing nothing."

"Deal. What are you up to tonight?"

"I just finished a big chunk of homework and conference prep, so I think I'll give myself a glass of wine and maybe watch TV."

"Great minds think alike. I was considering downloading a movie and having a glass of wine. Why don't you come over here and we'll do it together?" His bantering voice held an undertone of seduction and I smiled drowsily while I considered the proposition.

Then a hundred excuses ran through my mind.

It's a school night.

What if someone sees us together?

It's late.

It's raining.

He laughed. "I still haven't convinced you, have I?"

I sighed. "I guess it's too late to undo a lifetime of caution."

"Now, now. Better late than never. Think about it." When I started to speak, he said quickly, "I won't take no for an answer. So don't tell me if you'll come or not. Drive over here if you want to join me. And if not, then why don't you let me take you out to dinner tomorrow night? We can talk about this modeling stuff."

Well, a dinner with Ike in a public place certainly sounded safer than going to his house. Safer? What was I thinking? "Okay. That sounds like a plan."

"Okay. Good night, Acie. Sweet dreams."

"Thanks, Ike. Good night." I hung up the phone, disconcerted he let me off the hook so easily. Then I chastised myself. Good heavens, I hadn't given the man any reason to care one way or the other for me, and here I was complaining he wasn't paying enough attention to me.

I curled up on the couch, tucking my legs to one side. Why was I worried about getting involved with Ike? Did I really care so much for what people might say? My mother's comment echoed in my mind, comparing me and Henrietta.

Henrietta pursued Ike with single-minded intensity. She was always the most sought after girl in school, queen of the Prom, cheerleader captain, head of the Honor Society. Ike was a perfect match for her, but Ike didn't want perfect Henrietta.

Ike wanted me. I sat up, feeling like I was on the cusp of a startling revelation. Ike wanted me. Well, why shouldn't I take him up on his offer? Why not? Take a chance. Live dangerously.

Live. That was the operative word. Don't be stuck by what you think you should do.

Live.

I sprang up and went to the bedroom and changed clothes, pulling on my good jeans and my favorite green sweater that matched my eyes. I undid my hair from its serviceable bun and loosely braided it, letting a few wisps curl around my face. Then I snatched up my purse and headed for the garage door before I could change my mind.

Fate conspired against me. The phone rang.

I wavered, considering ignoring it, but when I saw the caller ID, I picked up the portable unit near the mud room door. "Hello, Aunt Sherry. What's up?"

"I'm worried, dear. Your mother is missing."

I let my purse slide to the floor. "She can't be missing. I just talked to her."

"You did? When?"

"I don't know. This afternoon, I guess."

"She didn't come down to supper. You know Sunday night supper is special here. We always have pizza. Your mother and I always have a drink before supper, but she wasn't in her room when I went to get her. And I checked the parking area and her car is gone." Aunt Sherry sounded worried and I could imagine her in her little apartment at the Senior Center, peeking out the window. "Why would she take her car out? You know she hates driving after dark."

"Maybe she had to go someplace." Even when I said it, I knew how stupid it sounded.

"Where would she go? There's nothing open on Sunday night. Besides, it's raining. Why would she go out in the rain?"

I had a terrible suspicion. "Mom said you were at the police station yesterday."

"Yes, I went to find out about Charlie Baron's house and if—oh, no. You don't think she went there, do you?"

Visions of a pleasant evening with Ike vanished. I picked up my purse. "I'm not sure. I'll go out there and see if her car is there."

"She's absolutely convinced Charlie's death was

160

foul play. She might go out there to see if she can find any clues."

I bit back the curse that threatened to slip out. "I wish she'd get it through her head she's not a detective. Not every death is a crime."

"Don't be too angry with her, Annabelle. She and Charlie were very close. This has come has a shock to her."

"I appreciate it, but it doesn't mean she needs to go looking for a murderer under every rock." I grabbed my purse. "I'll see if I can find her." My phone buzzed me and I checked the small display screen. "Someone else is calling me, Aunt Sherry. Maybe it's Mom. Let me take it. I'll call you back when I know what's going on."

"Thank you, dear. I knew I could count on you. You're so reliable."

Reliable? All my life I was responsible, reliable, and dependable. Why did it come back to haunt me the one time I was throwing caution to the wind and being crazy? Maybe I was cursed. I transferred to the other call. "Doyle residence."

"Your mother is out here snooping around, Dr. Doyle. I'm going to call the police."

"Who is this?" I slung my purse over my shoulder.

"John Staples. She has no right to be in the Baron house. I'll see to it she's arrested for trespassing." He hung up the phone.

I slammed the phone receiver back into the base and snatched open the garage door. When I got hold of my mother, she would have hell to pay.

Chapter 10

It was cold. It was raining. It was dark. And I was so mad I could barely see straight as I drove east on Norwood past the Sibling Streets. I clutched my steering wheel tightly enough that my knuckles turned white. I muttered under my breath what I would do with my mother when I found her.

"You run away and leave me alone to deal with life then you expect me to follow around behind you and pick up the pieces." I could barely hear myself talk over the drumming of rain on the roof of the car. I checked the outside temperature indicator on my dash. Damn. It was only 40 degrees outside. If it dropped further, we'd have ice or snow.

"Thanks, Mom. Thanks for waltzing out on me and Dad. Thanks for leaving me to handle him. Thanks for sending me postcards on my birthday from somewhere else." I remembered those postcards. I hated getting them because it reminded me she had left, but I also loved seeing where she was. My mother always seemed like an exotic bird, flitting from town to town. Savannah, Chicago, Buffalo, Charleston, San Francisco, Boise. I would eagerly find the location in an atlas then scour the library for information about the latest town.

"Now here I am, chasing you while you're on a wild goose chase. Why do I bother? You didn't bother with me. I should just leave you to the cops to handle."

I peered ahead at the road. There weren't any streetlights on this end of town and the only indicator I had of my location was the landmarks around me when my headlights illuminated them. There was Main Street and the little bridge over the creek. Just beyond it was the Country Club on my left. Four blocks past the club, Norwood ended at John Staples' front door.

The house shone dimly through the rain and fog inching up over the bluffs from the river. I glimpsed a light in the front of the house and one upstairs in the back. I turned left to go down the gravel lane that led to Charlie Baron's house.

His house was thirty yards ahead on the right, a dark shadow on a small rise at the end of a rutted gravel road. I drove carefully along the uneven lane, eyeing the deep ditches on either side. The darkness was all encompassing, my headlights stabbing through the gloom like lasers which illuminated only the tiny patch of road in front of me. Then ahead on the right I glimpsed a yellow glow and used it to guide me the final few yards until I saw the lip of the driveway and the yard light shining over it.

The house was set far back from the lane. When I made the turn onto the driveway, my headlights bounced over my mother's red PT Cruiser then it vanished from sight while I navigated the twisting drive. I tried to remember if I had ever been there and if so, how the drive was configured. I gave up on it and just focused on what was in front of me.

I finally reached the house and parked to the left of Mom's car, breathing a sigh of relief that I found the place with no incident. I twisted in my seat and fumbled for my fold-up umbrella, tucked behind me under the passenger side. As I did, I glimpsed something on my left on the lawn, a shape moving quickly through the darkness.

I instinctively cringed back when the shape lunged at me, veering away at the last minute. I grabbed the umbrella but hesitated before opening my door. What could be out there on such a wet and cold night?

A garage light clicked on, probably activated by a motion detector. I put my hand on my car door handle and started to open it, but when I did the shape came at me again. I saw now that it was a dog, tall and rangy.

"Damn it," I muttered under my breath. "That's all I need. That's Moriarty." If he was here, then his pack was not far away. I've been around dogs all my life and I knew they could be unpredictable, but I didn't expect any trouble from him. The few times I was close to him or his pack they were cautious, not combative.

I swung my car door open and simultaneously thrust out my umbrella, pressing the button to activate it. My movement startled the dog so he backed away, head lowered. I swiveled in the seat and put a foot out of the car, and when I did, Moriarty growled.

I stopped. This was surprising. I expected him to back up, not stand his ground and glare at me. The rain had mercifully lightened so I could easily see the big dog, his long legs planted solidly in the overgrown, grassy lawn and his sleek black-and-brown body tense and rigid.

"Hey, Morrie," I said softly, still paused with one foot in and one foot out of my car. "Remember me? I've brought food to you guys now and then."

The animal's ears flickered but he didn't move. He didn't continue to growl, though, which I took as a good sign. I extricated my right leg from the car and set my right foot next to my left and started to stand.

Moriarty took a step forward. I stopped, my umbrella open and in front of me. It would be a poor shield against an attacking dog, but it was all I had. I eyed the front door, estimating my chances of getting there before the dog could get to me.

As if reading my mind, he took another step forward so he was now just a few yards away, his eyes fixed on me. He was tense but not poised to strike, or so I hoped. I debated: race for the door or drop back into my car? Then to my horror a side door near the garage opened and my mother looked out.

"Who's there?" she called in a quavering voice.

Moriarty's attention shifted from me to Mom when she emerged from the garage to stand in the spotlight of the garage's motion light. Without a second's hesitation, he turned and lunged upward, springing at Mom.

I anticipated his action and I jumped at the same time, tossing my umbrella in front of him. It was just enough of a distraction to throw the dog off-balance. He landed heavily, stumbling and twisting his right front leg underneath him, snarling when he fell.

I raced to Mom, waving my arms. "Back inside!" I shouted. "Get back!"

Thank God, she understood immediately what was happening. She whirled, disappearing into the gray depths of the garage. I was just a step or two behind, barreling into her then I turned to grab the door and slam it shut. I peered through the small panes of glass at my attacker.

Moriarty stopped where he fell, his head cocked to

one side. With a whimper, he struggled to all fours. He seemed confused, his gaze going from the door behind which I cowered to the road in the distance. Another whimper then he shook his head as if trying to shake away annoying flies or bugs. I heard barking in the distance, multiple dogs all giving voice to anger or frustration. Then Moriarty sat and raised his muzzle to the sky and did the same, letting out a drawn-out howl that raised the hair on the back of my neck.

"What's got into him?" Mom said from behind me.

I looked over my shoulder. There was a dim light on overhead so she was mostly in shadow, but I could see she was concerned, not frightened. For some reason, it made me angry. Good heavens, we were almost mauled. Couldn't she be just the tiniest bit upset?

"What are you doing? Why did you come out here?" I turned my attention back to Moriarty, who had gotten to his feet and now loped toward the woods lining the bluff over the river below.

"I told you earlier. I'm concerned about Charlie's death." Mom sounded as defiant and as angry as me.

I leaned forward out the doorway to check on Moriarty's progress. That's when I saw John Staples, striding up the driveway. I stepped out of the garage and raised a hand.

"What are you doing here?" he shouted. "Isn't it bad enough your mother comes out here trespassing, and now you have to do it, too?"

My previous fear and frustration morphed into anger at hearing my own angry words tossed back at me. "I came here at your behest, Mr. Staples," I shouted, leaving the garage to meet him.

I looked to my right, where Moriarty had disappeared, and I saw the dog standing at the edge of the yard, staring at Staples with an expression I thought I recognized. I had seen it before on abused animals when they saw their so-called masters approaching. "What have you done to that dog?" I accused, flinging an arm in the direction of the big pack leader.

"What dog?" Staples came to a stop in front of me. His blond hair was plastered to his head by rain, showing clearly how thin it really was. Two dark red spots of color were on his cheeks and the rest of his skin was pasty white, making him appear like a grotesque caricature of a clown.

"The pack leader, there." I turned to where Moriarty had stood but he was gone, vanished into the shadows. "He was just there a minute ago."

"I didn't see any dog. I think you and your mother should leave." He crossed his arms over his damp sweatshirt and glared at me.

"I have a right to be here," my mother shouted from behind me.

Staples dodged around me and made a beeline for her. "You most certainly do not."

"What's it to you, anyway?" Mom demanded.

I reached them in time to hear Staples say, "I feel an obligation to keep an eye on the property. It's the neighborly thing to do."

Mom gave a disparaging laugh. "Neighborly? That would be a first for you."

"What's that mean?" Staples thrust his head out to glare into Mom's face. His scrawny neck and bony shoulders gave him a pelican-like silhouette.

"Charlie told me about you." Mom wrapped her

red sweater more tightly around her and tucked her hands into her arms. "He said you were always badgering him about selling his land to those developers. You even had your sister try to talk him into it. Shame on you, Mr. Staples. Charlie knew what he wanted to do with the land and you did everything short of prostituting your sister to get him to change his mind."

I blinked in surprise. This was strong language even for my blunt-tongued mother. Then I remembered how Meryl Staples flung herself at Ike. Good heavens, did that woman throw herself at old Charlie Baron, too?

"That's outrageous," Staples sputtered. "How dare you imply Meryl—" He seemed unable to finish the sentence because his mouth worked but no sound came out.

"I think you should leave, Mr. Staples." I interposed myself between Mom and the choking pelican. Each of them looked like they might come to violence.

"I'm calling the police as soon as I get home." Staples turned to leave.

"Go ahead and do it. And while you're at it, will you tell them you eavesdropped on Dr. Adler and Miss Baron while they were arguing?" I asked.

He turned back to us. "What?" His face was even whiter than before, either from shock or cold, I'm not sure which.

"You said you heard them arguing. That means you were in the park the night Henrietta died." I regarded him calmly although my heart was racing so fast I had a momentary fear I was having a heart attack. "Did you tell the police you were there?"

"I wasn't there. I told you. I heard them shouting. They were so loud anyone could hear them."

"Why were you even outside? Why did you leave the clubhouse?"

He started to reply then stopped. For an instant he stared at me and I could swear I saw different responses pass through his eyes before he finally said, "If you must know, I was worried for Meryl. I saw the way Adler accosted her earlier. She was outside and I was concerned for her safety." He smirked at me. "I made sure to tell the police Adler forced his attentions on her."

I laughed out loud. "If they believe that, I have a bridge in New York City I'd like to sell them." I turned to my mother. "Let's go inside. It's cold out here."

"You haven't heard the last of this, Dr. Doyle," Staples said behind me. "You won't get this land for a sanctuary. I won't let you ruin our chances of selling this land."

"It's not up to you or me. It's up to the townspeople to vote on it. Good night, Mr. Staples." I urged Mom ahead of me with quick gestures. "Let's go. It's getting cold."

Mom looked past me. "Asshole." She hesitated and I thought she might go after him, then she shrugged and led the way into the roomy two car garage where only one car sat, presumably Charlie Baron's pale blue sedan.

"How did you get in here?" I asked. "Wasn't it locked?"

"I have a key." Mom walked past the car to a door at the far end of the garage and opened it, entering with the ease of long familiarity. I went back to the driveway door and peered out, verifying Staples was going away.

He stood in the drive behind Mom's car, staring at the woods. Even from this distance I saw how angry he was. The scowl on his face would have frightened anyone and his tense posture told me he anxious to hit something or someone given the slightest provocation. He stood for one long minute, poised for action then he strode away and disappeared from sight.

I went through the door Mom opened and entered a small tiled foyer with a powder room on my right and stairs directly ahead, leading downward. To the left were double doors set at an angle. Beyond them I saw a large bed with a bench at its foot and a dresser against a wall. Large windows filled one wall of the room.

Mom was a few steps ahead of me and on my left, stepping into a spacious living room carpeted in pale beige carpet. Two roomy blue patterned chairs faced a glass coffee table and a couch set against another wall of windows. A large brick fireplace and built-in bookcases filled the wall shared with the bedroom.

Mom picked up the stack of magazines and letters from one chair. "No one's stopped the mail." She took a seat on the couch near a wine glass half-filled with red wine on a nearby end table. "Have a seat and help yourself to wine. It's there on the counter." She gestured vaguely to her left.

I looked to where she pointed and spied a dining room opening into a kitchen. Beyond it was a set of patio doors which presumably led to a porch or deck. I sank onto one of the blue armchairs. "Do you think you should be going through his mail?"

Mom set down the letter she was reading. Her face was drawn and tired, and her eyes were red-rimmed.

"Charlie and I were going to get married."

I probably looked like John Staples for a moment when I opened my mouth and words refused to come. Finally I said, "Why?"

Her mouth twisted up in a lopsided smile. "It's odd that's the first question you ask."

I leaned back, struggling to corral my racing thoughts. "Okay. When did you decide this? When were you going to get married? When were you going to tell me?"

Mom sat back and picked up the wine glass, taking a sip before answering. "Why get married? Because we wanted to. We were both old enough not to care what anyone said and we weren't anxious to spend our final years alone."

"You're not alone. You have Aunt Sherry and everybody else at the center."

Once again she smiled, but it was sad this time. "I notice you don't say that I have you to keep me company, too."

My face got hot. I started to say, *Oh, of course you have me* then I thought better of it. If she wanted honesty, I'd give it to her. "We're not exactly close, Mom. So no, I guess it wouldn't come to mind for me." I met her gaze squarely.

She nodded then looked away, staring intently at the glass she held clasped in both hands. "The only regret I have about leaving with Jimmy Watson is I had to leave you behind. I was torn between my love for him and my love for you."

I drew in a steadying breath before answering. "I'm not talking about the past, Mother. I'm talking about right now and Charlie Baron."

When she raised her head to regard me, I saw bewildered hurt in her eyes. "Will you ever forgive me for leaving you?"

"I don't want to have this discussion right now. You're trespassing in someone else's home. It doesn't matter if you were supposedly engaged to the man. You have no right to be here and John Staples is probably calling the police right now."

"Let them come and get me then," Mom said with unruffled calm. "I don't care. But I suppose you do care, don't you?"

"Of course I care," I said, forcing myself to reply in an even, measured tone of voice.

"Because you care what other people think."

"That's not a crime," I said through clenched teeth.

Mom was silent for a moment, her eyes once again fixed on her wine glass. Then she raised the glass and finished the contents in two swallows. "No, it's not a crime," she said, getting to her feet and going to the kitchen. "It's just a pity."

I remained seated. "I don't need or want your pity."

"You don't need or want anything from me, do you?" She headed for the kitchen sink.

I waited until she had finished rinsing out her glass before speaking. "I have no idea if I need anything from you. I didn't have a mother when I grew up, so I have no idea what kind of role a mother might play in my life."

Mom paused while she wiped the glass with a kitchen towel, her head bowed. "I suppose you're right. I suppose I don't know what kind of role I could play, either." She carefully set the glass on the counter and came back to the living room. "I'll take the mail with me to sort through it. Just let me make sure the furnace is set before we leave."

I stood while she bundled the accumulated mail into a pile. "I'll take it," I said when she tried to gather it all into her arms.

"Thank you." She relinquished her hold on everything and turned away, still not looking directly at me. I was glad because I didn't want to face her, either. We were forty years past any reconciliation we might have affected. All we could hope for was politeness at this point.

I went to the kitchen and found a pantry and grocery bags. I dropped all the mail into the bag and joined Mom again in the small foyer, where she was inspecting a thermostat on the wall. "All set." She took her cane, which rested near the double doors leading to the bedroom.

I looked back into the living room. "Don't you want to turn off the light?"

"I have them on timers. Charlie and I always liked to have a light on when we came home at night." Mom paused with her hand on the doorknob to the garage, staring back into the living room, a wistful expression in her eyes. Then she closed her eyes briefly, turned, and left.

"Did you mean what you said to Staples? About his sister?" I'm not sure where the thought came from, but I was uncomfortable with the silence between us and tried to fill it with the first thing that came to mind.

"Charlie told me about it. That woman came over here every night, begging him to sell the land." Mom stopped at the outside door. "I've watched them together. It's not natural."

"What's not natural?"

"The way Staples and she act. It's creepy."

I shot her an exasperated glare. "Mom, tact is not your strongest quality. Why don't you just spit it out and say what you mean?"

She glared right back at me. "I think they're sleeping together."

"Sleeping together? Euw." I made a face. "Incest?"

She looked thoughtful. "Or—how do we know she's his sister?"

I started to toss off a reply then I stopped. She was right. The Staples had moved to Grimper shortly after Charlie did, five years earlier. "But why would they lie about it?"

"Good question." Mom pulled open the outer door and we emerged into the night. "The rain has let up, at least." She held out her hand. "I'll take the mail."

"I'll follow and make sure you get back okay." I ignored her outstretched arm and opened the back door on my car to deposit the heavy sack on the seat.

"I'm old, Annabelle, I'm not stupid," she snapped. "I can find my way back to the Home."

"It's dark, it's wet and the roads might be slippery. I'll follow you." I got into my car, not giving her time to complain.

She glared at me then she stalked to the driver side of her car and disappeared inside. A minute later her lights came on and she backed up, turning the car so she could drive out facing forward. I waited until she was at the lane then I did the same. When the arc of my headlights swept the lawn I saw Moriarty at the far end. He and several other dogs were watching.

I flipped the headlights to bright and they seemed

to melt away, disappearing into the shadows of the trees. I made a mental note to mention Moriarty's behavior to Maggie. She and her husband would need to be cautious when they interacted with the big dog in the future.

Mom drove two blocks west then made a left turn onto Elm Street. The Senior Home was five blocks south, situated opposite the hospital and clinic. The Home was a three-story building shaped like a wide-mouthed C, with a lobby in the middle. The fifty senior apartments in the middle and far left wing varied from three bedroom units to claustrophobically small one bedroom units. The far right wing of the building was a nursing facility for those people who required more care.

Mom and Sherry had apartments on the top floor in the middle, over the main entrance. Mom drove to the side entrance for the underground garage. I parked in front and called Sherry while sitting in my car.

"We're back," I said. "She was out at Charlie Baron's. She's parking her car now."

"Where are you?" Sherry asked.

"In my car out front. I have a bag of Charlie Baron's mail with me. I'll take it to her apartment."

"I'll meet you there."

I said quickly, "Did you know they were getting married?"

Sherry sighed. "I knew they talked about it."

"I had no idea they were so serious." It sounded lame but I couldn't think of any other way to articulate what I meant. It just sounded foolish to say *they were in love* when they were both in their 80s.

"Your mother has been very lonely," Sherry said.

"She's one of those women who feel she's better off if she has a man in her life. She needs someone to fuss over, I think."

I had no response because I wasn't like that, so I had no idea how it felt. "I'll meet you at her apartment."

"Acie? Try to be patient with her. Charlie's death hurt her a great deal. She's very upset."

I stared ahead at the hospital across the street, several responses going through my head. "You know, Sherry, it seems to me we all make excuses for Mom. Maybe it's time she grew up and learned to face life."

"I'm sure that's how it seems, dear. I'll see you in a few minutes." She hung up the phone.

I got out and grabbed the bag of mail from the back seat. I hurried to the building, looking up to the third floor to see Sherry peering out at me. I waved and went inside, heading for the elevator on the left. The night watchman at the front desk smiled in greeting when I passed. He was in his mid-thirties and his duties usually consisted of answering questions about malfunctioning microwaves or refrigerators.

I checked my watch while I rode the elevator upward. No wonder I was exhausted. It was after ten o'clock. So much for a quiet night with a glass of wine and a movie—and Ike. I slowly exhaled, trying to banish the flare of resentment that tensed my entire body. By the time the doors opened, I was calm again.

Sherry waited for me. "Thank you for checking on her."

I left the elevator car and we started walking down the hall. "Staples threatened to call the police. I don't think I had much choice."

"He's such a pest. Your mother told me how he badgered poor Charlie about his land."

We passed an apartment with the door open. I glanced inside and caught a whiff of fresh paint. "Is Louisa doing remodeling?"

"She went to the other side," Sherry said without breaking stride.

Her matter-of-fact tone caught me by surprise. Louisa had been Sherry's bridge partner for years. "She died? When?"

Sherry snorted. "She went to the nursing home side. Of course, that's just one step away from dying, so I suppose you can say she's getting ready to pass over." She walked by two more doors then stopped and knocked once on Mom's door before opening it and going in.

Both Mom and Sherry had large one-bedroom apartments. We entered into Mom's kitchen area with the small dining table on the left. Straight ahead was the living room and to the left was the bedroom. Mom was just coming out from the bedroom. "Thank you for bringing that up," she said when I set the sack of mail next to her chair.

"No problem. I suppose someone should stop at the post office and get the mail changed."

"To what?" Mom sat in her favorite recliner and Sherry took a seat on the couch. "Henrietta was Charlie's only relative except for a cousin he hasn't seen in years." She appeared tired and she sounded dispirited.

"I suppose you can talk to the lawyers," Sherry said.

"Why?" Mom touched the bag of mail. "Nothing in

here matters anymore."

I stood nearby, not sure whether to sit down or not. Mom seemed depressed and it wasn't something I had ever seen with her. "You shouldn't go out to his house without letting us know where you're going," I said in what I hoped was a conciliatory tone.

"I don't enjoy asking for permission every time I want to do something." Her peevish comment told me Mom was rallying out of whatever funk she'd been in.

"I don't enjoy being called by the neighbors," I pointed out.

"You're not responsible for me." Mom picked up her remote and aimed it at the TV.

"Tell that to John Staples and Lee Street."

Mom snorted. "Lee Street. He can't find his ass with both hands in a closet with the light on."

I shared Mom's evaluation of our local police detective but I wasn't about to tell her. "It's late and I need to get home. I have class tomorrow." I turned to Sherry, who watched us with a worried frown. "Don't forget to use the garage door entrance when you come over this week to check on Sprite and Houdini."

"I will." Sherry joined me while Mom flipped through channels on the television.

"Good night, Mom."

"Good night, Annabelle. Good night, Sherry." It was a clear dismissal.

I hesitated, not sure what I could say to break the tension. In the end, I didn't say anything. Sherry and I exited, the door locking behind us. "I told you she's upset," Sherry said as we walked to her apartment door.

"We argued earlier," I said. "She's still just mad."

"The funeral's tomorrow. I don't suppose you can

come, can you?"

I shook my head. "I have class."

Sherry opened her door and turned to regard me. "I wish you two could forgive each other."

I stared at her. "What does Mom have to forgive me for?"

"You've hurt her, too, you know." Sherry leaned forward and gave me a quick hug. "You really are a lot alike in many ways." She disappeared inside before I could protest.

I stalked to the elevator and stabbed the button. Why was it I could never get the last damn word in? I fumed all the way to the lobby.

Chapter 11

By the time I arrived at home, my anger had cooled and I was merely tired. No, let me correct that. I was exhausted. I let Conan out briefly to do his business then I dropped into bed. I slept soundly until filtered sunlight awakened me in the morning, shining through the trellised patio outside my bedroom.

I reviewed my agenda for the day while I performed my morning ritual of puppy-potty, shower, hair dressing, clothing selection, and lunch-packing. I had a ten o'clock meeting followed by two classes. Because I would be gone for the rest of the week, I was anxious my students knew their assignments for the so-called 'free' time. We were at mid-terms and in theory my students would be busy working on research for their end-of-class papers which I counted as sixty-percent of their grade.

I knew in actual fact they would simply enjoy the time off. I didn't begrudge them the break. I trusted when we all returned to class the following week, we'd be refreshed and ready to dig in for the second half of the semester.

I chose a pair of dark blue slacks and a pale blue sweater set for my attire for the day. After consideration, I twisted my hair into a chignon and secured it with a large clip, leaving a few stands free around my face. I'm not sure why, but I didn't want a braid that day. For some reason, I felt it was important to be more…flexible.

While I ate breakfast and made my lunch, I debated what to do with Conan now that Sprite could free him. In the end, I left the mud room door open and hoped for the best. Conan had been a good indoor dog so far. I prayed his record would continue. I drove to school with only one worried backward glance.

I spent the morning immersed in academic matters and didn't get a break until one o'clock. As I expected, I ran into Ike in the faculty lounge. He and I often had coffee together while we ate our lunches. He gave me a wary smile when I entered and took a seat next to him at the table in the middle of the spacious room with windows to the campus outside.

"I was disappointed you didn't come over last night," he said in a low, confiding voice even though we were alone. He pushed a cupcake across the table to me. "I made fairy cakes and I was going to ply you with cakes and wine."

"I'm sorry I missed it. I'll save this for dessert." Ike's so-called fairy cakes were delightful spicy little cupcakes. He claimed the recipe came from his English grandmother. "I was on my way to see you but I got diverted." I told him about my mother's adventure the evening before at Charlie Baron's house in between lunch bites of sandwich and chips. "She said they were going to get married."

"Really?" Ike snitched a potato chip from the small sack I brought, munching it thoughtfully. "How do you feel about that?"

"Surprised. Bemused. Exasperated," I said with a shrug. "Of course, it doesn't matter since he's dead."

Ike sat back in the worn armchair. "No wonder she's so upset about his death. Obviously he had everything to live for, so it must seem like a cruel joke to have him die so suddenly."

I hadn't really considered it from that point of view. "It still doesn't explain why she thinks he was murdered. I think she's being irrational."

"I don't know." When I stared at him in surprise, he said, "Think about it. From what I can gather, he was found outside his house, near the driveway."

"Where did you hear that?"

Ike took another potato chip. "I asked around. You'd be surprised what kind of information you can get at the Dart-and-Drink Coffee Shop. Did you know that John Staples found him?"

Now that I thought about it, I knew as little about Charlie Baron's death as I did about him, period. However, if he and Mother were close, I suppose it would behoove me to find out what I could about his death. "Why was Staples at his house?"

Ike shrugged. "He said he was walking by and saw the light on outside the garage and went to check. It was a cold night, so why was Charlie Baron standing outside?"

"Mother said he told her he was expecting someone." I nudged the potato chip bag toward Ike. "Go ahead, finish them." I broke off a bite of the fairy cake and nibbled, letting the sharp flavor of cinnamon settle on my tongue. Ike's house had probably smelled delightful while they baked. I added it to my growing list of grievances against my mother. "I wonder if the police checked."

"Checked what?"

"Checked to see if Staples really could see the light from the road. I was out there last night. The light over the garage is a motion light but it wasn't on when I got there. Why was Staples out walking? Charlie Baron's lane dead-ends at a drop-off over the river. There isn't a walking trail out there, is there?"

"I don't know. I still can't figure why Charlie Baron would be standing outside waiting for someone. If somebody called and said they were coming, Staples would see them drive by the house. Why wouldn't Charlie just wait inside until somebody rang the doorbell?"

"Maybe he wasn't waiting outside," I said. "Maybe he went out because he saw someone or—" I remembered Moriarty, appearing out of the shadows the night before. "He saw something. Last night when I was out at the house getting Mom, the leader of that pack of dogs almost attacked us."

"What?" Ike's causal demeanor changed abruptly. He leaned forward, his hand closing around my wrist. "He attacked you?"

"Almost. It was odd. He showed up in the front yard. When Mom came out of the house, Moriarty leapt at her. I tossed my umbrella at him and it diverted him, but I think something else stopped him." I visualized last night's scene in my head. "I could swear he wasn't interested in me. It wasn't until Mom came out of the house that he moved."

"What stopped him?" Ike's warm hand was still on my wrist.

"I'm not sure. But he halted dead in his tracks when he could have continued the attack." A thought struck me. "Where did Moriarty come from?"

"Probably the woods." Ike gently caressed the underside of my wrist.

The soft touch made goose bumps spring up on my arm. "No, I meant here. Where did he come from? All of a sudden one day he showed up in the woods. Nobody in town knows where he came from. The other dogs have been around for a while, but Moriarty just appeared out of nowhere. The way he acted last night made me think he used to be somebody's pet."

"Why do you think so?" Ike continued his mesmerizing touch.

I struggled to remember how Moriarty acted, but Ike's actions were more interesting at the moment. "I don't know," I murmured. "Just the way he acted."

"So you were on your way over to my house, hmm?" Ike's startling blue eyes were fixed on mine, preventing me from evading his gaze.

I nodded. My tongue was stuck to the roof of my mouth, preventing me from speech.

"Maybe you could come over tonight instead," he suggested, his fingers now sliding over the top of my hand.

"I don't think I can," I managed to say. "I have to pack for my trip."

"How long does that take?" He turned my unresisting hand over and ran two fingers along my palm, light as a feather.

I shivered. "I need to do other things, too," I whispered, but for the life of me, I couldn't remember what it was I had to do. Prep my notes? Get Conan ready for his stay at the kennel? Really, those things weren't that important, were they? How long would they take?

The lounge door behind me opened. Ike sat back, his hand slipping away from mine. His eyes shifted from me to whoever had entered and he smiled. "Hello, Dr. Bell."

I folded my sandwich wrapper and stuffed it back into my lunch sack then turned in my chair to regard the college president, who was paused inside the doorway. She beamed at me then at Ike. "I was hoping you two would be here. The department secretary said you usually eat lunch together."

"Not really." I turned to look at Ike, my cheeks hot with color. "I mean, we both have a break at this time so we often lunch together, but—"

Ike interrupted my babbling. "Is there something we can help you with, Dr. Bell?"

She came to the end of the table so she could regard us both. "I just talked to the fashion editor of the magazine, and I have to say, I am so excited. So excited." Despite her sedate dark skirt and jacket, I was reminded of a child on Christmas morning who peeked around a doorway and was now anxious to share fantastic news.

"About what?" I asked cautiously. The last excitement Dr. Bell shared with me was the news that I'd be part of a photo shoot on campus.

"I just learned Dr. Adler is going to be included in the photo session. Isn't it exciting? Two of our faculty members *and* our campus, all in a national magazine. It's marvelous."

I glanced at Ike, who kept his face carefully neutral. I could tell he was struggling not to laugh. "Exciting," I agreed. "Very."

"Oh, I'm sure this is tame to someone as

experienced as you. But I think it's so amazing." Her plain face suffused with joy. "This is our brush with fame. I can't wait to see how it's done."

"How it's done?" I repeated. "What?"

"The photo session. This will be such an educational experience for us all. The Journalism Department, the Business Department, the Art Department—they're all using this as a teaching opportunity. It's a chance to see a real world scenario in action."

My jaw sagged open and I hinged it back up with difficulty. "These are usually closed sets. I don't know if the photographer will want people watching what he does." I was pretty darn certain the photographer would not tolerate a crowd on the set.

Dr. Bell waved her hand. "I discussed it with the fashion editor and she assured me accommodations could be made."

But the photographer sets the rules, not the fashion editor. Dr. Bell was obviously swayed by a conversation with a nameless paper-pusher at a national magazine in a skyscraper out East. Little did she know those New York functionaries had no clout when it came to an actual photo shoot.

I smiled weakly. "Well, we'll see." Ike shot me a distrustful look. I narrowed my eyes at him in warning lest he comment on my standard default reply. "I heard there may be news regarding Miss Baron's estate." I put a hint of a question into my statement.

Dr. Bell looked at the closed door to the lounge then said in a low voice, "I can't discuss it in detail, of course, but I don't think it will be a secret much longer. The college is the main beneficiary in Miss Baron's will."

Ike frowned. "It's odd there's information about her will but we haven't heard anything about her uncle's will." Both Dr. Bell and I stared at him, the same surprised expression on each of our faces. "He died a week ago. The last time I talked to Henrietta, she said she started probate on her uncle's will. There hasn't been any talk about it in town. People seem more interested in Henrietta's will."

The last time he talked to her about it. Was it the night she died? "When was that?" I asked in what I hoped was a casual tone of voice. "When did you and she talk about it?"

"I don't remember. A few days ago. Of course, it's only been a week since he died. I suppose these things take time. Although if her will is already being discussed, then you'd think his will would be public knowledge now, too."

Dr. Bell cleared her throat. "I believe there is a, uh, problem about his will. That's one reason I was asked to attend a meeting at the Franks law offices last week. It appears Miss Baron was named the executor for her uncle's estate, but although she started the probate process, she also filed an objection to certain parts of his will. Therefore any processing of her will must wait until Mr. Baron's estate is handled because she was one of his beneficiaries."

"What a mess," I said sympathetically. "It could take months."

Dr. Bell appeared sheepish. "I admit it. I was concerned about the endowment fund. I spoke with Miss Baron's attorney about it and that's when he told me the college was named a beneficiary and there is an objection. Miss Baron set up her will with Lawyer Franklin. Franklin Three," she added. "Mr. Baron used Franklin Two."

I grimaced, remembering the tedious process of settling my father's meager estate after his death. "Good heavens, what sort of objection could she have? It was Charlie Baron's estate to do with as he pleased." I couldn't imagine complicating an already complicated process with a legal objection to something in a will.

"I wasn't given details. I was assured, though, that the endowment fund was not in jeopardy. Mr. Baron made a separate provision for it in a codicil to his will. The court has already examined the will and they agreed the endowment can go forward. The rest of his estate must be decided in a court of law."

"Well, if the Franks have anything to do with it, then it will probably drag on for years." I popped the last of Ike's fairy cake into my mouth.

"You said an objection was filed." Ike glanced at the wall clock and pushed away from the table to stand. "That means the will is public record." Dr. Bell and I once again had the same look while we stared at him, this time one of confusion. "Once probate is started and the court accepts the documents, the will is made a part of the public record. The only way to file an objection is if the document has been accepted by the court."

"How do you know so much about it?" I asked, getting to my feet.

"My aunt died a month ago and my cousin is the executor. He told me about the process. It sounds complicated, but I think it's usually a formality unless there's an objection filed. Like in this case."

We all left the lounge together, Dr. Bell leading the

way. "I'm sure things will get straightened out eventually. My main concern was with the endowment fund and I was assured it will continue as planned. I believe Frank Three will present the check to Dr. Doyle at the ceremony." She turned her attention to Ike. "I'm glad you agreed to help with the photography assignment, Dr. Adler."

"I'm looking forward to it." Ike smiled at me, a mischievous twinkle in his blue eyes. "I can't wait to see Dr. Doyle in action."

"It will be fascinating, won't it?" Dr. Bell started to stride away down the hallway.

I held up a hand. "You said beneficiaries. In Charlie Baron's will—you said beneficiaries, plural."

Dr. Bell paused in mid-step. "Yes, I did, didn't I?"

"Who else was a beneficiary?" I was starting to have a bad feeling about all of this. If my mother and Charlie were serious…

Dr. Bell shrugged, her gaze going from me to Ike then back to me. It was an oddly helpless movement from a woman who was usually so decisive. "I don't know for sure. After all, nothing has been made official, really." She headed for the stairs, obviously in a hurry. "Keep me posted about the photo session, will you? I asked the fashion editor to keep me in the loop, but she sounded incredibly busy. Let me know if there are any changes."

"I'll do that." I watched her bustle away then I turned to Ike. "What if Charlie Baron named my mother in his will? Wouldn't she be told?"

"Your mother?" Ike nodded thoughtfully. "Yeah, he might have done it if they were getting serious. I'm not sure if she'd be notified. I think she should be. But if there was an objection filed, maybe she wouldn't be. Maybe they won't tell her until it's all resolved."

I felt a burst of indignation on Mom's behalf. "That's not fair. She has a right to know if someone is slandering her or something. Objection, my ass." I glowered at Ike.

"A minute ago you were ready to disown her. Now you're going to bat for her. Make up your mind, would you?" He grinned at me. "Did I talk you into dinner tonight at my place?"

I shook my head. "I have too much to do."

"Rats. I thought my fairy cakes would win you over." He checked his watch again. "I have to get going or I'll be late for class. I'll call you later, okay?"

"Okay." My mind was miles away, specifically in downtown Grimper. I wondered if I could get a peek at Charlie Baron's will. How did one look at a will?

I was shocked out of my legal musings when Ike kissed me quickly then walked away. He looked back over his shoulder at me and winked when he saw my outraged expression. I hurried to my office, relieved no one had spied us in the normally busy hallway.

I spent the next hour preparing to leave my office for the rest of the week. I tidied my papers, set my out-of-office on my email, changed the voice message on my phone, and turned my bedraggled philodendron over to the department secretary for care in my absence. When I finally shut out the light and locked the door behind me at three o'clock, I was confident everything was handled to my satisfaction.

I drove home on another glorious autumn afternoon, the sun peeking through the multi-colored leaves and the sharp air reminding me of apple cider and bonfires. The change of seasons always awakened in me a sense of promise, an anticipation of what was to come. Of all the distinct four season in Iowa, autumn was my favorite. It meant football games, chilly air, gorgeous foliage, and apple pies. The new school year had begun so it also meant new beginnings, new challenges, and new students to work with.

Autumn also meant winter was ahead and unlike many people, I enjoyed our longest season. Winter meant cozy fires, the smell of bread baking, and languid days lounging on the couch reading a book while snow swirled outside. Of course, it also meant slipping and sliding on icy streets, the back-breaking work of shoveling the sidewalk, and cold so intense you could lose a finger or toe.

But I have always been able to overlook the bad and focus on the good, so any negatives were amply balanced by the positives. It was that attitude which stood me in good stead throughout a challenging adolescence and allowed me to come through it with few scars.

Yes, I decided, you can have your pretty spring days any time. Give me a chilly October day, a blue sky, and the promise of mulled wine at the end of the day. I drove home, filled with a heady feeling of anticipation about everything: the upcoming conference, a possible relationship with Ike, and even (dare I hope?) the resolution of my many conflicts with my mother.

My phone was ringing when I walked into the mud room. I grabbed the receiver just before the answering machine kicked on. "Doyle residence." I let my briefcase and purse slide to the floor and walked into the house. Conan galloped out from the living room to greet me.

"Hello, dear. I just thought I'd check in with you before you leave and see if you have any last minute instructions for me."

I leaned over Conan and gave him a good head rub. "It's Aunt Sherry on the phone," I told him. "She's going to be checking on your buddies while I'm gone." I straightened and did a quick survey of the house while I chatted with my aunt, escorted by Conan. "I can't think of anything special. Just make sure to come in the garage like we talked about, bring in the mail, and check the water dishes. I'll leave the dishes out on the kitchen counter. You know where the cat food is."

Houdini thumped to the floor to follow me when I went to the kitchen then my den. So far, everything seemed fine. Conan's day of freedom appeared to be a success. Sprite jumped out of my den window onto my desk chair, spinning around and causing the papers on my desk to go flying. I lost control of the phone while I steadied the chair.

"…expected. Lunch was nice, but the church ladies always do put on a good spread. Your mother made sure they had those little egg sandwiches Charlie liked so much."

"I'm sorry, I didn't catch that, I was corralling a cat. What did you say?" I went back to the mud room and the critter dishes and doled out food while Sherry talked.

"I said the funeral was well attended, better than I expected."

Funeral? I thought immediately of Henrietta then I realized my aunt was talking about Charlie Baron.

"That's nice," I said automatically. "Where was it?"

"At the funeral home. Charlie wasn't much of a church-goer, although he did attend now and again. You know, your mother is still upset about it all. Maybe you can give her a call before you leave town tomorrow."

It wasn't a question but a command. "I will. Do you know if she heard from one of the Franks?"

"About what?"

I hesitated. If Mom got a letter from the Franks, Aunt Sherry would have heard about it. "Just wondering."

"About what?" she persisted.

"I thought since she was taking in Charlie's mail, maybe there was something in there from the Franks about the endowment," I ad-libbed. "I talked to Dr. Bell today and she said she thought it would go forward as scheduled. Mom asked me about it yesterday."

"Well, that's nice. I don't know if she's gone through all of the mail or not. There was a lot of it. I'll ask her when I see her."

"I suppose since there was a funeral that means the police have figured out the cause of death. At least, I guess that's what it means."

"Your mother was told it was a heart attack. She doesn't believe it, of course."

I rolled my eyes. Of course she wouldn't believe it. "He was elderly."

"But he was in good health. He had no history of heart problems. He walked every day all around his property, he golfed twice a week, and just the week before he was out in the woods behind his house, working with a chain saw to clear up a few fallen trees."

I had to admit, it sounded impressive. "Maybe it all caught up with him," I said, although it sounded lame even to me. I glanced at the clock. It was cocktail hour. "You girls aren't having a drink before dinner?"

Sherry sighed. "I told you. She's upset. She's lying down. Planning his funeral took a lot out of her."

I walked back to the kitchen. I didn't know Mom planned Charlie's funeral. Somehow I figured it just happened but now that I thought of it, someone did have to take responsibility. If Mom was missing cocktail hour, she truly was upset. I put a slice of leftover pizza into the toaster oven and poured myself a glass of wine.

"We're at an age where the death of a friend can be tough," Sherry continued. "And Charlie was more than just a friend."

"So I heard."

"No need for that snide tone of voice, young lady," Sherry chided. "Old people are allowed to fall in love, too, you know."

"No, I didn't know." My voice was just as snappish as hers. "Mom didn't bother to tell me."

"Maybe if you spent more time with her or called her now and then, you'd know what was going on in her life."

I started to fire back a retort but stopped myself in time. There was no use arguing who was to blame. "I need to go, Aunt Sherry. I have a lot to get done before I leave tomorrow. Thanks for keeping an eye on things for me." I tried to keep a conciliatory tone in my voice.

I must have succeeded because she answered with an equally serene tone. "No problem. I enjoy visiting the cats. Have a good trip." She hung up and I had the distinct feeling she was anxious to be done with the call.

So Mom was upset? I ate my pizza and considered calling her. No, I decided. It would probably be best to put some time between us. To be honest, I wasn't able to muster any sympathy for her and I knew it would come out in any conversation we had. Mom got along for years without me. I was sure she could manage for a few days.

I took Conan out for a long walk in the twilight then turned my attention to packing and trip preparation. I am not a quick decider when it comes to choosing clothing for a trip. I also wanted to be sure everything was in order for my housesitter, so I wasn't surprised to see the clock read 9 by the time I was done with everything.

I had a celebratory second glass of wine then showered and fell into bed. I just closed my eyes when I remembered Ike said he'd call.

The thought barely made it to consciousness before I was sound asleep.

I was munching on a slice of toast at 7:30 the next morning when a car pulled into my drive. I peeked through the side window and saw Ike getting out of his dark red Acura sports coupe, a red gift bag swinging jauntily from one hand. He wore black sweat pants and a faded sweatshirt with the Stoneyburst emblem in the school colors of purple and gold. Even with his hair tousled and in such casual wear, he looked elegant.

"What are you doing here?" I asked, ushering him into the foyer.

He set the bag on the table near the door. "I got

busy last night and couldn't call, so I thought I'd stop by before you go."

"How did you know what time I'd be leaving?"

"I know you, Acie. The conference starts this afternoon, and you won't want to miss a thing. If you're taking the Hell Hound to the kennel for boarding, you'll need to get him there early so you can get on the road."

"Am I so predictable?"

Ike leaned close to me. "Yes. And I'm glad of it. Besides," and he straightened, "I was on my way to the gym and I wanted to see you before you left." He handed me the gift bag. "Just a little something to remind you of me while you're gone."

I started to peek inside but it was closed with three strips of tape.

"No, you don't," he said with a laugh. "You can look at it tonight when you get to the hotel. Not before."

"Why not?"

"This is one surprise I want you to anticipate. Trust me." He put his arms around me and I looked up into his intent gaze. "Drive carefully. I'll call you tonight to see how you like my present."

I had my arms around him, and I jiggled the bag against his backside. "Is it breakable?"

He leaned forward and his lips met mine in a long, dizzying kiss. Warmth, anticipation, and desire seemed to surge from him to me—and then back again. When he pulled away, I was weak at the knees. "It's not breakable," he whispered. "But my heart is. Take care of it, okay?"

I nodded dumbly, so bemused by his kiss I was speechless. He pulled open the door. "See you on

Friday. I'll call you and we'll decide what time, okay?"

"Friday?" I had no idea what day today was, much less what was happening on Friday.

"For the dinner, the dance and for our photo shoot. Can't wait." He left, tugging the door closed behind him.

I stared at it then at the gift bag in my hand. I really didn't like surprises. What was he doing? I considered opening it, but I stopped myself just short of peeling back the tape.

Trust me.

If only Ike knew how hard it was. I walked to the kitchen and peered out the window, watching him drive away. I looked at the gift bag then at the window.

Trust me.

Okay. I'd give it a try.

Chapter 12

I resisted the urge to peek all day, adhering to Ike's admonition to wait until evening. It was easy during the four-hour drive to Chicago because I tucked the bag in the trunk along with my briefcase, roller suitcase, and garment bag. Out of sight was indeed out of mind.

The conference was held at a hotel on the west side of town, thank God, which meant I didn't have to drive through horrible traffic to find it. A spot of construction caused me an unintentional detour, but didn't delay me overmuch. By two in the afternoon I was sitting with colleagues from other colleges, deep in discussion about the recent Jane Austen fad and bemoaning the fact the Victorians got so little good press.

I joined a panel at three-thirty to discuss the influence of the Victorians on the so-called "New Generation" authors such as Hemingway and Fitzgerald. It was a topic which generated a great deal of lively debate that continued through dinner and migrated to the bar afterward for a postprandial drink.

Thus I didn't have a chance to consider Ike's present until I retired to my room at nine in the evening. The little gift bag sat on the room's desk and was the first thing I saw when I entered. I set all my gadgets to charge then I quickly checked my personal email on my laptop.

Paul sent a copy of the shooting schedule which I

skimmed. It appeared that they weren't going to start any interior shooting until Friday evening at the Harvest Ball dance. That meant there was no rush for me to get back. I just had to be there by 6:30 on Friday evening for the pre-dance dinner and ceremony.

I had an email from Maggie. She had turned in the article and it appeared in the newspaper with very little editing needed by the newspaper staff. She assured me Conan was enjoying his stay at Doggie Day Care with an attached video showing him romping with other dogs in the enclosed yard outside Maggie's office. I knew Conan would be fine, but it was nice to have confirmation. I had no worries about Houdini or Sprite. Cats are quite capable of doing without a human as long as someone refills the food dishes and makes sure there's fresh water. They probably wouldn't even notice I was gone until I returned.

Email handled, I poured myself a glass of wine from the bottle I had brought, having learned long ago to bring my own booze to conferences in order to avoid exorbitant bar tabs. I sat down, kicked off my shoes and curled up on the bed with the wine glass and Ike's sack.

I pulled out the red-yellow-green-blue polka dot tissue paper and found a flat square box tucked inside. I opened it. A gold necklace lay on a bed of red velveteen. It had a delicate-looking but heavy gold chain at the end of which dangled two gold words in script, one atop the other, about a half-inch square:

We'll see

The apostrophe was a small faux diamond which sparkled in the light. I laughed softly. Where did he find it? I clasped it around my neck and went to the bathroom mirror to examine it. The words hung just at the top of my breasts, so it would be hidden most of the time, unless I wore a more revealing top than I normally did.

I touched the words and could visualize Ike's laughing eyes when he purchased it. I sat back on the bed and when I did, the sack tipped over, spilling out an envelope. I opened it and found a card with a beautiful floral watercolor on the front. Inside was a quote in Ike's spiky handwriting:

Deep experience is never peaceful

I smiled. It was one of my favorite Henry James quotes, from one of his very earliest novellas. I touched the necklace again where it dangled outside my sedate pale green sweater. It was years since a man gave me a gift of any significance. Trust Ike to come up with such an appropriate item.

And the quote—how did he know? Ike was a Renaissance man, not a Victorian scholar. I thought of another James quote, this one from his later work:

Live all you can; it's a mistake not to. It doesn't so much matter what you do in particular, so long as you have your life. If you haven't had that what have you had?

What indeed? I thought, tugging on my nightgown. The quote seemed to sum up the dilemma I was facing. A part of me longed to *live*, to be with Ike and forget convention. That part was willing to fling aside my doubts and simply enjoy the moment.

But another part of me was still a young girl from long ago who was forced to grow up and become responsible in order to survive. Why couldn't I leave that girl behind? Why couldn't I relegate that child to the past and let the future take over my life?

I took off the necklace and put it back in its little box. Ike Adler was fast becoming a mystery who I wanted to solve and along the way I was discovering things about myself I hadn't considered, ever. Was that his intent? Woo me via my curiosity?

I brushed then braided my hair and considered myself in the mirror. Why would someone like Ike—talented, handsome, accomplished—woo someone like me? Yes, I was still beautiful, with good bones and skin. But I was such a klutz compared to him in other ways. I was a homebody with few hobbies and meager talent when it came to the things at which Ike excelled. Good heavens, he and I would be so mismatched it would be—

My iPhone chimed. I hurried to the desk and picked it up, glancing at the display. "Thank you for the present," I said before he could speak. "Wherever did you find it?"

"Online." I could hear the laughter in Ike's voice. "On the Etsy web site. I think you can find anything you want there."

"I love it. And the card is perfect, too. How did you know Henry James was one of my favorite authors?" I unhooked the phone from the charger and went to the bed.

"I wish I could say I know you so well I intuited he would be, but I actually overheard you talking with someone in the hallway one day." Now his voice sounded rueful. "I confess. The only Henry James I've read was what I was assigned in college. I really don't enjoy his work."

I laughed and sank back on the pillows. "Then I have a confession, too. I don't read Shakespeare. I find him boring."

"Then we're even," Ike said. "Good. I was afraid I'd find you had a secret life as a Marlowe scholar. It's nice to know you aren't perfect in all ways."

"I'm not perfect in any way, Ike."

"Oh, don't be so sure about that. How's the conference going?"

I snuggled under the covers and we talked about the various workshops I attended and would attend. It was nice to chat with someone who had the same professional background as I. He knew exactly what I meant when I said the moderator of my discussion group was too much Hemingway and not enough Fitzgerald.

"Someone given to putting others in their place?" he said.

"Someone who preferred to view authors as working class, rather than aristocrat. Not that they should be put on a pedestal, but I think Arthur Conan Doyle deserves more of a description than *he made the serial novel popular and spawned several imitators of his work.* From the way she said it, you'd have thought Doyle produced dime novels."

"You're just prejudiced because you share the same name."

"Perhaps." I sipped more wine and viewed the suburban Chicago night sky out my window. The conference hotel wasn't too far from O'Hare Airport and I saw planes lining up to land in the distance. "Did you get a copy of the photo schedule?"

"No. Your agent said he would send a copy to you and you would guide me through it all." I heard definite amusement in Ike's voice. "I think he knows this isn't a long-term career choice for me. I'm only in it because you are."

"He sent a copy to me. We're not needed until later in the evening, so I'll be able to go to the dinner and the endowment ceremony. I was concerned about it."

"Don't be. There's no way Dr. Bell is going to let it slip through her fingers. What time should I pick you up?"

"For what?"

"For dinner and the ceremony on Friday."

I yawned. "I didn't know you were picking me up."

"You're my guide, remember? Why don't I come to your house at six? I think there are pre-dinner cocktails, so we can mingle. It should give you plenty of time to get nervous about your speech when you accept the endowment."

"If it was Henrietta doing the presenting, I might be nervous. Knowing her, she would have stabbed me with a cocktail pick if she could. But I think I can handle one of the Franks."

There was an uncomfortable silence. "She was such an unhappy person. I'm sorry we argued like that before she died." Ike's voice was low and sad.

He sounded guilty, too. "It's not your fault, Ike. She told you she didn't need your help. You're not to blame that she died."

"I know. I just wish—it's just too bad we argued. If we hadn't, she would have walked back to the club with me and nothing would have happened to her."

"You don't know that," I said quickly, although he was probably right. "It's like saying it's too bad you weren't in love with her. If you'd been in love with her, you wouldn't have argued in the first place."

"When I asked her if she wanted me to walk back with her, you know what she said?" He continued without waiting for my reply. "She said, *I suppose it's time I get used to not having a man around. If Annabelle Doyle can do it, I can.* She was so anxious to compare herself favorably to you. She did it all the time."

"What?" This was news to me. As far as I knew, Henrietta Baron only cared about me as a potential adversary regarding the animal sanctuary. Why would she bother to compare herself to me on that or any other account?

"She didn't come out and say it, but a few times she mentioned remembering you from high school. I had the feeling you impressed a lot of your classmates."

A vivid memory of a high school dance flashed into my mind. I didn't have a date but I went anyway and I wore a pant suit I made myself. All the other girls had on frilly dresses, but my sewing skills weren't up to anything elaborate.

The pale yellow fabric was on sale at the local dime store and I made the elastic-waist pants and a sleeveless tunic top out of lightweight velveteen material. Those were easy clothing items to sew because they didn't involve any buttons or zippers. I splurged and also bought a length of dark gold tablecloth lace, which I used as a shawl. Even then I had long hair and the shawl matched my hair color perfectly.

I don't know if it was at that dance or another one, but Henrietta was Prom Queen and sat on the stage in the gymnasium, resplendent in a store-bought satin gown that fit her like a glove. Her glittering tiara sat atop her stylish hairdo and she truly looked like a Queen while she smiled at us peons mingling on the dance floor in front of her.

"I don't remember her very well at all from high school," I said. "Just bits and pieces of memory. She was a couple of years younger than me and that's like decades when you're in high school." I took a swallow of wine, washing away the taste of anger the thought of my adolescence provoked.

"She said you scared everybody with how you took care of yourself without any help from anybody. I think it impressed your classmates. I think she was jealous of you."

"Jealous?" I dropped my wine glass but caught it before a spill happened. "Good Lord, why? She had a fancy condo in Chicago, an upper management job with a big law firm, and an uncle who doted on her and was going to leave her buckets of money."

"You were a model," Ike said. "That's pretty glamorous. She said once a few other girls in your high school class went to modeling try-outs but they were turned down. I think she did, too, but she didn't get a job offer. You did it for years. Then you put yourself through school, got a PhD and became a college professor. It's pretty impressive, Acie. Her parents paid for college and her father found her the job with the law firm and he paid for her condo. Nobody helped you but yourself. I think that's what intimidated Henrietta." Ike paused then he said thoughtfully, "Well, that and your looks."

"Oh, for heaven's sake." It certainly wasn't an impressive accomplishment that I had done all those things. I simply had no choice. If I wanted something, I had to get it for myself. "Henrietta was an attractive woman, too. Modeling is a business, just like any other one. They wanted me because I look like the girl next door and I know how to smile on demand." I paused. "And, of course, I don't have any visible tattoos. It's a real problem in the business. Models get a tattoo then it has to be airbrushed out of the picture."

"You have a tattoo that's not visible?"

"Well, it's not visible for the assignments I take. If I was a swimsuit or lingerie model, it might be an issue."

There was a pause and I thought I heard him mutter something.

"Ike? Are you still there?"

"Yeah. I'm just imagining you as a lingerie model."

"I did a few test sessions, but I wasn't happy with the result. I just don't think I have what it takes to model lingerie."

There was another pause. "Oh, I don't know. I'm not having any trouble imagining it."

"I think maybe I'm just too girl-next-door for it. Anyway, there was nothing for Henrietta to be jealous about."

"You look like a beautiful girl next door," he corrected. "I think she was envious you were happy. I don't think she knew how to be happy unless she had someone with her. And there you were, alone, but you were happy. I know it sounds dumb, but no matter what happened, it seemed like it wasn't quite what she wanted. I don't know why she was so sure she and I— you know. She would never have been happy living in Grimper. Did she think I was going to quit my job and move to Chicago with her?"

I felt sorry for him. He sounded honestly bewildered. "I doubt if she really thought it through, Ike. After all, every time she was in town, you and she did something together."

"Only because she asked me," Ike said quickly. "I never asked her out. It was always her calling me and asking me if I wanted to do this or that."

"You mean you and she never—were never—weren't, um, intimate?" I longed to ask *Did you sleep with her,* but, really, was it my business? A small voice in the back of mind said, *Damn right, it's your business. If you sleep with him you better know where he's been.* But I still wasn't sure I would be going down that path with him, so maybe it didn't matter.

Did it?

"God, no. I think maybe I kissed her once or twice. I already knew then she and I weren't cut out for each other, even if I wasn't already in love with you."

I let out a breath with a whoosh of relief and hastily moved the phone away from my face lest he hear. "This whole love thing has caught me totally by surprise." I decided to get it into the open once and for all.

"You're the only one it has surprised." I heard that wry self-amusement again in his voice. "I'm sure most people in the department know I've been mooning around about you and I'm certain your mother guessed."

"Mooning?" I grinned. "You were mooning?"

"You know what I mean. You can sometimes be the densest woman on the face of the earth." I heard a jangling noise in the background. "Someone's at the door. I can't call you tomorrow, it's my bridge club night and Thursday I have classes until 9."

"That's fine. I'll see you on Friday at 6."

"You'll go with me?" He sounded delighted.

"I have to lead you around, remember?" I heard the jangling noise again. "You'd better get the door. I'll see you on Friday."

"Okay. Good night, Acie." There was a brief hesitation then he said, "Sleep tight, honey."

"Good night, Ike." I ended the call and dropped the phone next to me on the bed. Like receiving the necklace, it was a long time since man called me 'honey'.

I decided I rather liked it.

I wore the necklace the next day while I hobnobbed with my colleagues. It was tucked discreetly out of sight under my high-necked pale green blouse, but I knew it was there. I touched it now and again, reminding myself of Ike. I suppose that's why he bought it. If that was his purpose, it worked.

The day was the usual conference flurry of workshops, luncheon with new and old friends, then more workshops followed by dinner. I didn't get back to my room until after eight o'clock and by then I was exhausted. I checked my home and professional email then dropped into bed to consult the two phone messages on my iPhone.

The first was from my mother, just a brief, "It's me, Mom. Give me a call when you can. Something's come up that's bizarre."

Knowing Mom that could mean anything from gossip about one of her Senior Living neighbors or the discovery her car insurance was out of date. I decided she could wait until morning, when I could return her call and end it quickly because I had to make a presentation.

The other call was from the woman who ran the town meeting the week before. "Dr. Doyle, this is Marge Crandon. I need to talk to you immediately. It's absolutely critical you call me as soon as you get this message. It doesn't matter what time of day or night. Please call. It's about the sanctuary."

The message was only two hours old and was left while I was at dinner and my phone was set to mute. I considered postponing a return call, but any news Marge had about the sanctuary was probably important, so I redialed her number.

She answered immediately. "I'm so glad you returned my call, Dr. Doyle. I suppose you know Henrietta Baron has left her estate to our local college."

"I heard a rumor to that effect," I said cautiously. "Has it been made public knowledge?"

"Not really, but I was told about it because the mayor came to me. He was talking with the City Council and then they talked with Dr. Bell, at the college. It's about the sanctuary."

My stomach dropped. This didn't sound good. "What about it?"

"They all think it's a great idea, but the town has to get something out of it." She rushed on before I could insert a word of protest. "We agree it's a fine thing to give all those animals a place to live and roam. But we have to think about the money it will take to maintain the facility."

That was a detail that had me worried, too, but I wasn't going to admit it. "I know we'll have to do fund-raising and we'll rely on volunteers for—"

"Here's what we thought." She overrode my words without pause. "We'll have the sanctuary, as planned, but we'll also have a viewing area. There's a bear sanctuary up in Minnesota. We can use it as a model."

"Bear sanctuary?"

"I'll send you a link to it. What they do is they have this visitor center, where people can come and learn about bears. Some of the bears come to the center in this viewing area where visitors can see them—all behind glass and safe and all. The bears are fed there or something. I'm not sure. Anyway, the visitor center teaches people about bears and raises money."

"But it would cost money to build it," I said.

"We have Charlie Baron's house," Marge said. "It's big enough. At least, we think we have it. Or, rather, the school has it. Of course, it might be tied up in court for a while, but it looks like your mother was going to inherit the land and the school will get the house and the rest of the estate. That's the preliminary estimate, of course."

"What?" I managed to wedge a word in through the simple expedience of shouting it.

"Haven't you talked to your mother? Henrietta was going to inherit the house and the money. And since the school is Henrietta's heir, it looks like the school will get the house and the money. Your mother hasn't changed her mind about donating the land, has she? I mean, we just assumed she would."

"I haven't talked to her about it."

"Dr. Bell thought the school could donate the house. She thought she'd talk to the Architecture Department and see if they can use it for a remodeling project. They'll put on a new wing and viewing area.

The house overlooks the meadows and the forest, so it's perfect. And the mayor said the town would pay for the fencing and the upkeep as long as they get a portion of the revenue. We could have different stores in town selling things to tourists to promote the center."

"It wasn't quite what we had in mind," I interjected, slowing the flood of words. Charlie Baron left the land to Mom? That explained her earlier phone call. And it also explained Henrietta's objection to Charlie's will. Good heavens, how long had Henrietta known about it? Did she know about it when we had the town meeting? If she did, then she had no right to pretend she could stop the sanctuary by refusing to give us the land.

That bitch. My old animosity with Henrietta flared up again with a vengeance. But she was dead now, so who would get the land? I rubbed my forehead where a headache was starting to blossom. Good Lord. What a mess.

"I know it's not what was planned, but I'll be honest," Marge said in a tone of voice normally called *brisk* but which I think of as *shut up and let me talk, will you?* "The town isn't on board with the sanctuary. John Staples has folks worked up about it."

"Staples?" Why was I surprised? John Staples had become my Moby Dick, my white whale, my own private Hound of the Baskervilles who haunted and taunted me. It seemed like everywhere I turned, he was there, opposing me.

"Of course, everybody knows he stands to make a lot of money if the land is sold to a developer, so what he says isn't taken very seriously. But he's made good arguments against the sanctuary. Oh." She stopped and

I heard a gasp of breath.

"Are you okay, Marge?" I asked into the sudden silence. Perhaps she was taking a break to gather her strength.

"It reminded me of Meryl Staples. I saw her with Dr. Adler today. They were having lunch and they looked, well, chummy. I thought you and he were—you know."

Good heavens, did the entire town know Ike was 'mooning' for me? "Dr. Adler and I are good friends. I know Miss Staples asked for his help with problems she has with her brother. Maybe they were discussing that."

"Maybe." Marge sounded doubtful. "Anyway, back to the sanctuary. I think most of the townspeople like the idea but what's in it for them? I've talked to people and that's the feeling I'm getting. But if we combine the sanctuary with a tourist attraction, that's something people can support."

"I'll have to talk to the other committee members." I was barely aware of what I was saying. Ike and Meryl? Really? How could he be wooing me with cards and jewelry then have lunch with that woman? I was impatient for Marge to wrap up this talk so I could give him a call and give him a piece of my mind.

"…They want to meet with you as soon as you get back in town. When do you get here?"

"I had planned to return Friday afternoon, but—"

"Why don't I set up a meeting for two o'clock on Friday? I'll get the committee together, the mayor, the council, and Dr. Bell. We'll all sit down and discuss this idea."

My plans for a relaxing lunch with colleagues evaporated. "It should work okay," I said. "I need to consider it more, though."

"You think about it and we'll start working on details." Marge laughed. "I've wanted a big project to tackle. You don't mind if I help, do you?"

"Heaven's, no. That would be great."

"Good. I'm sure we can come up with a plan that will make everybody happy. Oh, this will be so much fun. Come to the city council chambers on Friday. I'll make sure everybody's there. Bye!"

I tapped the End icon on the phone and tossed it on the bed beside me. Ike and Meryl Staples? Damn it, how could he?

I poured myself a glass of wine and sat on the edge of the bed. Okay, I reasoned. So they had lunch together. Big deal. It didn't necessarily mean anything. I went to the vanity area outside the hotel bathroom and found the jewelry box where I had tucked it into my makeup bag. I took off the necklace and put it on the velveteen base.

We'll see.

My iPhone chimed again. I stowed the box back in my bag and grabbed the phone, glancing at the display. "Hey, Mom," I said, pacing over to the window.

"I suppose you've heard the news."

"About Henrietta's will? Yes, I did. She left everything to the school."

Mom gave a short, snorting laugh. "Yeah, except she didn't have anything to leave. Oh, she had her own stuff. A condo and a 401K. But anything Charlie left her is all screwed up. Did you hear about that, too?"

It looked cold outside. I had been insulated all day indoors and had no idea what the weather was doing. I glimpsed people scurrying past the hotel's front entrance, their heads bowed low to avoid the wind. "I heard something about it, but I wasn't sure what was what."

"I found out about it today. I had to go to Frank Two's office because he sent a letter to Charlie about the will."

"What? How do you know he sent Charlie a letter?" I sipped more wine. After a conversation with Marge and now one with my mother, my head was spinning. Or maybe it was the news about Ike and Meryl. *No. Don't go there.*

"It was in the stack of mail we brought from the house on Sunday. It's so typical of the Franks, isn't it? They sent Charlie a letter about the objection Henrietta filed to his will. But Charlie was already dead when they sent it. They're so disorganized. I went to see Frank Two about the letter and guess who was there?"

I was having a hard time keeping her story straight, so I just murmured, "No idea," which echoed my sentiments about the entire conversation.

"That stupid John Staples was there. He and Frank Two looked like they were in cahoots."

Cahoots? I smiled. I hadn't heard the word in years.

"I wouldn't put it past that odious little man to hire one of the Franks to sue me. Anyway, Charlie left the land to me. And Henrietta apparently filed a—hold on, it's here someplace." I heard her rummaging through papers. "Oh, shit, I can't find it. It's something with a Latin phrase on it. What it means is Henrietta pitched a fit and claims I coerced Charlie into changing his will."

I heard the telltale rattle of ice in a glass. I joined my mother in taking a sip of my alcoholic beverage of choice. "Now that Henrietta is dead, what will happen with the objection?"

"Good question. Frank Two made vague comments about the possibility of a lawsuit. You know how he is. He'd file a lawsuit against his mother if he thought the case was interesting. I wonder if that's why Meryl Staples was hanging all over Ike Adler today."

I took another swallow of wine, found my glass empty, and went back to the desk to refill it. "Go ahead, Mom," I said while I poured.

"Go ahead with what?"

"I'm sure you want to tell me all about Ike and Meryl."

"It's none of my business. If you don't care that he and that woman were sitting in public, holding hands, then I don't care either."

"What do you mean, sitting in public? Where?"

"At Barrymore's Cafe. I saw them. She left when Sherry and I came in. He looked surprised to see us and he made a comment about going to class then he left, too, not a minute or two after her."

The implication was obvious. *They didn't want to be seen leaving together.* "I'm sure it was just a friendly chat," I said.

"Uh-huh," she said doubtfully.

"So what are you going to do about Charlie Baron's land?" I dragged the conversation away from the dangerous topic of Ike Adler.

"Not much I can do until this whole will business gets settled."

"Will you donate it to the sanctuary?"

"Of course I will. What use do I have for four hundred acres of land? I just wanted you to know about it in case you were still worried. Once all this nonsense gets legally settled, the sanctuary will have its land."

"Thanks, Mom." I recognized a peace offering when I saw it. "I appreciate you calling."

"And don't worry too much about Adler," she said. "You know what they say—a woman needs a man like—"

"A fish needs a bicycle. Yes, I know. I'll see you on Friday."

"Okay. Good night, dear."

"'Night, Mom." I started to set the phone to mute but instead I powered it off. I didn't want any more phone calls. And I didn't want to make any phone calls. I didn't want to call Ike and perhaps be disappointed.

I sipped my wine and stared at my reflection in the window. I had gotten by this long in my life without a man. Why change now? Why expose my heart to heartache? I really didn't need the grief, did I?

I visualized Ike's mischievous smile; the sadness in his voice when he talked about Henrietta; the easy laughter we shared whenever we were together.

Was it already too late?

I heard his bantering voice in my mind. *We'll see.*

I sipped my wine. Yes, we would.

Chapter 13

Thursday was too busy to give me time to worry about Ike. Right after breakfast, I was sidetracked by a colleague who wanted to discuss American fiction at the turn of the last century. That kept me occupied until it was time for my presentation.

As I expected, my talk generated a lively question-and-answer session which carried over to luncheon, where I sat with several workshop attendees. We continued our talk while consuming salad and sandwiches, then I spent the afternoon in other workshops. They kept my mind firmly on academic matters and away from the tricky subject of love.

Because I was leaving earlier than anticipated on Friday and had to cancel a planned luncheon, I spent Thursday evening with friends. Thus I didn't get back to my room until past ten o'clock. I checked my email and found the final shooting schedule from Paul. I double-checked the timing and was relieved to see I wouldn't be needed until 8:30 the next night for makeup, with shooting scheduled to start at 9:30 or possibly later. The banquet was from 6:30 to 8:00, so I would have time for the endowment ceremony but very little time at the dance.

Oh, well. I didn't need to dance, anyway. Ike probably wouldn't be needed throughout the entire shoot, so he could spend time at the dance if he wanted.

I shut off my laptop and stowed it away, then checked my phone one last time. I had checked my phone throughout the day but I had no more messages from Mom, Marge, or Ike. I got ready for bed and poured the last of my wine into a glass. I thought about calling Ike. *But what if he's not alone? What if someone is with him?*

My imagination galloped ahead to envision him in a passionate embrace with beautiful Meryl Staples, her arms around him and her dark head resting against his chest. For an instant my heart beat frantically and I was doused with hot then cold, probably a combination of panic and hot flashes.

Pragmatic common sense soon took over. Why would Ike go to the trouble to seduce me then turn around and have an affair with Meryl? Despite his seeming indifference to public opinion, he still had to be careful about his professorial reputation. Loose behavior, while not specifically prohibited, was definitely frowned on. Granted, we were all adults, but a man seducing or wooing two women was, generally speaking, considered bad behavior.

What about Meryl? What did she stand to gain? Of course, the coldly logical reason was if she snagged Ike, she could get out from under her brother's thumb. She didn't appear to have any means of support except him, so maybe she was one of those women who had to rely on a man for a living.

I swallowed my wine and grimaced at the thought. What a terrible way to live, to always be dependent on someone else's good graces. It seemed to go beyond that, though. Meryl was somehow unformed or a shadow. I nodded. Yes, that was the term. She wasn't a distinct personality but was an adjunct to her brother. What was it Ike said? *She seems to need someone.*

Mom said something, too, about Charlie. I drained my wine glass and sleepily considered brushing my teeth. Oh, well. *One night won't plunge me into decay. Live dangerously.* I turned off the light and started to drift off to sleep when I remembered.

Mom accused John Staples of pimping out his sister, or words to that effect. Why was Staples so bent on selling the land? I let my drowsy mind take over. Maybe there was a body buried there. Maybe buried treasure. Maybe…

****

I had time in the morning to attend the breakfast and listen to the speaker. By ten o'clock I was checked out of my hotel and on the Interstate, heading west. I resolutely pushed thoughts of Ike, Meryl, the sanctuary, and legal matters out of my mind. Instead I focused on the simple pleasure of driving on a relatively uncrowded highway with just the occasional slowdown for a toll booth. I turned my XM radio on loud and channel-surfed my way to Iowa.

I arrived home a little after one o'clock. I hauled my bags into the house, waking up Sprite and Houdini who were sprawled in the middle of my bed. They yawned when they saw me and resumed sleeping. I skimmed through the stack of mail Aunt Sherry left on the kitchen counter then I departed after grabbing my Wild Cat Freedom Committee file from the den.

I was relieved to see it was a clear, albeit cold, day. If this persisted throughout the weekend, it would be a perfect Homecoming with quintessential football weather. Clear and cold, sunny skies, a stadium full of cheering fans, and a campus awash in alumni, family, and friends.

Nothing could be better for a photo shoot, even though most of it would take place indoors. Bad weather always affected temperamental artists like photographers and models, although it really didn't matter to me. My hair and skin didn't react to the elements like it did for some models. I remember one poor girl with naturally curly hair who was constantly fighting humidity to keep her career alive.

I drove through dappled sunshine to City Hall, a somewhat modern two-story building which shared a visitor's parking lot with the Police Station. When I got out of my car, Lee Street was leaving that building, striding to a dark sedan parked nearby.

He paused when he saw me across the parking lot then he came toward me, obviously trying to intercept me before I entered the municipal building. I considered making a dash for it then I decided it might be rude.

"Dr. Doyle, I have a few questions for you. Do you have time to answer them?"

"I'm going to a meeting so I'm afraid I don't." I kept my voice disinterested, trying to discourage him from persisting.

"It won't take long." Street's ferrety face looked very pale in the bright sunlight. His pallor, combined with his slouched posture and slicked-back hair, reminded me once again of a cartoon gangster. All that was missing was the zoot suit.

I struggled to keep a smile from escaping at the mental image of Lee Street in a zoot suit, a cigarette dangling from one corner of his mouth. "I'm sorry, but

I'm running late as it is. Perhaps later?" I moved to the sidewalk leading into City Hall.

"Why didn't you tell me you and Dr. Adler are involved in a romantic relationship?"

I stopped and turned to face him. "Because we are not."

"That's not what I was told."

I silently blessed all those long hours of interrogation by social workers during my youth. "I appreciate the fact you sometimes must listen to rumor in order to gather information, but I think you really should take my word for it." I met his gaze without flinching. "After all, if I was involved with Dr. Adler, I think I'd know it."

I wasn't lying. Ike and I were *contemplating* a romantic relationship. We hadn't yet embarked on it. I had a great deal of experience in interpreting words to find a truth I could support. Lee Street was sadly mistaken if he thought he could trip me.

"Your mother is the heir to sizable estate." Street's shoulders shifted in his loose dark suit coat, twitching like he had an itch.

"My mother is an heir if—and it's a *sizable* if—the court decides in her favor. It will undoubtedly take months, or maybe years, to figure out." I looked at my wristwatch. "I'm sorry. I need to go."

"Were you aware of the contents of Mr. Baron's will on the night you argued with Miss Baron?"

I sighed loudly. "Of course I wasn't. If I was aware of it, why would I argue with her?" Really. The man was an idiot.

"Perhaps to provide yourself with an alibi."

I regarded him for one long second. "Really?" I

said in my best imitation of a sarcastic freshman. "I think the speech I was giving was probably a better alibi."

His lips pursed and a bright spot of color tinged his ears. "We haven't ascertained the exact time of death."

"I was either with a large group of people or with Dr. Adler the entire time Miss Baron was gone." I turned once again to go into City Hall.

"Yes. Dr. Adler."

This time I didn't even pause. I just said over my shoulder, "I'll be happy to answer your questions when I'm done with the meeting."

"I thought you had an endowment ceremony and dance tonight. And modeling."

I stopped at the entrance to the building and turned. "I'll make time for you if needed."

Street stared at me and his shoulders twitched again. "Good to know, Dr. Doyle."

I jerked open the heavy glass-and-wood door, pausing inside to look back at him. He still stood near my car, staring at the door behind which I lurked. Then he twitched his suit coat again and went to his car.

Alibi? I needed an alibi? I shook my head in disgust. The man was either an idiot or he was grasping at straws. Probably the latter. Henrietta's death was an accident. Why try to make it out to be something it wasn't? I consulted a directory on the wall and proceeded to the council chambers. I was halfway there when an idea stopped me in my tracks.

What if her death wasn't an accident? What if they had proof it wasn't? The thought led me to the next question.

What kind of proof? Why were they focused on

Ike?

The knowledge washed over me like a cold ice bath. He was the last person to see her alive.

"There you are!"

I was shaken out of my trance-like state by Marge Crandon, who leaned out of a doorway to my left.

"I was afraid you were delayed," she said, gesturing me inside. "We're ready. Dr. Lippincott couldn't be here, but everyone else from the committee is here. We're so excited about this new idea of an open sanctuary. We can't wait to talk about it."

I had hoped Maggie could attend, but she was understandably busy. I reluctantly shelved my anxieties about Henrietta's death. Right now I had an animal sanctuary to get approved.

****

Three hours later, we had hammered out a rather detailed compromise. Legal details had to be finessed, but overall it was a workable plan. The mayor called the editor of our local newspaper and she promised to hold a spot for us on the front page so we could explain our plan. Marge volunteered to draft the new article for the newspaper and I promised to review it first thing in the morning so it could make the Saturday afternoon paper.

I hurried to Maggie's office to inform her of the afternoon's events and to get Conan, who was boarding with her while I was out of town. I managed to grab a few minutes of Maggie's time just before she was due to examine a large cat crouched in a cage in the waiting room with an equally large woman in charge of him.

"It's the best of both worlds," I told Maggie, restraining Conan from making friends with the cat, who eyed us balefully. Maggie, Conan and I stood near the doorway to the exam room. "Assuming all the legal problems can be ironed out we should be able to get things open by next year. Imagine it. Won't it be exciting?"

Maggie smiled. "That's great news. You know, I wasn't sure if we'd get a vote passed or not. The longer people had to think about it, the more they were wavering." She gestured us away from the exam room door. "Move Conan over there and keep him on a short leash. Mrs. Selden's cat can be mean."

I did as she asked, making sure Conan stayed near me while the woman manhandled the big cage across the waiting room. "Thanks for taking care of Conan," I said, watching the woman lug the cat into the exam room. "He seems to love it here."

The cat hissed at Conan, who drew back in obvious surprise. "He's not feeling well," the woman said with a reproving look at my puppy. She plunked the cage on the exam table and bent over to peer inside.

Maggie rolled her eyes. "He's always grumpy," she said in a low voice. "I'll see you tonight at the dance. Now we really have something to celebrate." She turned to her patient and I heard her say while she closed the door, "What did he swallow this time, Mrs. Selden?"

When I drove home with Conan we passed Ike's street and I was tempted to stop by his house and ask him about the rumors I heard. Good sense prevailed, though. I would see Ike in an hour or so, and I could ask him then. I had primping to do before he arrived. I continued on to my house and entered to find Sprite waiting expectantly near the garage door. When she saw Conan, she pranced happily to butt heads with him and they immediately were off, romping through the house.

"Looks like she missed him more than she missed me," I commented to Houdini, who sat near the food bowls with a reproachful look.

I fed everybody then went to the bedroom to consider my wardrobe for the evening. I had a nice mid-knee-length black dress which would serve for the endowment ceremony and dance since I would be changing clothes later for the photo shoot. I pulled out the black dress and a small gym bag, which I packed with jeans, sweater, and sneakers for after the shoot.

I showered quickly but didn't wash my hair. It would take too long to dry and day-old hair was easier to style, anyway. I plaited it into a simple braid and pulled on thigh-high nylons before slipping on the dress.

The doorbell rang as I considered my shoe choice. I looked at the clock, momentarily panicked, but it was only 5:30, so it couldn't be Ike. I went to the door and peeked out to see my mother standing on the front step, dressed in a dark purple dress with a glittery lavender jacket.

"Hi, Mom." I pulled open the door while trying to keep an eye out for Sprite. She must have been busy elsewhere, though, because she mercifully didn't make a break for it. Conan trotted out from the living room while Mom slipped inside quickly.

"I thought I'd stop by and see if you need any help for the modeling thing tonight." She patted Conan's head and his tail beat a hearty tattoo against my legs in appreciation.

"Nope, all I have to do is show up." I walked back to the bedroom and Mom followed. Conan decided we were boring and went back to whatever he was doing.

"You're not wearing that, are you?" she asked.

I looked at my black dress. "Yes."

"It's old."

"No one knows that."

"Of course they know it. You always wear the same dress." Mother went past me and opened my closet door.

I ignored her and went to my dresser to look over my jewelry choices. I touched Ike's necklace in the small box but reluctantly set it to one side as being not quite dressy enough.

"How about this one?" Mom called out.

I sighed and turned. She was holding out a form-fitting dark green dress with a slit up the side and a matching see-through jacket decorated with multi-colored beadwork. "That's too dressy." I returned to my jewelry appraisal.

"No, it isn't. You have an important role tonight. You're accepting an endowment on behalf of the department. You're the senior department faculty member in modern British fiction. It's one of the reasons Charlie wanted to give the school an endowment."

"What?" I looked at her over my shoulder.

"He loved all those authors you're always talking about." Mom shook the dress, making it ripple and sparkle in the light. "You know, Conrad and Dreiser and whoever. I tried reading that *Portrait of a Lady* book." She shook her head and the dress rippled again. "Too slow and too boring. Isabel Archer, the heroine, wasn't very smart. But Charlie loved it."

I started to give argument to this dismissive treatment of one of Henry James' finest characters, but I saw the perplexed look on her face. I probably looked the same way when I skimmed through one of the banal romance novels my mother frequently insisted I read.

I subdued my criticism and said, "It's one of my favorites, too." I felt camaraderie with the dead man, not just because of his taste in literature but because of his patience in dealing with my mother.

"Charlie specified you accept the gift. You should look the part. Try it on."

Charlie specified you accept the gift. I heard a faint sadness in her voice. I suppose that was what made me relent so quickly. "You won't let me rest until I do this, will you?"

"No, I won't. And while we're at it, maybe I could do your hair."

"Nothing's wrong with my hair. It's going to be re-styled later anyway." I took the dress from her and went into the bathroom. I hung the dress hanger on the wall hook and unzipped my black dress, letting it slide to the floor.

"It's just plain, dear. I have a great idea for what we could do. You get changed."

"I don't know why I should change anything," I protested half-heartedly. "I'll be changing again in a few hours for the photo shoot anyway. That's when the important clothes come out." I eyed the green dress, hanging near the door. It had a halter collar neckline, leaving the back bare and covered by the flimsy beaded jacket.

"It won't hurt you to dress up. Good heavens, you

act like you're the 80-year-old. Live it up. Have fun. Act your age."

"My age is fifty-five," I said. "I think I am acting my age."

"Buy a sports car. Have a few flings."

I unhooked my bra and dropped it to the floor then pulled the dress up over my hips. I was wearing the flimsiest panties I owned, not quite a thong, but close, and I'm glad I did. The dress fit like a glove. I bought it on impulse several years ago because it reminded me of a memorable photo shoot in Paris. I wore it once to a charitable ball with a man I dated. The gown was the talk of the party.

I surveyed myself in the mirror. "This is too dressy," I called.

Mother appeared behind me. "It's perfect. Let me do your hair." She picked up my hair brush from the sink and my hair doo-dads in the jewelry box where I kept the barrettes, bands, and accessories.

"What are you going to do?" I asked suspiciously.

"Humor me. Come on." She led me back to the bedroom and the chair next to the window. "Sit."

I sighed and sat down. "What do you mean I should buy a sports car? What's wrong with my car?"

"Hold this." Mom handed me my hair box. "You drive a six-year-old Toyota sedan," she said, deftly undoing my braid. "All I meant was you should live it up a little."

"What's wrong with my Toyota?"

"It's a very adequate car, but it's rather staid."

"Staid?" I tried to look up at her but she had my hair in grip like a vise.

"You and Ike have been keeping company now for

a while. Are you sleeping with him?"

This was so typical of my mother. Her tactic was to start one subject then shear off to another one. I tried to swivel my head to look at her but with her firm grip on my hair, I was unable to move. "Of course I'm not sleeping with him."

"Why 'of course'? He'd like to sleep with you," she said with a smug sureness in her voice. "Hold still." She began a slim braid on the left side of my head, starting level with my ear.

"I can't help but hold still," I grumbled. "You have me in a stranglehold. What are you doing?"

"Hush." She braided the right side, repeating the process. Then she began brushing my hair, pulling it back behind me to take long strokes and looping the braid up, forming it into a hair band that held most of my hair back.

"Ike and I are just friends."

"Don't you want to be more than friends? Hold up the box." I balanced the old jewelry box on my palm and she leaned over, peering inside. "Don't you have...oh, there we go. That's what I want." She plucked out several large pale gold hairpins, a black elastic band decorated with pearls, two gold pins with butterflies on the end, and two gold combs. "Hold still." Her voice was muffled, probably the result of several hair items sticking out of it.

"I am holding still. Just because Ike and I go out now and again, it doesn't mean—"

"You didn't answer the question." Mom twisted the long tail of my hair, pulling it tight against my scalp then she twisted it again. She stuck the combs into my hair against the back of my head then she tucked the pins in on the top.

"What question?" I had no idea what she was doing with my hair, but a quick glance at the clock told me I'd have time to re-braid my hair if needed.

"Don't you want to be more than friends with Ike?"

"I—no, I don't think—I mean, he's a colleague, and I—we—can't—"

"Go look in the mirror." Mom gave me a little push on my shoulders.

I tilted my head experimentally but my hair was securely in place. I went into the bathroom and stopped in front of the mirror over the sink. How had she done it? My long white hair was held back by two thick braids, the mass of hair bundled into a loose chignon accented by the dark gold combs. The butterflies and other cleverly hidden pins held the chignon securely in place with the pearls encircling the top.

"That's better, isn't it?" she asked from the doorway.

"It's more appropriate for this dress." I saw her hurt expression, quickly hidden when she saw me looking at her. "Thank you," I said.

She smiled. "I never had a chance to do your hair when you were little."

I stared at her in the mirror, not willing to turn and confront her directly. "It was your choice."

Her eyes took on a faraway look of memory. "Yes, it was. There were times when I deeply regretted it. I missed you."

So you left me with my father, who really wasn't capable of raising a child. I guess you didn't miss me that much. "Why didn't you just get divorced?" I blurted, the old question bubbling up and out.

"I did. In absentia."

"But you could have divorced him and stayed here. You could have stayed in town." I looked at the sink, at the box of hair accessories, at the floor—anywhere but at her. *I could have lived with you. I wouldn't have had to live with my poor alcoholic father, who could barely keep a job and a roof over our heads.*

"No, I couldn't," Mom said softly. "If I stayed here, I would have been trapped, unable to break away. I was thirty-two years old, Annabelle. I had never been anywhere further away than Des Moines. Don't you understand? Haven't you ever wanted to run away and join the circus? Haven't you wanted to just kick off your shoes and go wherever your feet take you?"

She made it sound like it was a crime I didn't feel that way. All my old anger, stuffed into the background of my mind with those questions, now started to bubble. "Someone had to stay behind and take care of Daddy." I struggled to keep my voice even.

I heard her make a choking sound, like she had gasped and strangled the noise. "I'm sorry. I didn't think he'd be allowed to keep you. I thought you'd be sent to your Uncle Roman's to live. He could take better care of you."

I drew in a long sigh, forcing away years of bitterness, relegating it once again to the background. "It didn't work that way. I stayed until Dad died then I had the chance for a modeling job and I left."

"But why did you come back? Surely you could have found a job in another college somewhere else."

I wasn't about to go into the complex emotions which led me back to my hometown, the town where I was pitied by my classmates because of my drunken father. The town where I excelled in school during the day and cleaned offices at night in order to put food on the table. Despite my past, or maybe because of it, I had special ties to this place.

"It's home." I brushed past her, picking up the beaded jacket from the bed and grabbing the matching green shoes from the closet. "Why did you come back?" I asked while I drew on the jacket. "You didn't have to stay in town after Daddy's funeral. Why did you?"

She looked thoughtful, her green eyes distant while she considered the past. "I suppose I was looking for home, too," she finally said. "Jimmy and I never stayed in one place long enough for it to feel permanent. When I came back here for the funeral, it seemed right to stay. I thought you would be staying, too, though."

I turned back to the bathroom to continue my contemplation of my jewelry box. "I couldn't wait to get out of town. Dad was sick the whole last year of school but he wouldn't go to a doctor. I think he knew he had cancer and he didn't want it confirmed." I chose a pair of plain gold earrings and managed to clip them on even though my hands were trembling.

"I'm sorry." Mom stood in the doorway, watching me. "I honestly didn't think you'd have to live with him. I thought Sherry or Roman would get custody and I knew they'd be a better parent than me, because I just didn't want to be here." She took a deep breath, and it sounded ragged. "Will you ever forgive me?"

I regarded her in the mirror. "It's long in the past, Mom. Why revisit it?"

"I know you can't forget it, but can you forgive it?" She smiled and it looked like her eyes were bright.

With tears? I wasn't so sure. Mom could be a good actress when she needed to be.

"I'm not carrying a grudge. I wouldn't have come back to Grimper if I was." I brushed past her and picked up my gym bag. The doorbell rang, interrupting the moment. *Thank you, God.* "That must be Ike," I said brightly.

"I'm sorry." Mom headed for the door when I did. We had a brief comedic moment while we jockeyed for position then I let her go ahead of me. "I didn't know Ike was picking you up. I thought we might drive together."

"Isn't Sherry going?"

"She isn't going to the banquet but she's coming to the dance later. I think paying twenty dollars to dance is more her speed. Besides, I wanted to watch you at the ceremony. It's an important night for your department and a great honor for you. I wanted to be there."

That surprised me. Mom never really cared about my academic achievements. But the more I considered it, I realized I was wrong. In very small, subtle ways, Mom always managed to attend any public function where I had to speak or any events where I was featured. I guess this was just the first time she said it.

"I don't blame Sherry for not coming." I reached for the front door. "It's probably going to be boring. If you want to ride with Ike and me, I'm sure it would be fine."

"Oh, no," she said with an adamant shake of her head. "I'm not interrupting your date. But if you don't mind," and she leaned closer to whisper to me, "I'd like to see his face when he sees you." Her green eyes were twinkling, this time with mischief, not tears.

"Sure." I pulled open the door.

Ike stood on the threshold, a corsage box in one hand. He wore a tailored black suit that emphasized his broad shoulders and a pale gray shirt with black-and-white tie that highlighted his gray-and-black hair. His blue eyes widened when he saw me. "Holy crap," he breathed.

Mom and I both burst out laughing.

Chapter 14

Ike was holding a corsage box. "I'm sorry, I didn't get you a boutonniere," I apologized. "I was so busy today." I gestured him into the foyer and closed the door quickly behind him.

Conan raced into the hallway to greet the newcomer, knocking into me with his energy. Ike leaned over to give the puppy a good head rub, holding out the box to me. "There's one in there for me, too," he said, straightening up. "I told them to go ahead and put something in." His eyes went to Mom. "Are you joining us for dinner?"

"No, I just stopped to see if Annabelle needed anything. I know she was busy today what with travel and meetings and all."

"Meetings?" Ike quirked an enquiring eyebrow at me.

"We had a special meeting today about the sanctuary. I'll fill you in later." I opened the flimsy white cardboard box. Inside was a white orchid with a pale pink blushing center. Nestled in the tissue with it was a white carnation tipped with pink. "It's so pretty, Ike. I don't remember if I ever had a corsage before."

"Surely for Homecoming you did, didn't you?" Mom asked.

I shook my head, avoiding eye contact with her. I didn't want to spoil the moment. "No, I usually just went with friends to dances when I was in school." Actually, I don't remember ever going to Homecoming when I was in high school. I went to few parties because I was always working. "And by the time I went to college, I was too old to go to dances and Homecoming." I gently extracted the delicate flower from the box.

"Do you want me to help?" Mom asked.

The wistful tone in her voice alerted me and stopped me from saying *No, that's okay, I can do it.* "Sure," I said. "Pin me up."

Mom stepped forward, taking the orchid from me. "They usually have straight pins which can be tricky to get in right. Maybe we'll need a safety pin."

"Pin it on the jacket. I don't want pins in the dress, but the jacket is heavy mesh. It can handle it."

"Good thinking." Mom busied herself with the corsage, adjusting it on my right shoulder so it was displayed nicely.

I handed her the small carnation. "You're good at this. You do Ike's."

It was the right thing to say. I could tell by the pleased look she flashed me while she fussed with Ike's lapel, smoothing the fabric when she was done. "You kids look like you're all ready to go to a dance."

Kids? Ike and I exchanged a smile. Mom picked up her small purple handbag from the hall table where she left it. "I'll see you two at the dinner."

"Are you sure?" Ike said. "You can certainly ride with us."

"No, you'll be busy later on and won't need to be bothered taking me home." She was pulling open the door as she spoke but I caught of glimpse of her waggling eyebrows. "I'll see you in a few minutes. 'Bye."

Ike closed the door behind her, deftly blocking Conan from nosing his way outside. "I have to tell you, your dress is amazing." His arms went around me.

"Wait a minute." I slipped off the jacket and laid it on the table. "I'm not going to crush my flower." I eased my way into his embrace while Conan snuffled around our feet.

Ike's hands slid over my back. "Oh, my God," he whispered, his eyes intent on mine. "You're naked back there."

"You might say so," I murmured.

He pulled me closer to him. "Does this mean I might get lucky tonight?" His lips were close to my ear and I shivered in his arms.

I put my lips close to his ear, brushing the side of his jaw in a kiss. "We'll see."

Our kiss was long, deep, exploratory, and left me trembling and left Ike red in the face. "This is one time I'm pretty sure *We'll see* doesn't mean no," he said when he released me. "Will I get a chance to see your tattoo?"

I held out my jacket and he helped me slip into it. I regarded him over my shoulder. "Maybe."

"Hot dog!" He looked at Conan, who regarded us eagerly. "No, not you."

"Speaking of which—" I considered my puppy. "Be good while we're gone."

"You're not going to lock him up?" Ike asked, picking up my little duffel.

"I let him have the run of the house the other day and he did fine." I gave Conan a brisk head rub. "Don't let me down, guy."

Ike crooked an elbow. "Shall we?" He nodded at my bag. "What's that?"

"I thought I'd change back into street clothes when I'm done with the shoot. I'm usually pretty tired by the end and all I want to do is kick back and relax."

He winked at me. "I hope you won't be too tired."

I felt a brief qualm at the thought of an intimate encounter with him. It was so long since I was with a man. What if I didn't live up to his expectation?

"We'll see," I said.

Ike tossed my gym bag in the back seat of his car and we drove to Stoneyburst's Student Union. For the first time I paid attention to Ike's sleek sports sedan with its leather interior, wood trim, and powerful engine. Perhaps Mom was right. Maybe I could get a sportier car. This was certainly a nice one.

Of course, I had a dog to transport, too. "I wonder if anybody who owns a car like this owns pets," I mused.

Ike glanced at me. "Sure. I used to have a dog and I had a Mustang. Just because you have a sports car, it doesn't mean you can't use it to move groceries, animals, and garden supplies." He jerked a thumb at the back of the car. "I've hauled bags of manure in the trunk and plants in the back seat, so I think a puppy won't hurt anything."

I touched the leather wrapped console between us. "Mom thinks I need a sportier car."

He laughed. "Your mother would probably drive a Ferrari if she could afford it. I don't think it matters how sporty the car is. I think it does matter how you feel when you drive it."

I hadn't considered that. "How do you feel when you drive this?"

"Comfortable. Content. Youthful." His shoulders lifted in a shrug. "I'm not trying to recapture my lost youth, but I like a car with gumption. I can afford a nice car, so I buy one. It's not the fountain of youth, but I like to have nice things around me." His right hand briefly caressed my hand where it rested on the console. "Like my garden. My house. You."

"You have a beautiful garden. I'm flattered to be compared to it."

Ike turned into the faculty parking lot next to the Union. "You're more beautiful than anything in my garden."

I blushed at his praise. "Thank you," I murmured.

The parking lot was nearly full. Ike found a spot near the exit between two SUVs. He parked the car then turned to me. "You are the most beautiful woman I've ever known. I know you don't want to talk about this, but I do love you, Acie." His eyes searched mine for a clue to my feelings.

I longed to look away but I didn't. "I care for you, Ike," I said carefully. "But it's been a long time since I let myself love anyone." I touched his face, running one finger gently along the angle of his jaw. He must have just shaved because his skin was smooth to the touch. "I think if I learn to love anyone again, it's going to be you."

Ike pressed my hand to his lips. "I'm happy to hear that." His kiss was soft against my palm, sending shivers down my spine.

He got out, hurrying around the car to open my door for me then grabbing the little gym bag from the back seat. As we walked to the building, I saw a line of people in dress clothes going into the front entrance leading to the ballroom. The side entrances had the usual collection of students going in and out and, since it was Homecoming weekend, there was a large number of presumably parents or alumni bustling around, also.

The banquet was held in a room adjacent to the ballroom, actually two large meeting rooms with the separating accordion wall pushed back. We stopped at the concierge desk and Ike left my gym bag with the porter on duty, then we continued on to the ballroom. Dr. Bell, resplendent in a dark purple dress with purple-and-gold jacket, was keeping an eye on the doorway and she spied us as soon as we entered. She gestured us to the front of the room where a small stage, podium, and microphone were set up in front of a table with a *Reserved* sign.

Ike and I eased through the crowd, pausing now and again to talk with someone. I kept my arm through his and I fell into my Model Role, keeping a faint smile on my face and adding sway to my hips. I straightened my spine, edged my shoulders back and lengthened my walk slightly, making sure to keep my toes pointed straight ahead. Those small, subtle movements made a real statement, and I could see it reflected in the faces of those who watched us.

"Such an exciting night," Dr. Bell said when we reached her. She had an amber-colored drink her hand. "Are you ready, Dr. Doyle?"

Ready? Good Lord, how did she know? I looked at Ike then at her and then I remembered: the endowment. I prayed my embarrassment didn't show on my face. "Absolutely," I said. "Can't wait."

"Why don't I get us a drink?" Ike squeezed my hand gently. I could tell he was struggling not to laugh.

"Thank you," I said faintly.

"I spoke with Miss Lyons, the production manager," Dr. Bell said. "They're setting up in two of the large conference rooms near the ballroom. I assured her they can use it for the entire weekend, so they can leave their wardrobe and makeup and"—she waved a hand—"things there. The photographer has already been here and examined the lighting in the ballroom and we've had to make adjustments." She looked concerned, her eyebrows drawing together in a worried frown.

"That's not unusual," I assured her. "I can't remember a single photo session I had where the lighting wasn't changed at least four or five times."

"Oh, that's a relief." She took a long swallow from her glass. "I was worried perhaps we hadn't done something correctly."

My mother materialized at my side, wine glass in hand. "You and Dr. Adler made quite an entrance. People are saying what a well-matched couple you are."

"We are, aren't we?" I murmured. "He's so handsome and I'm glad you made me wear this dress. It was the right choice."

"Stunning dress," Dr. Bell said firmly. "You are doing your department proud, Dr. Doyle."

Mom looked pleased. "She was going to wear just an old black dress, you know, but I talked her into changing." She nodded. "Yes, you and Dr. Adler are quite the couple. He's smart, handsome, and a great cook. The trifecta. You're lucky he hasn't been snagged yet. Speaking of which, I wonder where Meryl Staples is tonight. I don't see her."

I turned, scanning the room and the two hundred or so people in it. "You're right. I don't see her obnoxious brother, either." Ike was working his way through the crowd, a glass of wine in each hand. I was familiar with the cash bar at events of this type, and I was surprised to see the glasses were quite full. "I never did ask him about that."

"About what?" Mom asked, sipping her wine.

"You said you saw Ike and Meryl together the other day." I smiled at Ike when he finally reached us and handed me a glass of wine. "Thank you."

"I got a double," he said, holding up the full glass. "It saves time standing in line."

"Good idea." I took a sip then said, "We were just saying that Meryl Staples and her brother aren't here."

"I talked to her the other day," Ike said, a disapproving look on his face. "She's so afraid of her brother but she won't go to the police. She asked me for help and when I told her I'd go to the police with her, she agreed she would. But she didn't show up on Thursday like she said she would."

"Afraid of him? Is he abusive? If she's being threatened, maybe you should go to the police without her." Mom looked from me to Ike as if challenging us to act.

"There's no proof." Ike shrugged. "All I know is she begged me to make sure Henrietta would sell the land. Of course, this was before Henrietta was killed and we knew you were going to get the land." Ike looked at me. "That's what she was doing in the parking lot last weekend. She was desperate because Henrietta had died and she wasn't sure what would happen with the land."

"That damn land." Mom shook her head. "It's not good for anything, really. Even if they want to build houses there, it's going to take a lot of work to make it usable. Why is John Staples so anxious for a subdivision to go in there?"

"He'll make a lot of money, probably," I pointed out. "I wonder how much?"

"Dr. Doyle, Dr. Adler—it's time to take our seats." Dr. Bell pointed me to a table near the front. "You're with me, Dr. Doyle, because you're speaking, and I believe Dr. Adler is in the center." She smiled at my mother. "Each of our faculty members is hosting a table, so to speak, since this is a fund-raiser for the scholarship fund."

"I know," Mom said, grabbing Ike's arm. "You're at my table, Dr. Adler."

"Looks like I'm being kidnapped," Ike said with a grin. "I'll see you later." He allowed my mother to tug him to an empty seat at a table in the middle of the room filled with Mom's Elm Grove cronies.

I followed Dr. Bell to the table near the front. She sat on my left and 'young' Frankland Franklin, a.k.a. Frank Three, sat on her left. "Mr. Franklin is presenting the endowment on behalf of Miss Baron's estate," Dr. Bell said. "It's such a pity she died so young. Asthma is a terrible thing, just terrible."

"Asthma? I thought, well, I assumed the fall was the cause of death." I shook out my napkin, using my action to check Ike, who was the center of attention amongst seven octogenarian ladies.

"The fall probably precipitated the asthma attack," Frank Three said in the whiny, nasal voice both he and his father shared. He was short and stocky but his suit was cut in such a way to minimize both his paunch and his drooping shoulders. I suppose a lawyer could afford good tailoring. "The cause of death was officially suffocation due to complications of asthma."

"Really?" I'm sure my voice reflected my disbelief.

"It's sad, regardless how she died," Dr. Bell declared. She smiled but I clearly saw *Okay, don't pursue this topic* in her look.

I took the hint and focused on my meal, making polite conversation with others at the table while the meal progressed through salad, the predictable chicken with rice pilaf, and a rich chocolate dessert I left mostly untouched.

I snatched covert glances at Ike and mother throughout my meal. They appeared to be having the time of their lives, laughing with the other ladies at the table. Ike was dispatched at least once to get refills on drinks. I prayed my mother would be sober enough to drive home. I had visions of a DUI call from the lockup later that night.

As soon as coffee was served, Dr. Bell touched my wrist. "This is our signal," she said, pushing back her chair.

I dabbed my lips and set my napkin on the table then followed Dr. Bell and Frank Three to the left of the small stage. I walked cautiously up the three steps, conscious of the large glass of wine I consumed and the tricky swirl of my dress around my legs. I made it to the middle of the stage without any mishaps and took a seat next to Frank Three behind the podium, which Dr. Bell commandeered.

She tapped on the microphone and the room quieted. "Thank you all for attending this fund-raising event for the English Department Scholarship Fund. I trust our faculty members have entertained you throughout dinner with amusing stories from academe."

I glanced at the crowd. My mother's table certainly looked like they'd been entertained, but a few other tables looked bored. As I noted before, our faculty is not known for its conviviality, so I wasn't surprised.

"I won't delay you overly long because I know we're all anxious to get to the dance and the, um, other events of the evening." She looked back over her shoulder at me. "It gives me great pleasure to introduce Mr. Frankland Franklin, who is acting on behalf of the estate of Mr. Charles Baron."

Nice wording, since nobody knows who really has the estate anymore until all the legal wrangling is done. I applauded politely with the audience as Dr. Bell took Frank Three's seat.

Frank Three approached the podium and after tugging and adjusting, finally maneuvered the microphone within speaking distance. "As we all know, a series of tragic events has led to me being here to speak with you today," he began, his voice fading in and out when his head moved, causing his mouth to drift away from the microphone's sweet spot.

He droned on in the same vein for five boring minutes, speaking about a life cut short and a young woman who wanted to honor her uncle's wishes. While he spoke, I watched the crowd and I began to notice my mother was sitting straighter and straighter in her chair, her chin jutted out in what I recognized as a prime snit fit.

She touched Ike's arm and he bent his head to listen to her while she spoke, her cheeks pink with anger. He nodded, his face sympathetic then he took her hand and held it, turning his gaze to me. His blue eyes, so intense and compelling, seemed to reach out to me across the room. I knew he was trying to tell me something, but what? What message was he trying to convey?

Frank Three mercifully ended his speech to faint applause. I rose and came forward to accept the over-sized faux check for three-hundred thousand dollars. I smiled while pictures were taken by people in the room and by a student photographer from the art department. Then I handed the big piece of cardboard to Dr. Bell and I took my place at the microphone.

I viewed the sea of faces, most of whom looked bored or tired, with a few stifled yawns here and there. I shifted my gaze to the middle of the room and saw my mother staring hopefully at me. *Hopefully? What about?*

I searched my memory for the rehearsed speech I prepared then hastily edited when I realized Henrietta would not be presenting me with the check on behalf of her uncle. It had required finesse on my part because of the legal mess caused by her uncle's death then her death.

Wait a minute.

Her uncle.

This wasn't about Henrietta. No one had given Charlie Baron credit yet. It was all about Henrietta and her death.

But really, it was about her uncle.

I adjusted the microphone to give myself time to

mentally adjust my speech. *Was this what Ike was trying to tell me?* I smiled at the crowd and took a chance. "On behalf of the Department of English, I want to thank Charles Baron for this gift. This endowment fund will help us make certain that students are given the opportunity to study at Stoneyburst without worrying about financial hardship."

I turned slightly to acknowledge Frank Three. "I'd like to thank Mr. Franklin for standing in for Henrietta Baron, who had planned to present this check on behalf of her uncle."

I faced the audience again, meeting my mother's gaze. "I think one thing we've all forgotten, perhaps, is if circumstances were different, *Mr. Baron* would be here to present this check to us himself. While it is truly tragic Miss Baron met with an untimely accident, it's also a tragedy that Mr. Baron died so unexpectedly, too."

I saw the surprise on many faces in the audience. We had all forgotten about Charlie, I realized. I was as guilty as anyone. I completely forgot Charlie was originally going to present the check to the department. We pushed his death to the back of our minds. Everyone was upset that Henrietta, who was younger, died, and most people relegated Charlie to a subsidiary role of *the uncle she inherited from*.

"It's because of Mr. Baron's largesse this scholarship can be funded. He was a relative stranger to our town, having moved here just a few years ago. But he believed in education and he believed in giving opportunities to those who are less fortunate and who may have to struggle to attain that education."

Like me, I realized. I was unable to go to college

right out of high school, even though I had exceptional grades. I could have gotten merit aid and perhaps a scholarship, but I still would have gone deeply into debt.

Good Lord. For the second time that night, knowledge hit me like the proverbial ton of bricks. *Charlie Baron donated this money because of me.* I held on to the podium with both hands when the realization made me go momentarily mute.

My mother told him how I lived when I was growing up and how I couldn't afford to go to school. Charlie Baron did this to help my mother make up for what happened to me.

I knew this was the truth as sure as if Charlie Baron was standing in front of me, telling me. I knew this deep down in my soul, in my heart. This was why Mom was so anxious for me to act the part. This was why Charlie's death hit her so hard. They planned this. They wanted to pay me back.

He loved her and he wanted to help her.

She wanted to make amends.

Disjointed thoughts spun through my mind and I struggled to push them aside so I could continue. I took a deep breath and scanned the audience, seeing only rapt attention and no sign my epiphany was noticed by anyone. My gaze swung back to Mom's table and I saw Ike's approving nod.

He knew. He guessed. Dear God, what a man. He still held my mother's hand as he nodded to me. I think at that moment I loved Ike Adler more than I have ever loved anyone else in my life. *What did I do to deserve such a man?* Whatever it was I did, I made a swift vow I would continue to do it so I could continue to have him with me, far into the future.

"Charlie Baron was a self-made man and he understood the value of education. He wanted to do what he could to help a deserving student reach their academic goal. And not only that. He was willing to help make an animal sanctuary a reality, not because it would benefit him, but because he knew it was the right thing to do."

I heard Frank Three's muffled exclamation behind me. I wondered if Dr. Bell dug an elbow into his ribs to stifle him.

"The future of the sanctuary is in the hands of the citizens of Grimper, who will vote on its existence next week. There's been a change in plans that I know would have made Charlie very happy. A compromise plan is being designed which will let the town benefit from the sanctuary." I held up a hand when a buzz broke out in the crowd. "You'll be able to read all about the plan tomorrow in the newspaper. I think the news would have made Charlie Baron very happy."

My mother nodded, her eyes shiny with tears. Ike put an arm around her shoulders and gave her a little hug. She leaned against his shoulder, her smile as bright as her eyes.

"I didn't know Charlie Baron well at all, but I was told he loved Henry James, which of course would endear him to me because James is one of my favorite authors. I'd like to end my thank you to Mr. Baron with this quote from Henry James: *I call people rich when they're able to meet the requirements of their imagination.*"

I paused to let the words soak into the minds of the people listening. "Charlie Baron was one of the richest people I think anyone could hope to meet, because he allowed his imagination to soar, and he provided us with the means to meet the requirements of his imagination." I nodded to the crowd and stepped away from the microphone. "Thank you."

Applause broke out then Dr. Bell stepped forward, still holding the faux check. "We hope you'll all join us at the dance in the ballroom. Thank you!" She brandished the check, almost knocking over Frank Three in the process.

I saw Ike pushing through the crowd, heading for the stage. Mom stood next to her table and she made a little wave when she saw me watching her. I went to the steps but didn't get far before Frank Three accosted me.

"That wasn't fair," he said in a low voice. "You know as well as I do the use of the land is legally under review. You have no right to make an announcement."

"This is a small audience and I doubt if the information will get far tonight," I said, trying to edge by him.

"That is not the issue and you know it. You made a public announcement about something which is in legal contention. There may be serious consequences for you."

I don't know why—maybe it was the way he was all puffed up and acting so officious. Maybe it was my elation at finding a measure of compromise with my mother. Or maybe it was the sight of Ike, waiting for me at the foot of the steps. I'm not sure what made the devil enter me. I said, "For heaven's sake, grow up. There's more to life than contesting a few hopeless lawsuits. Get a life."

He gasped and glared at me when I swept by him

to the steps. Ike held out his arm and I took it without a backward glance.

Ike did look back, though. "If looks could kill, you'd be frothing at the mouth and gasping now," he said while we made our way through the congratulatory crowd.

"Stupid little man," I muttered. "If he's not careful, I'll sue him."

Ike pushed open the doors to the hallway leading to the ballroom. "I'll give you the money to do it."

"I may take you up on it." We joined other diners who were meandering their way to the ballroom and the dance music heard issuing forth. I noticed a fellow colleague, Joel Harris, with a drink in hand as he sauntered toward the ballroom. His wife wasn't with him but I did see her talking with Ted Dreyer near the side of the hall.

"Good Lord," Ike said. "Look at that. I can't believe they're out in the open finally."

"What?"

"Dreyer and Mrs. Harris. They've been having an affair for a year. What the hell do they think they're doing, flaunting it?"

I looked at Joel, who didn't appear to notice his wife was engaged in a rather serious flirtation with another man. "I don't think Joe cares."

"That's because Joel is banging his twenty-year-old research assistant," Ike said, his tone clearly reflecting his distaste. "He needs to act his age instead of his shoe size."

"Why Dr. Adler. Are you jealous?" I teased.

Ike and I entered the ballroom just as the band launched into the Fray's *Never Say Never*. Ike swept me into his arms. "I'm here with the most beautiful, most desirable woman in the room," he said, looking into my eyes. "They're all jealous of me."

He led me out onto the dance floor and we began to dance.

Chapter 15

Was it the wine? Was it the heady feeling that we were the subject of all the eyes in the room? Or was it the fact I was in the arms of a man I was perilously close to loving with all my heart and soul?

I'm not sure what it was, but that dance was magical. Ike was a strong partner, leading me surely and adroitly through a heady two-step that had my dress swirling and me smiling up at him while he guided me around the floor. I felt like we were spinning through clouds, buoyed up by our love and our intuitive grasp of what the other was feeling. I could have closed my eyes and still danced with him without a stumble or hesitation.

The poignant lyrics added to the effect. I had never really listened closely to the song before but the words seemed to echo in my head when Ike held me and our bodies moved together in rhythm. I knew exactly what he was feeling and I know he knew how I felt, too. I closed my eyes briefly and when I opened them his blue eyes were locked on mine.

"Thank you," I whispered, my hand in his tightening. "I forgot how much I love to dance. It's been so long since I had a good partner."

"I'll always be your partner, Acie. As long as you want."

"Why?" It was a question which haunted me from

the moment he said he loved me. "Why me, Ike?"

"Why does the sun shine?" He smiled, those delightful dimples appearing at the corners of his mouth and small creases lining his eyes. "It just does and I just do."

The music faded to silence and our steps slowed until we were stopped at the edge of the dance floor. "Thank you," he whispered, his lips close to my ear.

I turned my head slightly so his lips brushed my jaw. "We need to do this more often."

"We will, I promise." His voice was a caress, making me shiver in his arms.

"Very good, but the lighting wasn't quite perfect." The brisk, businesslike voice interrupted the hazy warmth of the cocoon around Ike and me.

We broke apart slowly to regard the man facing us, a sleek silver camera in his hands. "I beg your pardon?" I asked, my voice clogged with—lust? Desire? Bemusement? I was still lost in clouds. I wasn't even aware of lighting much less that it wasn't perfect. As far as I was concerned, everything was perfect.

"It's a nice shot but the lighting was wrong. And of course it's the wrong dress. It's a good dress but it's hard to get it right without reflections. Too shiny." He regarded me critically. "I remember you. I need to light you from the left because you have that odd bump on your collarbone." He stretched out his hand.

Ike stepped in front of me. "I'm not sure who you are, but you may want to ask first before you touch a woman."

The hazy dream of the dance was fading. I put a hand on Ike's arm. "It's okay," I said shakily. "This is our photographer for the night." I vaguely recognized the man. He was small and thin to the point of emaciation. His long legs and arms gave him a spider-ish appearance. His thick thatch of black hair was now liberally laced with white, but I think it was artifice, not reality, because he was my age. I was a model in my twenties and he was an up-and-coming photographer. Despite his relative youth in the business, he was a little dictator but he got away with it because he was talented.

What was his name? I struggled with memories tucked away in my distant past. It had something to do with the 'spider' aspect that always made us models cringe. I remember one memorable shoot session where one of the models had us all in stitches when she compared him to Spiderman.

It triggered a recollection. "Sebastian, right?" I held out my hand. *Sebastian Doron the Spider Moron,* we used to call him. He was easy to get along with as long as you did exactly what he asked. I leaned slightly against Ike. "This is the lead photographer for the shoot."

Sebastian regarded my hand then me. "You're not changed."

I thought at first he meant I hadn't changed in all the intervening years. Then I realized he was talking about my outfit, which he was eyeing critically. Ike tensed next to me. "He's not being rude," I said, lowering my hand. "He's just being busy."

As I expected, my words bounced off the scrawny man. He shifted the camera to his other hand and looked around the dance floor, now filling with couples when the band started playing a Beach Boys song that invited enthusiastic dancing.

I moved to the side of the room, keeping my arm through Ike's to steer him with me. "I didn't realize you were getting started so soon," I said to the photographer. "We were told we had time before we had to get ready."

"Why not get started? There's nothing else to do." Spider followed us but continually evaluated the people around us. I recognized his look. He was setting up shots in his head, envisioning how it would appear through the lens-finder.

"Maybe we have something else to do," Ike snapped. "Like enjoy the party."

I gently shook his arm. "Now, now. You know the photo shoot is the most important thing in the world right now." I kept my voice light and teasing. "I thought you were setting up out of the way," I said to Sebastian.

"We are. I just wanted to get a feel for what's here. I'll be using some of it later. I may want a few crowd shots. I can add those in the background." He eyed me again. "They're waiting for you in makeup."

I sighed. I doubted anyone was waiting for me, but when Spider Moron was ready to shoot, the models needed to be ready, too. "Come on." I tugged Ike's arm. "We're being paged."

"Is he always that rude?" Ike glanced back at the photographer who stood in the middle of an aisle, forcing people to walk around him. "I thought we weren't supposed to start until nine-thirty."

We made our way past people who were taking seats at tables around the perimeter of the room. "Creative artists aren't very social. That passes for polite for him. The final schedule said makeup at eight-thirty." I had tucked my watch into the duffel with the rest of my day clothes, so I had no idea what time it was.

"We have a few minutes, then." Ike slowed his pace.

I didn't argue. I decided to enjoy the dance while I could. Once we got started with the shoot, I'd be on call for the rest of the night.

"You look beautiful, just beautiful." Aunt Sherry and Mom appeared in front of us, each with a wine glass in hand. Sherry wore a pale blue silk blouse and dark blue pants. It was a simple outfit but very chic, especially paired with the sapphire-and-pearl necklace with matching earrings. "I told your mother you were the prettiest woman here. I saw the model they brought in for the pictures." Sherry made a dismissive gesture, nearly losing her wine glass in her enthusiasm. Luckily it was empty.

"Where did you see her?" I peered through the crowd, but it was dark around the fringes of the room and hard to pick out details.

"They came in the side door. I thought I'd be available in case they had questions."

"Did they?" Ike asked with an amused smile.

"No. Dr. Bell had people from the Art Department and the Business Department looking out for them, so I didn't get much chance to talk to anyone." Sherry frowned at Dr. Bell, standing near the stage talking to a distinguished looking gentleman who had a much younger woman hanging on his arm. "You'd think they'd want a local to show them around."

"Must be a trophy wife," Mom said. "Why else would a babe like her hang out with an old codger?"

"Hush, he's probably a big alumni donor or

something. I should find Laurie Lyons and make sure we're on schedule," I said. "It's close enough to eight-thirty that we can—"

"How dare you influence the audience like that!" The chilling, venomous voice was so close to me I thought I felt a drop of spittle hit my neck.

I turned and found John Staples behind me and to my right, pushing Ike aside by wedging himself between us. His ill-fitting black suit appeared as if it had been hastily pulled out of a closet where it was stored for a long, long time. The sight of him next to Ike was especially startling. Staples looked like he'd slept in someone else's clothes. Ike looked as though his suit had just been freshly pressed and fitted to him.

"You can't change the rules like this at the last minute." Staples' voice rose. "It's not fair."

I saw several startled expressions on other dance-goers. "Mr. Staples, I don't think I care to discuss this right now." I edged my way backward.

"I don't give a shit what you care to discuss. You've been acting like Miss High and Mighty just because you teach college and you can afford to prattle on and on about charity. You have no right to even be involved in this. The decision about the land should be in the hands of the people it affects and that's those of us who live near there." His voice kept getting louder and louder while he got closer and closer to me.

"This isn't the time or the place to argue about this." Ike put a hand on Staples arm to draw him away from me. I marveled at Ike's calmness until I saw the telltale glitter of anger in his eyes. John Staples was about a minute away from a punch to the jaw if he wasn't careful.

I admit, I was praying he wouldn't be careful.

"Mr. Staples, I only told the truth. I'm the chairwoman of the sanctuary committee and I recently discussed an alternate sanctuary proposal with the mayor. Marge Crandon is drafting a summary of the proposal and it will appear in the newspaper tomorrow." I took another step back but couldn't go far or I'd tread on Aunt Sherry, who regarded Staples with a look of disbelief combined with disapproval.

I don't think Staples even heard me. "Who are you to decide, single-handedly, what kind of proposal will be given to the citizens? The townspeople don't want this sanctuary in their back yard. The vote next Tuesday would prove it."

"Says who?" My mother shoved past me, her face taut with anger. "You have no right to say you speak for the townspeople. I've heard the lies you're spreading." She shook her finger at him. "You should be ashamed of yourself. You're nothing more than an abusive, hate-mongering, greedy little man who tries to bring everyone else down to his level."

Oh, good work, Mom. I silently applauded her gusto even as I realized we were becoming the focus of unwelcome attention. I was pretty sure this was not the kind of publicity Dr. Bell wanted for the school.

Mom's words bounced off of Staples' righteous indignation but it did have one effect. It turned his attention from me to my mother. "You coerced that old man into giving you his property. You're a fine one to talk about shame. What did you do to get him to agree?" Staples stuck out his chin and glared at her.

"Now just a minute." Ike put out his arm and gently pushed my mother back. "Mrs. Watson, calm down. And you, Staples. There's no reason for you to act like this."

"Don't tell me to calm down, young man." Mom's tone was snappish but she did take a step backward. "That sanctimonious prick can't yell at my daughter. I won't stand for it, do you hear me?"

Staples apparently decided my mother was no longer worth his attention. He turned back to me. "I'm going to see to it your underhanded dealings are exposed." He lowered his head and for a minute I thought he might charge into me. "You can't just change things at the last minute."

"I suggest you leave us alone." Ike's voice was low but with an edge to it that even a moron like Staples could hear.

"I hate to interrupt, but I believe Dr. Doyle and Dr. Adler are needed elsewhere right now." Dr. Bell appeared next to Staples. Behind her I saw a campus security guard who watched Staples with the sort of alertness I usually saw on the faces of students when they neared the end of a class. "Miss Locke is looking for them."

"Locke?" I asked, grateful for the interruption. If anyone could diffuse Staples' temper, it would be our authoritative Dr. Bell.

"The fashion editor. She came out from New York City to oversee this project." Dr. Bell glowed with pride. I didn't have the heart to tell her the "editor" was probably an intern or maybe an assistant who just wanted to make sure they didn't go over budget.

"We were just on our way." I tried to inch my way around John Staples, but he was rooted to the floor like the proverbial immovable object.

Dr. Bell took Staples' arm firmly in one hand. "I'm sure we can discuss this another time. Right now, though, my faculty members are busy."

Staples struggled to pull his arm away but she had him in an iron grip. "Let me go! I have every right to talk to that lying bitch about—"

"Okay," Ike said. "I've heard enough." He grabbed Staples out of Dr. Bell's grip, took aim, and leveled a punch at Staples' jaw which sent the man reeling backward toward a table. Luckily, the people sitting there saw what was coming and scattered before he could land.

"Ow." Ike winced and shook his hand. "I forgot how bad that hurts."

The security guard caught hold of Staples before he could fall and spun the nasty little man upright. "Come with me." He jerked Staples' arm behind him.

Staples sagged in the man's grip, his gaze bleary. The lower right side of his face was flaming red and I could already see a garish purple bruise starting to form. "He bro ma ja," Staples mumbled. "Assho bro—"

"That's enough." The guard tugged, none too gently. "Come along quietly, sir." He manhandled Staples, muttering and stumbling, out of sight.

"Good work, Ike," Sherry saluted Ike with her glass. "Nice punch. Pity it didn't knock him unconscious. Someone needs to hit that idiot with a tranquilizer dart. He's much too excitable."

Mom still glared at Staples, who was being dragged, unresisting, out of the room. "Charlie should have tasered him when he had the chance."

"What? Charlie tasered somebody?" I took Ike's hand and looked at the knuckles. "Are you okay?"

"Yeah. Just bruised. The son of a bitch's jaw was harder than it looked." He smiled ruefully at me. "It's been a long time since I hit somebody, but if anybody deserved it, he did."

A murmur of approval from the crowd around us told me the onlookers agreed. Dr. Bell bustled forward. I hastened to apologize but she waved it away. "He's a disagreeable man and he was probably drinking before he came." She spoke just loud enough for others to hear. "I'm sure the campus security people will sort it all out."

"I'm sorry, Dr. Bell," Ike said. "I tried to get him to leave, but when he started using foul language, I felt—"

Dr. Bell held up a hand. "I understand. The security people will handle it. We have students from the Art Department acting as liaison to the production coordinator for the photo session and they mentioned you are needed. Both of you. Now."

I took the hint. "Absolutely. We were on our way before we were so rudely interrupted." I looked around. "Where are they set up?"

Dr. Bell gestured and a young black man with multi-colored dreadlocks and mismatched coat and pants stepped forward. "Over here," he said, making a beeline for an area to the right of the dance floor.

"I'll see you later," Dr. Bell said then she turned her smile on a woman bedecked with jewelry standing nearby. "I'm so pleased you could come. Wasn't the endowment ceremony…?" Her voice faded as she and the woman vanished in the crowd.

I breathed a sigh of relief. For a minute I was afraid Dr. Bell would insist on coming into the changing room with me. "Let me check in with the production coordinator first and I'll see if you can come in," I told Mom.

I expected her to argue with me or insist on coming with us, but instead she just nodded, looking thoughtful. "You go ahead," she said with a little wave. "We'll be over by the bar."

"Bar?"

Sherry pointed to a corner near the entryway. "See you later, honey." The two old ladies toddled off.

"I'm surprised," I said to Ike while we followed the young man through the crowd. "I thought for sure Mom would insist on coming with me. She wanted to see a photo shoot."

"Maybe she's had enough excitement for one night." He nodded at our guide, who waved to us from a door at the back of the ballroom. "I'm guessing he's from the Art Department. I don't think anyone from the Business Department would dress that way."

"They're set up in here," the multi-colored young man said, pushing the door open. "Did you see the photographer? He's out on the dance floor. I get to assist him during the shoot."

"I'm sure Sebastian will be glad to have you help him." I followed him through the door.

"Wow. You know him? He's, like, famous." The young man stopped and regarded me with new interest. "He does all these celebrity people. They did a feature on him in *Rolling Stone.* You know him? Wow. Thanks for getting him here."

I murmured a *You're welcome* as we left the relative busyness of the dance behind and entered a world of chaos. The student hurried away and I saw where his path was leading. Straight to Sebastian the

Spider, who entered by another door and was in conference with a group of people in one corner.

Ike and I stopped to survey the large space. It was about half the size of the ballroom and one of the corners was blocked off by using large dark cloth screens to provide a semblance of privacy. In another corner was the essential ingredient for any photo shoot, a table with coffee urns, bowls of fruit, a tray of sandwiches, and water bottles in an ice-filled tray. The air was filled with the babble of dozens of voices as people darted here and there, a few pushing racks of clothing, others carrying bags or boxes, and still others just walking with a purposeful air and talking loudly.

"Over there." I nodded kitty-corner across the room where I saw a row of chairs set up under portable lighting. "Makeup. That's where we start."

"Is it always like this?" Ike's head whipped from right to left while he surveyed the ebb and flow of people.

I smiled at his bewildered look. "No. Usually it's a lot more crowded and a lot noisier." I paused when a woman hurried across the room toward us, clipboard in hand. She had a healthy sprinkling of freckles, brown hair styled into licks and spikes, and a purposeful air which told me she was Someone In Charge. "I think she's Laurie Lyons. Our leader." I walked forward and held out my hand.

"Doyle and Adler, right?" the woman asked, glancing at the clipboard while she gave my hand a brisk shake.

"Yes," I said. "I'm Doyle, he's Adler."

"Female makeup left, male makeup and clothing right, female clothing in the next room. We start in sixty." She wheeled and walked away, pulling out a cell phone as she moved.

"Is it all right if my mother and aunt watch during makeup and dressing?" I asked quickly before she could get too far.

She paused, staring at her phone screen. "If principles agree, it's good." She left us with the phone pressed against her ear.

"What did she mean?" Ike asked, following me through racks of clothing and boxes.

"I go for makeup now and you go behind that screen for makeup and a clothing change." I nodded at the screen on our right. "This is a woman's fashion shoot, so you're not a principle model, you're—" I almost said *arm candy* but I didn't want to hurt his feelings. "You're an extra, so I doubt you'll have a lot of clothing changes."

"I wasn't sure if I'd have any," Ike said. "Do you mean I change clothes right here?" He looked around the bustling room.

I thought of the shoots I'd been in where men and women changed clothes in the middle of a crowded area. "Behind the screen." I nudged him to the blocked-off area. "I'll have to find the women's changing room. There are usually alterations to do, so I'm not surprised they moved it somewhere else to get space. They want us to get started in an hour but I doubt we'll be ready so quickly."

I led him to the right side of the room and peeked around the screen. A salon chair was positioned in the center of a space about the size of a small bedroom. Portable mirrors faced the seat and lights were positioned behind it. A man and a woman were busily arranging bottles and tubes on a small table near the mirrors. They looked around when we neared them.

"Adler," I said, giving Ike a little push toward the chair.

"It's about time." The man rolled his eyes. "Sit down."

"He's a first-timer," I said.

"Why the hell do they send us people who don't know what they're doing?" The man approached Ike and eyed him. "I suppose there's something there to work with."

Behind him, the woman mimed a talking puppet hand and rolled her eyes. "Take off your coat and shirt and let's get started. I'll hang them up for you."

Ike shot me a wild look. "What?"

"Don't worry. They won't bite." I eyed the man. "Right?"

He smiled artificially. "Of course not. Get undressed. Now. We're running late."

"They're always running late," I said dismissively. "Don't worry and don't hurry." I turned to go but stopped when Ike put a restraining hand on my arm.

"Will I see you later?" he asked hopefully.

I leaned over and gave him a rather abbreviated kiss, but one which held promise for the future. "You will," I said softly.

The woman laughed. "Glad to know where we stand," she called after me while I left.

I went to the "women's side" of the room, which wasn't screened. Like Ike's side, a salon chair was positioned with portable mirrors facing it. A young woman with long, luxurious blonde hair sat in the chair facing the mirror while a man dabbed foundation on her face. She wore a white shirt that covered most of her body except for her long legs, which were bare and ended in impossibly tall high heels.

FMP, I thought with a grimace. I well remembered those so-called Fuck Me Pumps we used to have to wear on the runway. They were a bitch to balance on and uncomfortable to boot but they gave a model the right strut if she could use them right.

The stylist glanced up. "Doyle?" he asked in a husky bass voice which was at odds with his slender frame.

"Reporting. Is it okay if my mother and aunt look on? They're curious about the whole process."

"As long as they stay out the way, I'm fine. I'll be done here in five." He turned back to the girl who watched me in the mirror, an evaluating look in her pale blue eyes.

I smiled at her. "I'm the mother in the shoot."

She eyed me coolly. "I'm the daughter. We can talk when you're out of makeup. I still have a few minutes to go until I'm sure we have the look right."

The makeup stylist raised one eyebrow at this abrupt dismissal. "You should be nicer to your mama, honey." He rolled his eyes and I could tell from his pained expression he had a diva on his hands.

I shrugged. "No rush. Sebastian said he's ready when we are."

As I expected, the mention of the photographer's name made the girl sit up straighter. "You talked to him? He's ready?"

I held up a hand in a *calm down* motion. "Not to worry. He and I have worked together before. He'll be patient."

The girl snapped her fingers. "Get me finished. I need to talk to him before we start shooting."

The stylist nodded somberly. "Sure thing." He dabbed at her face and I could swear he was moving slower than before.

"I'll go get my audience." I left before I laughed out loud. A stylist could make or break a model and it didn't pay to piss them off. I learned that a long time ago. This girl had a ways to go in this trade.

I glimpsed the young man who guided us before, standing with a group of people. I gestured him to me and sent him looking for Mom and Aunt Sherry, giving him firm instructions to make sure they left their drinks at the bar. I peeked around the corner of the Men's Screen and saw the male stylist working on Ike, dabbing powder on his face. I dodged back before anyone spotted me.

By the time Mom and Sherry arrived, the makeup stylist was ready for me after ushering out the younger model through a side door, which probably led to the changing room. "I'm doing hair and makeup both," he said when I took my seat in the chair. "I'll bring in an assistant tomorrow for the full shoot."

"That works for me." I took off my jacket and held it out to Mom to hold then I helped him drape a white sheet over my front. "To keep my dress clean," I explained to Mom, who took a seat on my left, turned so it faced me. "Where's Sherry?"

Mom looked over my shoulder. "She's talking to the photographer. I hope they don't come to blows. Sherry read him the riot act for interfering with the dance and getting in the way. The last I heard her, she was telling him he needed to mind his manners."

The makeup stylist stifled a laugh. "I'd like to see that." He walked around my chair, evaluating my hair style. "I'm glad you didn't braid your hair. It leaves it wrinkly."

"Wrinkly?" Mom asked, looking at the array of tubes and jars on the nearby table. I could tell she was itching to touch them and I gave her a little *no, don't you dare* look.

"You know, all wavy and wrinkly. I love this style. It's fine for tonight because this is the dressy event. I may just leave it as is and only change a few pins."

I glanced to my left and saw Mom's pleased smile. "My mother did it."

He nodded approvingly. "Well, I'll just have to hire you. You know what flatters your daughter, that's for sure."

Mom glowed at the praise. "Thank you."

The stylist turned so his back was to her and winked at me. "You're her mother? I thought you were another model."

"Not unless they hire old ladies," Mom said with a laugh.

"Oh, you'd be surprised. Some of the models I work on—" He tsked while he swabbed makeup remover on my face. "They need so much work you wouldn't know they were young. Of course, you don't have to worry about that, do you?"

I held still, knowing no answer was required. When a man was fussing around me with cleanser or foundation, I knew enough to keep quiet.

"Yes, you've been taking care of your skin. Good for you." He winked at Mom. "I can see where she gets it. You have gorgeous skin. At least I won't have to cover up anything. All I need to do is highlight and make sure the lighting is kind to you."

He kept up a patter of conversation while he cleaned, dabbed, outlined, and highlighted. It didn't take long then he turned his attention to my hair, patting a few stray strands into place and replacing my rather plain clips with more elaborate, faux-jeweled ones. When he finished, I was a more dramatic version of myself.

Laurie Lyons reappeared with her clipboard, looked me over, then nodded and moved off to the Men's side of the room.

"Whew." The stylist blew out a relieved breath. "She's been tough tonight. I had to redo one of the other models twice before she passed inspection. Okay, you're off to clothing." He drew off my sheet covering then herded Mom and me to the nearby door.

Sherry hurried over to join us. "I heard you're pissing off my photographer," I joked as we entered a big room full of clothing racks and more boxes. The door we passed through was on one side, with another door opposite and one on the right which probably led to an outside hallway.

"He was being rude. He just needed someone to remind him of his manners." Sherry pulled me to one side while Mom examined the dresses hanging in racks against the wall. "She wants to go out to Charlie's house tonight."

"What for?" I held out my arms and one of the female assistants quickly stripped off my dress. I stepped out of the fabric, shivering in the cool room when it drifted over my mostly naked body, clad only in panties and nylons.

"Good God, aren't you afraid someone will walk in?" Sherry asked, her eyes so wide it looked painful.

"If they do they won't see anything they haven't seen on a million shoots before," I said. "Mom can't go out to Charlie's house. It's late."

"She wants to look for something." Sherry darted little glances at the three other models who were also in various stages of nakedness as they were being dressed. "Where are the men? They don't do this to the men, do they?"

"Do what?" I eyed a stocky middle-aged woman in a dark blue business suit who approached me with a dark red gown in her arms. "That can't go over my head," I warned.

She stopped and looked me over, top to bottom. "Wrong color for you. Let's go with the autumn brown." She handed the gown to a young woman, who dashed away. "Sorry. I'm Beth Locke, assistant editor for this project. You came highly recommended by Paul Wardlock."

I was impressed. Locke wasn't a callow intern or junior assistant. She had the air of a professional woman who knew her way around a shoot. Maybe this was a bigger gig than I gave it credit for. "Glad to meet you. I've been out of the game for a while but I'm hoping to get back in now and again."

Her gaze once again swept over me. "You have the kind of look the agencies want. And you're going to be perfect for this. You're just the right mix of beauty and hometown pretty." She took the new gown the breathless young intern handed her, this one in a gold/brown tone. "Let's try this one. Hold out your arms."

Sherry watched this whole process, her gaze skittering from me to the people walking past me, most of them oblivious to my naked state. "They don't make the men stand like this and have people dress them, do they?"

The editor and I exchanged an amused look. "Oh, it depends."

"Doesn't it feel odd to have these people touching you?" Mom asked, rejoining us.

"You get used to it after a while." I kicked off my shoes and balanced with a hand on Mom's shoulder while Locke helped me into the clinging dark gold gown with long sleeves and a plunging neckline.

"That's bit fancy for a dance like this, isn't it?" Mom asked doubtfully when I straightened.

Locke shrugged. "There're four or five outfits for tonight. I'm not sure which one we'll use in the final layout. Besides, no one will know how fancy the party is. It'll be what we show them." She turned to the young girl who was her 'fetcher'. "Black shoes, size eight."

"Ready?" Lyons called out from the doorway to the hallway. Without waiting for a yea or nay, she turned. "Let's go."

I smiled at Mom. "Show time."

Chapter 16

We emerged from the costuming room and Laurie Lyons led us along a hallway filled with dance guests and students who were obviously hanging out, hoping for a glimpse into the glamorous life of a model. Our little contingent continued past the main doors to another set of doors at the far end of the hallway.

We entered a relatively quiet area where several tables and chairs were pulled off to one side. The photographer had set up his lighting so it was a bubble of brightness at the side of the dimly lit room. Crew members, set stylists, props and photography people formed a semi-circle around the tables like onlookers at a fight, effectively blocking any dancers from getting too close.

Dr. Bell stood to the left of the photographer, out of the way but near enough to keep an eye on the activity. Beth Locke noticed her, too, and nodded a greeting. I spied Ike talking to the young woman acting the part of my daughter. They were seated at a white-linened table with drinks in front of them and flowers in the center. Ike now wore a dark gray tux with a starched white shirt and dark gray bowtie. The formalwear accented his classic good looks. I have to admit, he was amazingly handsome.

When Ike saw me, he started to rise from his seat but Sebastian shouted, "Stay seated! This isn't a party.

You don't move until I tell you!"

Ike sat so abruptly I thought I saw his teeth rattle. I gestured Mom and Sherry to one side, near the door. "He's in a pissy mood so just stay out of the way," I murmured.

"Where's my principle model?" Sebastian snarled without lifting his head from the viewer on the top of his camera.

Beth Locke started to move forward but I forestalled her by working my way through the crowd of assistants, stylists, and lighting techs who acted like a guard of honor around the photographer. "I'm here, Sebastian, so don't pitch a fit. Where do you want me?"

His head jerked up and he glared at me. I glared back. His sallow face relaxed into a grudging smile. "Thank God there's one professional, at least. Let's get this done with." His gaze swiveled around the crowd of people watching. "You. Stay there."

I followed his gaze and saw Aunt Sherry, peering around the body of an assistant dresser who stood near a rack of clothing. Aunt Sherry nodded quickly. "I'll be good."

Sebastian grunted. "I don't know who let that old biddy in here, but if she talks to me again, I'll brain her with a tripod."

"It's a pleasure to work with you again, too, Sebastian," I said pleasantly, moving to stand slightly behind Ike. "Here?"

Sebastian nodded then gestured to his left. "Move over a tad. Good. This might not be a disaster after all."

I arranged the dress so the lighting shone fully on the long sweep of the skirt. Poor Ike was frozen in place, his hands flexed like claws on the table. I put a hand on his shoulder. "You can relax," I said, bending over to speak to him.

"They put makeup on me," Ike grumbled, his head still tilted down. "I look like a clown."

"Look at me." He peered up and I touched his face lightly. "You can't even tell. Don't worry, nobody will see it. You can wash it off in an hour or two."

He smiled wryly. "I didn't think it would be like this."

"Like what?" I looked at Beth Locke, who watched us from Sebastian's side. She made a pinching movement with her fingers. I moved closer to Ike, bending over as far as the décolletage on the dress would allow.

"That guy just yells at us all the time."

"All photographers are like that," the young girl said. She flashed a smile, more for the camera than for me. "I'm Margo."

"I'm Anna," I murmured. "And this is Ike." I moved my hand so it rested near Ike's breastbone. He covered it with his hand. "Turn your face a tad to the left."

He looked confused but did as I asked. "It's not so bad now you're here. I know you'll protect me."

"Of course I will." I shifted position so the lighting accented Ike's face. "Really, all you do is go where they tell you, pause when they tell you, and smile when they tell you. It's easy."

"Good!" Sebastian yelled. "That's a good series. Let's set up for the next one."

Ike looked around in confusion. "He took pictures?"

I laughed. "He took quite a few."

"Now what? Is that it?" Ike asked hopefully.

"Oh, I doubt it." I saw Sebastian and Beth Locke in deep discussion. "I'm sure we have a few more pictures ahead of us."

****

Three hours, two set changes, and four clothing changes later, I was in my street clothes, my makeup was washed off and my hair was brushed out and braided loosely. The makeup stylist had even given me a brief shoulder and scalp massage, which felt fabulous.

"You go home and get some rest," he said, pulling a towel over his brushes, tubs, pots, and tubes. "Don't forget your puppy. I can't wait to meet him. And make sure to bring that aunt of yours tomorrow, too. I had a blast watching her harass Sebastian."

Aunt Sherry and Mom had left an hour or so earlier, and Sherry promised to make sure Mom went home and didn't go to Charlie Baron's house. I never had a free moment to find out the details about why it was so important. Since I didn't have my mobile phone with me, I had no idea if she ignored our advice and was now languishing in jail, arrested for trespassing. I decided not to worry about it for now.

"I hope my puppy behaves better than my aunt," I told the stylist when I picked up my small duffel and left the staging room. I had earlier made the mistake of mentioning my bulldog puppy to Beth Locke and Sebastian overheard.

"Bring him to the shoot tomorrow," he ordered. "It'll add a nice touch of homey realism."

"I wouldn't take a puppy to a football game," I pointed out. "I thought we were shooting at the stadium tomorrow."

"We're shooting all over campus. Bring him," Sebastian said. "Maybe we'll use him, maybe we won't." He handed his camera to an assistant and strode off.

So now I was committed to bringing Conan to a photo shoot. I prayed his social skills would be up to the task. I emerged into the hallway and went left to the foyer of the ballroom where Dr. Bell and Ike stood to one side. The dance was still going strong but a glance inside the room told me the crowd had thinned out considerably.

Ike was once again dressed in his own suit, but with the coat slung over his shoulder and his sleeves rolled up. As I approached them I was acutely conscious of the fact I wasn't wearing a bra, it was chilly in the open area, and my sweater was rather thin.

Ike immediately saw my dilemma. He strode to my side and draped his coat over my shoulders. "You look cold." His eyes flickered to my chest.

I shivered dramatically. "I forgot a coat. Thanks." I handed him my gym bag and put my arms into the sleeves, feeling the residual warmth from his body.

"You know, you were right," he said. "Modeling is a tough business."

I stifled a yawn. "It's like teaching, I guess. You have a few minutes of intense work and a lot of time getting ready for those few minutes."

"I think everything went well, don't you?" Dr. Bell asked. "The editor seemed happy with the night's work."

I nodded agreement. "I think they got what they needed for that part. It sounds like we'll have a full schedule tomorrow. Have you heard the weather forecast?"

"Thank goodness, it's supposed to be clear. So that's one thing we don't have to worry about. You know, I didn't have a chance to say this earlier, but I wanted to thank you for your speech when you accepted the endowment for the department. You were right. We all somehow forgot poor Charles Baron and how untimely his death was. Thank you for reminding us."

"Is that what Mom was talking to you about?" I asked Ike. "I saw you two with your heads together when Frank Three was speaking."

"Yeah. She was pretty upset nobody was talking about Charlie. I'm glad you picked up on it." Ike stifled a yawn, too.

"Well, I'll let you two go, you have a busy day tomorrow," Dr. Bell said. She seemed energetic enough to go for another hour or two of dancing. "I'll see you in the morning for part of the activity then I have an alumni brunch to attend before the football game. I'll try to join up with you in the afternoon. Oh, and I also wanted to let you know the campus security escorted Mr. Staples home. He was none the worse for his encounter with you, Dr. Adler."

Ike grimaced. "I forgot all about him, but now that you mention it." He held up his hand and I saw his knuckles, faint purple splotches on the ridges.

"He's bruised but not broken, so to speak. I'm sure he'll be blustering about legal action, only because he has the Franks for his lawyers and they love to file lawsuits. But we have enough witnesses to squash any action on his part, I'm sure." She beamed at us. "Such an exciting evening, wasn't it?"

I repressed a yawn. "Yes, indeed. Exciting."

"See you first thing tomorrow." Dr. Bell bustled away, back into the ballroom. The last sight I had of her was making a beeline for the bar.

"Ready to go?" Ike asked. "Hey, wait. What about your dress? You changed clothes."

"It's in the changing room. I'll get it tomorrow when we come back to prep for the morning's work."

We left by the front door, going out into a clear, cold night. The moon was an amazing shade of gold hanging fat and full, low on the horizon. It looked close enough to touch. "Harvest moon," Ike said, his breath puffing out in a small cloud.

I pulled his jacket tighter around me. "Thanks for the loan," I said while we hurried through the now empty faculty parking lot to his car.

"You looked like you needed it." He clicked his key fob and the car replied with a chirp. "I didn't have that much makeup on but it felt like another layer of skin or something. I don't know how women stand it."

"I'm lucky. I don't need as much as some models do, but there's still enough it feels so nice when it's gone." He opened the car door for me and I settled into the seat, the chilly leather making me huddle deeper into his coat.

He slid into his seat and turned to me. "Do you want to go my place for a nightcap?"

I put my hand over his on the console. "I thought you were coming to my house so I could show you my tattoo."

"I wasn't sure if that was still on for tonight or not."

I took a deep breath. "It's been a long time since I,

um, entertained a gentleman caller." I smiled hesitantly at him. "I hope you'll be—" I stopped, not sure what I was trying to say.

Ike leaned toward me and I met him halfway. Our kiss was long enough to warm me and short enough to make me want more. "We'll just get there and see where it goes," he said softly. "There are no expectations and there's no pressure." He touched my face gently.

"Okay." I leaned against my seat and watched him drive, his silhouette highlighted then darkened by shadow. His hair was tousled and his face had a faint beard, somewhat scratchy. The strong line of his jaw was briefly shown by a passing streetlight.

Ike was the handsomest man I'd ever known, but it wasn't just his physical appeal which so delighted me. I remembered the conspiratorial look he had when he and Mom talked during the endowment ceremony. Ike understood her concern, understood her outrage, and he empathized with it. He didn't just humor her. He agreed with her. Ike was a man I could not only love, but I could respect.

It had been a long time since I'd met a man like him. If ever.

He pulled into my drive and I didn't wait for him, but let myself out of my side of the car. Ike followed with my gym bag, waiting near me when I entered the security code into the garage door opener. We entered through the mud room and I kicked off my shoes. Ike followed suit, padding behind me in stockinged feet into the foyer near my bedroom.

Conan came trotting out from the rug near my bed, his tags jingling. "Were you a good kid tonight?" I asked, covering my shyness at the thought of Ike so near my bed.

Ike handed me my gym bag and I tossed it in the room, taking a chance to peer around. Houdini was sprawled on the bed and he greeted me by stretching then curling back into a ball. "Looks like Conan was a good puppy," I said, continuing into the living room. "When I first got him, he would have accidents in the bedroom, but we haven't a problem with that for a month or more. Still, I'd better not push my luck. I'll let him out for a potty break."

"Why don't I pour us a glass a wine while you do that?"

"Great." I waved at the kitchen. "You know where it is." I led Conan to my den and the patio door there. "Time to go, guy," I said, opening the door.

Conan was more than ready and he zipped outside, heading for his special spot near the trees bordering the right side of my property. It was far enough away I didn't have to worry about doggie landmines but close enough I could keep an eye on him.

"Hey, little princess," I heard Ike say.

I peered through the living room and saw Sprite escorting Ike into the kitchen, her tail upright and tapping his leg lightly. She would be happy tonight. Her favorite person was in the house. I smiled. *I* would be happy tonight, too. I turned back to watch Conan.

I didn't see him. "Conan?" I called out the patio door.

There was no answering yip, his normal way of saying *Hey, I'm busy here, lady.* "Conan?" I stepped outside onto the cold flagstones of the patio, the frosty night quickly penetrating my socks. "Come on, Conan.

Don't play hide and seek tonight, okay?"

No reply. I was starting to get concerned. We had the occasional marauding raccoon, and one of them would be big enough to take on my dog. I went back to the den where I kept a pair of rainy day sneakers and slipped into them. I flipped the switch for the outside yard light then went out, grabbing my flashlight from the hook near the door as I went.

The moon lent everything an eerie glow, casting shadows where I expected to see light and light in spots I normally only saw in sunlight. It was briefly disorienting. "Conan, you little poop, where are you?" I stepped out onto the grass, which was already wet with condensation.

Sharp, high-pitched whining broke out on my right, just beyond the boundary of the yard light. Beyond that yellow circle everything was an impenetrable black. I switched on my flashlight and shone it into the darkness.

"Acie? Is everything okay?"

I looked back. Ike was framed in the patio door, lights from behind showing me his silhouette. "Conan hasn't come back yet. I'll check on him."

"Do you want me to help?"

Another yelp sounded from the shrubbery then a low, throaty growl, far deeper than anything my puppy could produce. I broke into a run, jogging across the damp grass. "Conan! Get over here right now!"

"Acie, be careful!" I heard the patio door slam behind me but I didn't pause. I ran to the edge of the circle of light then kept my flashlight trained on the ground ahead of me. I was so focused on my footing I didn't see the fight until I was on top of it.

My light illuminated a snarling face, something from a nightmare or a surrealist painting. I caught a glimpse of a long snout with the skin pulled back, large teeth, and feral dark eyes. I faltered, not sure what I was seeing. It wasn't Conan. It was too big for that and it was too big for a coon. My momentum kept me moving forward and I was next to the woods when Ike caught up to me.

"Wait." He grabbed my arm, pulling me to a halt.

Another snarl broke out with growling then barking, yips, more snarls. I shone the light in the direction of the noise and it highlighted lunging, twisting figures. "Damn it!" I yelled. "It's the pack of dogs. They have Conan!" I started forward, but Ike kept me back.

"You'll be mauled." He pulled me so hard I stumbled backward.

"Damn it, Ike, it's my puppy in there. I need to—"

He grabbed the light out of my hand and strode forward. "Break it up!" he roared, snatching up a large stick and brandishing it overhead. "Now! Get out of here!" He sounded like the wrath of God and probably looked like it, too, when he moved into the melee of animals, swinging the stick right and left, hitting, poking, and yelling.

"Be careful!" I looked around for a similar weapon and found one, a nice hefty piece of tree branch which probably came down in the last storm. I joined him, hitting dog rumps and hearing satisfying yelps when my blows landed.

I glimpsed Conan, dodging a big dog while he angled in to nip the leg of another animal. "You get back here!" I shouted, reaching for his collar.

I was knocked aside when a huge dark shape barreled into me. I went down, landing heavily on my side. Conan immediately abandoned his attack and ran to me, standing over me when the pack leader, Moriarty, came at me, jaws wide-spread. I struggled to right myself and groped for the stick, which I dropped when I fell.

Ike joined Conan, looming over me and planting his legs on either side of my body. He brought his branch down so hard I was sure he would knock the big dog unconscious, but Moriarty dodged at the last minute and the blow landed on his shoulder. He bounded out of the way and stopped, staring at us, a snarl splitting his face.

Then he seemed to sag. His head tilted to one side and I saw the feral anger leech out of him like water running out of a pitcher. He began to shake and shiver. Conan abruptly sat like his legs wouldn't support him and he whined, pawing his face and twisting his jaw to the ground.

"What the hell—?" Ike stepped toward the big pack leader, but Moriarty bounded away, the other dogs following in his wake. In seconds, only Ike, Conan and I remained in the dense underbrush.

"What was that all about?" I staggered to my feet.

Ike shone the flashlight on Conan, who sat placidly, panting. "I'm not sure." He knelt next to my puppy, who submitted to a brief exam with enthusiasm, wiggling with happiness while Ike and I ran our hands over him.

"He's not hurt, thank God. Oh, Lord, are you okay?" Visions of rabies shots flashed through my mind.

"I'm fine. Just cold feet." Ike shone the flashlight on his socked feet, which were wet now with dew. "Let's go."

We hurried back to the house, Conan bounding ahead of us, tail wagging so hard it made it difficult for him to move. He appeared fine, but I was still nauseous with adrenaline and fear.

When we got to the house, I made Ike take off his socks. I dug out a heating pad and soon we were on the couch, wine in hand and Ike with his feet on the pad and Sprite resting on the top of the couch, near his shoulder. "The pack has never come this far east before," I said, my pulse finally returning to normal.

Ike looked at my windows, his expression thoughtful. "It's like they were waiting for him." He nodded at Conan, now being groomed by Houdini, who came out to see what all the fuss was about. Conan looked like he was ready to slip into a blissful coma while Houdini scrubbed his ears.

"It's just a pack of strays." I swallowed more wine, my hand trembling. "I never had any problems with them before."

"You said they attacked you the other night, right?"

"Moriarty almost attacked Mom." It felt perfectly normal to lean against Ike and also felt normal when his arm went around me, holding me close.

We sat like that for a long minute, each of us lost in thought. Ike moved his feet off the heating pad and switched it off, then sat back, his arm around me when I snuggled against him. My pulse began to race again, but this time it was in anticipation. I deliberately put all thoughts of the bizarre animals out my mind and focused instead on the man next to me. "Ike?"

"Hmm?"

Maybe it was exhaustion. Maybe it was the near brush with, well, maybe death from a pack of dogs. Maybe it was the wine. Or maybe it was the fact I was walking around, partially nude, in front of a bunch of strangers only hours before.

I'm not sure what it was, but something gave me the courage to say, "I suppose you're wondering about that tattoo." *Deep breath. Don't panic. This is Ike.* I stood and set my glass on the coffee table in front of us. My hand only trembled a little.

I stepped to one side then I unzipped my jeans and slid them and my panties off over my hips. I stepped out of the heap of fabric on the floor then I showed him my backside.

Ike set his glass down, too, and came around the coffee table. "I see what you mean," he said, his touch feather-light on my skin. "It might be a bit, well, provocative."

I turned and we were chest to chest. "Now you know why I don't do lingerie modeling."

Ike put his arms around me. "I guess it's only fair I show you mine, too."

My eyes widened. "You? A tattoo?"

He stepped back slightly and his hands went to his shirt buttons. "Not just one, I'm afraid. Two."

I watched in fascination while he undid his shirt and slid it off then pulled his white T-shirt off over his head. His chest was brown but lighter than his arms, showing off his golfer's tan. His wiry gray and white hair was scattered over his firm pectorals and when he turned there was only the tiniest crease of a paunch at his waist.

He presented me with a smoothly muscled back. It took me a second to get over the shock of seeing so much masculine flesh so close. When I could finally focus again, I saw words tattooed in flowing script high across his shoulders.

Pleasure and action make the hours seem short I ran my finger over the words and saw goose bumps rise on his skin.

"I got that one when I finished my PhD coursework," he said, twisting to look back at me. "*Othello*. I was ABD for three years and I had to work construction to get by. The guys on the crew really gave me shit about it." He turned to face me, smiling wryly.

"I'll bet they did." *ABD* was academic jargon for All But Dissertation, that awkward time between passing written/oral exams and finishing your dissertation and defending it in order to obtain a PhD. "ABD for so long? I was ABD for a year."

"It's hard to come up with an original subject for a dissertation for the Renaissance. I should have chosen American Realism and Naturalism, like a beautiful woman I know."

"How did you know I did my dissertation on the Americans?" This was not common knowledge in our department. I taught Victorian literature, which most laypeople assumed meant British fiction. Actually it included any author from the time period, including the American Realism authors, but I only taught one or two classes on the subject in the years I was at Stoneyburst.

"I read it."

He was so close to me I was warmed by his bare chest against my thin sweater. My body responded to his nearness, my nipples firming. "You read my dissertation?" I couldn't resist. I slipped my arms around his waist and leaned closer.

He sighed and enfolded me in his arms. I pressed my head against his warm skin and breathed deeply, inhaling a scent of makeup, man, and cologne. It was a strangely comforting yet erotic smell. "Acie, I swear, I've been in love with you from the minute you applied for the job here and I was on the interviewing committee."

I pulled back from him to stare into his eyes in amazement. "What?"

Ike shook his head. "You truly are one of the densest women on the planet. *Whoever loved that loved not at first sight?* I'll never forget how you looked that day. Your hair was done up in a twist at the back of your head and you wore a gray skirt and sweater set. You tried to look so demure and professional, but my God, you were so beautiful." He laughed shakily.

I did some quick math. "Ike, it was almost fifteen years ago. You don't mean you've, I mean, you can't mean you—are you saying you've cared for me, all this time?"

"I didn't pine for you, if that's what you're asking." He continually touched me gently, as if confirming I was really there, in his arms, just light little movements on my face, shoulders, back, arms, neck. "If you remember, I dated a few women here and there, and was serious about a couple."

My stomach lurched. I did remember and also remembered how I used to feel when I saw Ike with another woman. Why, oh why, didn't I realize how I felt? He was right. I truly was one of the densest women on the planet.

"We had to review the dissertations of all the candidates. Yours was the only one that was interesting and readable."

"Why didn't you say anything? I mean, why didn't you say something sooner?"

He tugged me closer, this time firmly pulling my lower body against his so I could feel his hardness. "I didn't think you cared for me. But then, when Henrietta started asking me out, I thought I saw jealousy." He bent his head and kissed the delicate spot below my ear, his lips warm and firm. "When I overheard what you said to her at the town meeting, I was sure you understood how I felt." He looked at me. "That's when I started to have hope."

I cradled his face in my hands and peered into his eyes. I saw only honesty, love, and trust there. A sure knowledge flooded through me, carrying me along on an exhilarating tide. "I think I did know, but I was afraid to show it. I've always been so afraid of what other people might think."

"Are you still afraid?" His face bent to mine.

I put my arms around his neck. "No," I whispered. "Not at all." I raised my face to his and I fell into the most seductive kiss I've ever experienced. It was as if my body, my soul, and my mind were trying to merge with his. Chaotic thoughts raced through my brain, but the one that finally won out was *This is Ike. Finally. Ike.*

We broke apart a breathless moment later. Ike explored me, hands moving up under my sweater to cup my breasts. "I think it's time we get horizontal," he whispered, his voice thick. "Either that or we use the couch, and I'm not sure I want the audience."

I glanced at my animals, who watched the crazy humans with bored curiosity. "Makes sense to me." I started for the hallway to the living room, leading him by the hand. "Hey. Wait a minute. What about the other one?"

"Damn." Ike's hands cupped my butt. "It's hard to walk when I see an invitation like this. Whatever possessed you to have those words tattooed there?" He squeezed gently.

I turned to lean into his embrace. It felt so good to have a man against me, thigh-to-thigh with only sweat and a thin layer of clothing separating us. "My ex-husband said I was too hard to understand, so before we got divorced, I thought I'd put instructions where it would be easy to find. I flashed him one last time before I walked out on him."

Ike's hands squeezed first one, then the other, butt cheek, *Kiss* on the left and *here* on the right. "Kiss my butt." He pulled me closer still. "I'll look forward to it." He lowered his head, but I put a light hand on his chest, keeping him away.

"Tell me. What about the other one?"

"Other one what?" Ike was moving now, angling his pelvis against mine in a most agreeable way.

"Your other tattoo?" I pulled away from him and put my hands on my hips in mock anger. "Where is it?"

His hands went to his belt buckle. I swallowed heavily when he undid his trousers and let them drop to the floor revealing powder blue boxer briefs and his penis, hard and clearly outlined by the fabric. He hooked a finger in the waistband then he stopped. "This might be better seen lying down."

We kissed our way into the bedroom, leaving a

trail of clothing behind us. By the time we landed on the bed, we were both naked. Ike lay on his back and stretched out his legs, crooking his right leg to the side. "Voila."

I couldn't see anything in the dark, so I switched on the bedside lamp then I got on my hands and knees and peered at his inner thigh, in the bare area where most men had no hair.

"Good heavens," I murmured. "A person needs to be quite close to read it."

"Yeah. How about that?" His voice was husky and low.

I examined the words tattooed inside his right thigh. *Make me immortal with a kiss.* "That's not Shakespeare, is it?"

Ike propped himself up on his elbows to regard me. "No. By the time I got this one, I'd moved on from Shakespeare and was into Marlowe. It's *Faustus.*" He touched the tattoo, his fingers brushing against my wide-spread thighs where I straddled him. "I did it on graduation night, as soon as I had my PhD in hand. It was a memorable drunk."

"Is it an invitation or a warning?" I asked, gently nudging his legs back together so I could hover over him, poised on my arms and knees.

"I guess you can take it however you want. But I have to tell you, if you keep doing what you're doing, then you'd better take it as a warning, because I won't be responsible for what you're doing to me."

I cat-walked up his body, my hands on either side of his torso so my breasts brushed against his thighs. "What am I doing that has you so hot and bothered?"

"Just looking at you has me all hot and bothered."

He put his hands on my breasts when I straightened on my knees, positioning myself over him. "I hope you're going to do what I think you're going to do," he said with a gasp.

I lowered myself. "We'll see."

Chapter 17

The next morning, I awoke to four pairs of eyes watching me. Ike was next to me, his head resting on his pillow. Sprite sprawled above him, sharing the pillow, one paw tangled in his hair. Houdini was at the foot of the bed, his paws stretched up toward me and Ike. And I sensed Conan on the floor in his usual spot, his tail thumping on the rug.

"It gets crowded," I said. "It's only a double bed."

"I like cozy. It's a better word." Ike tugged the blanket over my bare shoulder. "Did I mention I love you?"

I touched his face. His beard was definitely scratchy this morning. "Yes, you did. Did I mention I love you, too?"

His smile was like morning sunshine. "I can die a happy man," he whispered.

I felt an unaccountable twist of alarm. "Don't you dare. I'm not done with you."

"Okay. How about showing me what you have in mind?" He nudged Houdini and the big cat took the hint, dropping onto the floor with a thud. Sprite raced after him and I heard Conan's nails clicking on the hard wood floor.

"I'm not sure we have time." I turned over to check the bedside clock. "Hmm. Six a.m. We're due in makeup at eight. Of course, nobody shows up on time anyway." Something hard and insistent poked me from behind.

"That should be enough time for what I have in mind," Ike whispered, his hands slipping around me to hold my breasts. "Let *me* show *you*."

****

A little over ninety minutes later we were showered and sitting at my dining table, drinking our first cup of coffee, eating a croissant, and reading the newspaper with Conan gnawing on a doggie treat nearby. Sprite and Houdini were ensconced in my den, keeping an eye on the bird feeders.

Ike sat across from me, dressed in last night's clothing minus the necktie and suit coat. His beard was definitely scratchier than last night, giving him a rakish air when contrasted with his suit and dress shirt. Earlier, when I offered him my shower shaver, he declined. "They told me not to shave," he said while we soaped each other. "They want to see how the scruffy look goes over with the clothes they have planned."

I thought it would go over great, and told him so. That led to a bit of grope and tickle, which led to…well, you know.

Now we sat sedately at my table, him in his dress clothes and me in my usual Saturday uniform of jeans, a loose sweater, and sneakers. I lowered the newspaper section I was reading and tapped the page. "There's an article in the paper about the dollar versus the euro. You may want to exchange money now instead of waiting."

Ike lowered his section of the newspaper to regard me. "Does this interest mean you're taking a European vacation during over Christmas holiday with me?"

"I don't know. Do you want me to go with you?"

He shot me a *gee, what a moron look.* "I just wanted to be sure," I said. "I am worried about our peers, you know." I sipped coffee as I regarded him. "I can easily imagine no end of teasing if anyone finds out we're involved. And it may not be according to regulation."

"Hmm." He sipped his coffee, too. "I'll dig out my copy of the Code of Conduct and check. Of course, there's one easy way to solve it."

I heard a car pull in the street. I got up to check my visitor and saw Mom getting out of her red PT Cruiser dressed in her Saturday best, black Docker pants and a black-and-white blouse covered by a chic little black jacket, a black and white cane in her right hand. Aunt Sherry emerged from the passenger side wearing a red cardigan that matched the car and a pair of sharply pressed jeans which looked brand new.

"The girls are here." I went to the front door and pulled it open just as Mom was getting ready to knock. "Ike's here," I said by way of greeting, ushering her in.

"His car is in the driveway, dear," Aunt Sherry said, moving past me.

"And that explains why I didn't use my key." Mom dropped her black patent-leather handbag on the table in the entryway and came into the dining area. "Good morning, Dr. Adler. I thought you might be up." She paused. "So to speak."

Ike stood. "Good morning, Mrs. Watson, Mrs. Holms. Would you like a cup of coffee?"

"I don't think we have time." Mom eyed Ike's attire then turned to me. "I see you've been busy, dear."

I started to stammer an excuse. *Ike dropped by on*

his way to the photo shoot. It's not what it seems. Then I thought, *What the hell.* I sat down and picked up my coffee cup. "Yep." It was a very freeing feeling.

"As I was saying," Ike said, resuming his seat. "There's a simple solution to our problem." He ignored Mom and Sherry, who stood nearby, watching us with a bemused smile. "We can get married."

I set my coffee cup down. "Are you proposing?"

"Not really." Ike's expression was bland, unreadable. "I'm only saying if you're worried people will talk, one way to shut them up is to get married."

Sherry waved a dismissive hand. "Don't worry about them."

"I do worry about them, or at least, some of them," I said. "I have a career to consider, and so does Ike."

"Surely what two consenting adults do is nobody's business, is it?" Mom asked.

I sighed. "This is a college. Lord knows whose business it is." I tried a different subject. "Why are you two here this bright and early?"

"I want to go to Charlie's house and I remember how you read me the riot act the last time I went. I need to look for something that I think will prove his death was no accident or heart attack."

"You ladies shouldn't go alone," Ike said before I could speak. "After what happened last night, it might not be safe."

"What happened?" Sherry cleared her throat. "Besides the obvious."

I rolled my eyes. "There's nothing obvious about it."

"He's sitting there in the clothing he wore last night and he hasn't shaved. You glow like a bride on her wedding day. It's pretty obvious."

"I glow?" I touched my face.

"What happened last night," Ike said, bulldozing over all of us, "was that the pack of dogs roaming around the neighborhood almost got Conan and Acie."

"And you," I added.

"I was fine," Ike said in dismissal.

"You were not fine. Those dogs were attacking anything that moved, including you."

"The more I think about it, the more I wonder," Ike said. "It seemed like the pack leader was the one doing most of the attacking. The others seemed more to be joining in."

"That's why he's called a pack leader, Ike," I said patiently. "He leads, they follow."

"You were attacked?" Mom asked. "Here?"

"Yes, which is why we're not sure if it's safe to be out there. In fact, I wonder if we should call Animal Control." Ike checked his watch. "We can do it later. Why don't we go out to the Baron house, too? We have time before we're due at the Union for the morning."

"You need to change your clothes," I said around a last bite of pastry.

"Why? I'll just be changing again later." Ike saw my aggrieved look and held up a hand. "Okay, okay. Until we know how our relationship will be accepted, we'll be discreet." He drank the last of his coffee. "We can run over to my house and I'll change then we'll meet you at Charlie Baron's house. It won't take long."

"I know just where it should be," Mom said while Ike and I put our dishes in the sink. "So it won't take long at all."

"What are you looking for?" I clipped a leash to

Conan's collar. He wiggled in anticipation at the thought of a ride. Oh. Damn. A ride. "Ike, I'll have to drive my car. We can't take Conan in your car."

"Why not?" He was already walking to the hallway leading to the mud room and garage.

"He might get it dirty. And you don't have a doggie seat belt." I grabbed my iPhone out of my purse and stuck it in my sweater pocket.

"It's a short drive. We don't need one. We'll see you there," he called out. "Just wait for us in your car."

"No hurry," Sherry called back and I heard the front door open and close.

"Ike, are you sure you want a dog in your car? It's a very nice car."

"He's a very nice dog." Ike pulled open the door to my garage. "Do you need to lock up?"

"No, everything locks automatically. Are you sure?"

"Of course. So what do you think about my marriage proposal?"

I lifted the neck chain which held his gift. "We'll see."

He laughed.

****

It took slightly longer than I expected at Ike's house. Conan explored the place while Ike changed his wrinkled dress clothes for jeans, a black-and-white flannel shirt, and loafers. I suggested he pack his own shaving gear for later, just in case they decided they didn't want the scruffy look.

"I have room in the closet in my spare room," Ike said while he tucked shaving essentials into a small leather bag.

"Room for what?" I had never been in his bedroom before, although I'd seen most of the other rooms of his charming little three-bedroom house. I looked out the double doors leading to a patio, which in turn led to his garden. "Even in autumn, your garden looks beautiful."

"I make sure to plant the right mix of flowers so there's color all year long." He came to stand next to me, and put an arm around my shoulders. "I have room for clothes, if you'd like to stay over."

I turned and he put his arms around me. "We really have nothing in common," I said. "I mean, nothing important."

"Of course we do," he countered.

"I can't cook," I said.

"I can."

"I don't garden."

"I do."

"I'm terrible at sports."

"I don't care."

"I don't understand the first thing about card games."

"It doesn't matter."

I cast around for something else which would convince him we weren't suited to each other. "I adore my house," I blurted.

"I love my house, too," he admitted.

"Well, there, you see. We can't be together because—"

"We'll take turns visiting each other."

I gave up on logic and decided to finally face the question which had haunted me, lurking in the back of my mind, since Ike first kissed me. "You can do it all, Ike. What the hell do you want with me?"

His eyebrows drew together when he frowned. "What?"

I threw up my hands in despair. "I'm a klutz in the kitchen, I always forget the rules in bridge, I don't know a thing about football or golf, I kill every plant I touch. I tried marriage and a few long-term relationships, but somehow they didn't work out. Why would you want to spend any time at all with me, much less…" I swallowed hard. "Much less have a, um, you know, an, um, a—"

Ike drew me into his arms. "Are you asking why I love you and why I think you're sexy and why I want to have a wild, passionate, crazy affair with you?"

I tensed in his arms. "Is that what you're asking me to do?"

He kissed the tip of my nose. "Acie, I'll have any kind of affair with you that you want, but I do promise some of it will be wild and crazy." He drew back and regarded me with humor in his blue eyes. "At least a little bit wild and crazy."

"But why?" I looked away from him, my face getting hot from blushing. It just wasn't easy to look Ike in the eyes. He had a way of seeing deeply into my heart.

"Because you're intelligent, funny, loving, giving, and beautiful." He held me closer and I rested my head against his chest. "I can't say why I love you, Acie, but I do."

His heart was thudding against my ear, a deep drumming tone, ba-boom, ba-boom. It was warm and safe there in his arms. "You're too damn perfect, Ike."

His laugh made me jiggle. "Believe me, I'm not. I lose at bridge as often as I win. I'm good at golf because I practice. I've had plenty of plants die. And I didn't succeed in my marriage, either. I leave my dirty clothes lying around the house, I don't vacuum until the house is overrun with dust bunnies, and I can't get the hang of something as simple as making a good pizza. If you stick with me for even a little while, you'll find plenty to complain about, believe me." He lifted my chin with two fingers and stared into my eyes. "Just give me a chance to make you complain, please?"

I saw trust, and honesty, and a hint of worry, or fear, in his look. Ike, worried, if I would care for him? Ike, who was always so assured, so confident?

I think it was the hint of fear which made me throw caution to the winds. I was just as fearful as him, or maybe more. Perhaps between the two of us we could find a way to overcome our worries and make it work.

I smiled but before I could speak, he said, "I know." He kissed me quickly. "We'll see. Come on, Conan." He snapped his fingers to my puppy, who was busily sniffing in Ike's closet.

Conan trotted to us and we all went out to Ike's car. I stowed Conan in the back for the short ride to Charlie Baron's house. It was a perfect football weekend with a pristine blue sky, big puffy white clouds, and a chill in the air which made me look forward to a fire in the fireplace later.

We pulled into Charlie Baron's long driveway. I saw now how it angled to the right then to the left, the trees lining it giving it a tunnel-like air of secrecy. No wonder it was so disorienting the night I was there. Between the twists and turns, the rain, and the fog, I'm surprised I was able to navigate it as well as I did.

We were about ten yards from the house when Ike

slammed on the brakes. Conan yipped and slid off the back seat and I was thrown forward. "Damn that woman," Ike muttered.

I twisted in my seat to check Conan. "Why did you stop so fast?" Conan peered up at me from the foot well in the back. "I think he's okay." I turned around and that's when I saw who Ike was looking at.

Meryl Staples stood in front of the car, having apparently just appeared from the trees on the right side of the property. "What's she doing here?" The woman looked like an escapee from a bad B movie. Her black hair was tangled and her loose black skirt was twisted so she showed an amazing amount of leg and a hint of underwear. She leaned on Ike's car, her pose giving us a good look at her breasts when her blouse gapped open.

Ike shut off the car and got out. I got out, too, and let Conan out of the back, snapping on his leash so I could evaluate if he was truly okay after his spill. He bounced ahead of me, anxious to join Ike and Meryl who were—

"Oh, for pity's sake," I said.

Meryl had Ike in a passionate embrace. It was embarrassing. She was babbling, pawing at his shirt, touching his face, crying, and generally being an idiot. Ike looked over her head at me, his eyes wide while he struggled to push her away.

"Help me," she cried. "Oh, please. I didn't think he'd do this. It's so terrible. Help me, please. I don't know what to do."

Ike tried to grab her arms, which were like snakes, coiling all around him. "Calm down," he murmured. "Just calm down. What's wrong?"

Ike was being too gentle. I stepped forward, grabbed a handful of her black hair, and jerked hard. "Grow up and grow a spine. Men aren't the answer to every problem."

Meryl stumbled back, landing with a thud on Ike's car. I winced, more for the car than for her. She huddled there for an instant and I saw her face twist into anger, her mouth drawn into a snarl. Then she straightened and the weepy, ineffectual, helpless female was back. "Help me, please," she moaned, making for Ike again.

I stepped into her path. "Forget the histrionics and just tell us what's wrong."

"He's crazy, I tell you. Crazy. It was an accident." Meryl turned her pleading eyes on me and when she didn't see any sympathy, she tried to dodge around me to Ike. I dodged with her, blocking her. "He didn't mean to kill poor Mr. Baron, but they argued and Mr. Baron had a heart attack. I told him to go to the police, but he wouldn't."

I turned and stared through the shadows to the house. "Where's my mother?" I demanded, a bad feeling starting to form in the pit of my stomach.

Meryl talked around me, pleading with Ike. "You have to do something. He's so far into debt and the only way out of it is to sell the land."

Ike strode ahead. "Mrs. Watson!" he called. "Where are you?"

Conan surged forward, dragging me with him. We almost knocked over Meryl, who ran after Ike, trying to grab him. "I swear to God, I'm going to hit that woman," I said through clenched teeth.

We reached the house and Mom's red car, but there was no sign of her or Aunt Sherry. Ike went to the front door but before I could follow him, Conan dragged me to the right side of the garage and a thin strip of grass bordered by trees. Through a gap in the foliage I glimpsed the Staples house, not too far away and sitting lower than the Baron house. "Ike!" I shouted. "Here!"

We rounded the back of the garage and for the first time I saw Charlie Baron's back yard, which overlooked the land we wanted to use for the sanctuary. The lawn was as wide as the house and extended about half the length of a football field. It ended in a low line of shrubs, which marked where the yard ended in an abrupt drop-off.

I had seen the property on maps, of course, and seen photos, but it was impressive to be standing there high on the bluff, looking out over the plain and the river in the distance. I didn't have time to admire the view, though. Conan struggled against his leash, straining to reach my mother and Aunt Sherry, who were backed up to a large brown shed near the edge of the property. The pack leader, Moriarty, advanced on them, growling.

Mom stabbed at the big dog with her cane and Moriarty dodged. Aunt Sherry yelled, waving her arms, trying to look large. The dog darted first left then right, looking for an opening to attack. Then he heard us behind him and turned, fangs bared. I used both hands to restrain Conan, but his collar wasn't up to the strain of forty pounds of muscular dog who was anxious to break free. I jerked backward when Conan raced forward.

Ike caught me and broke my fall, lowering me to the ground, but he didn't pause. He sprinted after Conan, who aimed straight for the big Rottweiler.

Conan was just a foot or two away when Moriarty twisted, leaping high in the air then dashing away and heading for the woods behind the shed. Conan followed, barking. He and Ike disappeared from sight.

"He's so far in debt and he's so afraid," Meryl said behind me, grabbing my arm. "He had to borrow money and he can't pay it back. What will I do if he goes to jail?"

I turned on her and slapped her as hard as I could. She rocked back, stumbling three or four steps. "What's he doing? Where is he? Where's your brother?"

Meryl put her hand on her face where the imprint of my hand shone stark white then slowly started to flood with color. All pretense of helplessness vanished. "He's my husband, not my brother. He's probably over there." She gestured in the direction where Ike and Conan vanished.

I started in that direction but paused when Mom and Sherry joined us. "Are you okay?"

"The damn dog almost got me," Mom said. She looked pale and tottery. I held on to her arm, thinking she was faint then she jabbed at Meryl with her cane and I realized she was shaking with outrage. "I told you there was something fishy about those two. Out with it. Why the act?"

Meryl regarded us with cool hauteur. Gone was the sobbing, lost woman. In her place was a calculating femme fatale. "We needed money. We were hoping I could find someone to help us pay it back."

I glared at her. "Mom was right. He was pimping you out. That's why you hit on Ike."

Meryl didn't even flinch. "He's not bad looking and he has a nice car, a nice house. I figured he must have money."

Aunt Sherry snorted. "Yeah, right. He's a college professor. They aren't exactly rolling in dough."

"I was willing to try anything. John lost everything gambling. That's why we moved to this pissant town. We couldn't afford to live anywhere else. He bought the house and borrowed money based on selling that land. Then the old man moved in and decided to donate his chunk of it. We knew our piece would be worthless."

"Why attack my mother?" I edged away, anxious to find Ike.

"He said if she died, everything would be so screwed up in court nobody would be able to unravel it." Meryl's eyes kept darting around us, looking for escape. "The old man left the land to your mother, but it was contested. Then the person contesting it was killed. It would be tied up in court for years."

Aunt Sherry shook her head. "That doesn't make sense."

She was right but I couldn't put my finger on why it didn't make sense. I was too worried about Ike to think straight.

Mom jabbed her cane on the ground. I could tell she longed to stab Meryl with it. "What did he do? Did he hurt Charlie?"

"John said he'd get the sanctuary voted down by the townspeople." Meryl stepped away from us, turning to look at the trees and her house. "Once it's voted down, then there's only one logical use for the land. He already talked to the lawyers. They said once the land isn't in contention any more, they'd release that portion of the estate."

"I will never allow that land to be sold to developers," Mom said. "Never, do you hear me?"

Meryl turned, her cornflower blue eyes narrowed in anger. "The only thing in the way is you, you old bitch."

Mom, Sherry, and I took a step back from the small gun in her hand. "You're crazy," I said. "You can't shoot us. That's murder." *What am I saying?* A shouting voice in my head was at odds with the calm way I was talking.

"I'll say that awful dog of John's attacked. I tried to shoot it and missed."

Aunt Sherry took hold of Mom's hand. "You can't say you shot all three of us."

"Everybody knows you're meddlers." Meryl gestured the gun at Mom then at Sherry. "God knows what kind of accident could happen when that dog attacked you and I had to shoot to try to save your lives. That's what you get for sticking your nose in where it doesn't belong. Get over there." Meryl's face lost all pretense of civility, smoothing into a mask of harshness. She jerked the gun again to the left of the shed, toward the drop-off.

Mom and Sherry inched backward, clinging to each other. "This won't work," I said desperately. "Ike was with us. He'll know what happened." I couldn't stop staring at the gun. She held it very competently without any wavering or hesitation. *Just my luck she knows how to handle a gun. Damn it.*

"John and his fucking dog will deal with him," Meryl said. "Move."

"You're crazy." Mom sounded distracted and I glanced at her. Her gaze was fixed beyond Meryl, to the woods that served as a border between the properties. Meryl had her back to it and I was at an angle so I couldn't see beyond Meryl. The gun occupied my entire attention.

"You won't get away with this," Aunt Sherry said, also staring past Meryl.

I tore my gaze away from the gun to see what they were watching. That's why we three saw Ike chasing John Staples before Meryl did. They burst out of the woods behind her then everything happened all at once.

Meryl turned and fired her gun.

Conan leapt out of the woods at her, snarling. She staggered back, the gun flying out of her hand when Conan fastened his teeth on her arm.

Her scream mingled with John Staples' shout when Ike grabbed him, Ike's hand closing on something around Staples' neck. Ike yanked then flung something at me where I stood paralyzed. Moriarty lunged into the melee, rocketing out of the trees and leaping at Ike and Staples where they rolled on the ground.

Mom strode forward, lifted her cane like a baseball bat, and whacked Meryl Staples hard against the ribs. The woman went down with another scream. She kicked out when she fell and Mom flailed backward, her cane flying out of her hands.

Conan lost his hold but immediately jumped back on Meryl, his jaws clamped on her wrist, shaking his head back and forth until blood flew. Sherry waded in to kick Meryl, landing solid punches on Meryl's backside and ribs.

The sight of my mother and aunt fighting lifted my paralysis. I grabbed Mom's cane and went after Moriarty, knowing I had to prevent the big dog from hurting Ike.

I stopped. Moriarty had his jaws around John Staples' ankle. The man was on the ground under Ike, and he struggled to land a kick on the dog's face even while he staved off Ike's blows. I hesitated, not sure who to hit. Just when I had a clear angle at John Staples, he pushed hard, trying to dislodge Ike.

Staples, Ike, and Moriarty all slid over the drop-off and disappeared.

"Ike!" I screamed. "Ike!" I dropped the cane. *Oh, dear God.* I had one night of love and the man I adored was killed. I rushed forward. "Ike Adler, you'd better not die because I'm not done with you!" I yelled.

There was silence.

"Ike?" I peered over the edge.

"That sounds promising." Ike looked up at me from thirty feet downslope, John Staples lying in a heap nearby. Moriarty was crouched at Ike's feet. "Get the goddamn dog whistle and burn it, would you?" He leaned over and touched Moriarty's head. The big dog looked up at him and cringed then sat down, panting.

I sat back on my butt, so relieved I wanted to upchuck. The sun glinted off the silver of a chain on the grass nearby. I crawled over and picked it up. That son of a bitch Staples used the whistle to manipulate Moriarty. My one glimpse of Moriarty as an abused, cringing animal was confirmed.

I don't know which angered me more—that John Staples was an animal abuser or a murderer. The two weren't far different in my book.

"I think he broke a leg," Ike called.

Meryl was sprawled face-down on the ground. Mom sat on her butt and Sherry sat on her legs. The younger woman looked unconscious. "We've got her," Mom said, one hand curled into Meryl's hair. Conan sat near Mom, his eyes pinned on Meryl.

"Are you okay? Is Conan okay? What about the gunshot?"

"He's fine. She must have missed. Stupid bitch." Mom jerked Meryl's head then released it. The woman's face hit the grass with a thud.

I grabbed the cane and crawled to the edge of the drop-off then slid on my butt, landing near Ike. He helped me to my feet. I was careful not to step on Moriarty, who apparently had adopted Ike and was now pressed against his legs.

"It was an accident," Staples moaned. "It was all an accident. I didn't mean to kill him. We argued and he fell on the stun gun thing of his." The man was tangled in the middle of shrubbery, jagged branches and leaves covering him. His right leg twisted under him in a very unnatural position.

"I heard that!" Mom yelled. "Charlie bought a taser gun to protect himself from your dog, you son of a bitch!"

I placed Mom's cane tip very carefully on Staples' throat, in the indentation under his Adam's apple. "What do you mean?"

"It was an accident. He fell and he had one of those stun guns. It went off. He died. And she didn't have to run. The dogs wouldn't hurt her."

"You mean Henrietta?" Ike demanded, standing over Staples with clenched fists.

I looked at Moriarty, who gazed up adoringly at Ike. "What about Henrietta?"

"I couldn't help her. She had asthma and I couldn't

help her."

"Did you try?" I pressed the cane down.

He gasped and struggled feebly. Moriarty growled and Staples went still. "It was all an accident," he moaned. "I did it for Meryl. I love her. She needs nice things. I did it all for Meryl."

I shook my head. "*Men have died from time to time, and worms have eaten them—but not for love*," I quoted.

Ike grinned. "I love a woman who can quote Shakespeare in a crisis."

"It was all an accident," Staples moaned.

I moved the cane aside. "Trying to kill my mother wasn't an accident." I kicked him in the ribs.

"Meryl suggested that! I didn't want to! It was all her fault." He moaned and twisted on the ground.

"Go ahead, blame her all you want," I said. "She's unconscious and can't defend herself."

He moaned again and tried to sit up but the pain was too much. He collapsed back into the shrubbery.

"Is he dead?" I asked, peering at the broken little man.

"Just passed out," Ike said. "Where's Meryl?"

"She's still out like a light," Mom called.

"Mom and Sherry took her on." My iPhone, stuck in my pocket, throbbed insistently then chimed. "Damn it, now what?" I dug it out and looked at the display. "Shit." I put the phone to my ear.

"Dr. Doyle, I don't mean to be insistent, but you're late." Dr. Bell's histrionic whisper would have been funny under any other circumstance. "I explained that you and Dr. Adler may be—ahem—busy, but you need to get here soon."

"Dr. Bell, can you—"

"They're doing shots now at the football stadium. Did you know they have a student athlete alumnus acting the part of the young woman's boyfriend? It's all very realistic. He's in a football uniform and everything. The football coach is working with them and the team will be in some of the pictures. He was so happy to cooperate."

I'm sure he was, I thought. *Especially if the college president asked him to be.* "Dr. Bell, please, listen, we have a probl—"

"They'll need you here soon. You should probably just come directly to the stadium. The makeup person is here and—oh, wait a minute—young man, what are you—what—"

"Look, get your butt out of bed and get here and bring your hunky boyfriend." I recognized the husky deep voice of the makeup artist from the day before. "The editor is anxious and Sebastian is ready to pitch another fit. So get here, bring the hunk, and bring the puppy. Sebastian really wants the puppy. He Googled the puppy last night and he said the breed is perfect for the shoot. So bring the puppy. Now."

"Call 9-1-1," I said, finally getting a word in edgewise.

"Huh?"

"Call 9-1-1. Tell them to get to Charlie Baron's house. There's been an accident."

"Holy fuck. Are you okay? Is the hunk okay? What about the puppy? Is the puppy okay?"

"We're all fine. Just call 9-1-1 and tell them we need the police and an ambulance."

"Whew. Okay. I'll let Sebastian know you'll all be

here soon. Yeah, and I'll call the cops."

I shook my head. Trust a makeup stylist to worry first about the photo shoot. He must have handed the phone to Dr. Bell because she came back on the line. "What's this about the police?" I heard an excited babble of voices in the background.

"I'll explain it all later. We'll get there as soon as we can. Just make sure the police come out to Charlie Baron's house and call an ambulance." I didn't trust the stylist to get the details right, so I figured it wouldn't hurt to repeat my instructions.

She started to ask questions, and I did the only thing I could think of to cut her off. I pressed the End icon.

Ike moved next to me and I went into his arms. "Did you let our boss know we aren't AWOL without a good excuse?"

"I did." I held him tightly. It's true what they say. A person doesn't know what they've got until it's gone, and when I thought Ike was gone, a piece of me was ripped away. I vowed to never let him far from me again.

I put my arms around his neck. "You know, as soon as we're done with the police and the questions and the photo shoot, I know a nice private little spot over by the golf course where we could sit and watch the river. We could spread out a blanket, have a picnic and…" I stood on my tiptoes and moved my lips near his ear. "Maybe we could start being wild and crazy there." I brushed a kiss against the side of his face then waited to see his reaction.

His eyes widened in amazement. "Dr. Doyle, are you propositioning me?"

I put one hand on the back of his neck and pulled his face to mine. "You bet I am, Dr. Adler. What do you think about that?"

Just before our lips met I heard his whispered, "We'll see."

A word about the author...

J L Wilson writes mysteries touched with romance, time travel mixed with romance, and romantic paranormal fiction.

Do you see the pattern? Find out more at www.jayellwilson.com.

Check out the character list for J L's Remembered Classics Series: http://bit.ly/character_lists